THE

A wide white cha... there in the middl... lated carved wood, like something from a play written in about 1515. On the chair a man sat, his long legs stretched out, one arm gracefully raised a little, so a big, black-striped bird—a falcon, maybe—could sit in turn on his wrist. He was dressed, approximately, in how we—I—think of Italian Renaissance clothes. A dark red silk doublet, almost black, white linen shirt, lace cuffs—but also black jeans and black-red boots. His hair was long. Long red hair.

I'd never seen him before in my life.

I'd seen him a million times, in my brain, in my dreams.

It was him.

It was Silver.

He got up out of the chair, and walked easy and relaxed toward the camera. He smiled at us with his white, perfect teeth. His skin—silver. Amber-eyed.

"I'm here for you," he said. That was all. And your insides dissolved.

The bird flapped its wings. Was it a robot, too?

The camera had gone in very close, and every feather was visible. And every feature of his face. The skin was poreless, yet *real*. It was both matte and burnished. Metallic—but only as if under a first-class silver body makeup. Just as Jane described . . .

Bantam Books by Tanith Lee

●

The Silver Metal Lover

METALLIC LOVE

Tanith Lee

BANTAM BOOKS

METALLIC LOVE

A Bantam Spectra Book / March 2005

Published by
Bantam Dell
A Division of Random House, Inc.
New York, New York

All rights reserved
Copyright © 2005 by Tanith Lee
Cover art © Kinuko Craft
Cover design by Jamie S. Warren Youll
Book design by Rachel Reiss

If you purchased this book without a cover, you should be aware that this book is stolen property. It was reported as "unsold and destroyed" to the publisher, and neither the author nor the publisher has received any payment for this "stripped book."

Bantam Books, the rooster colophon, Spectra, and the portrayal of a boxed "s" are trademarks of Random House, Inc.

ISBN 0-553-58471-5

Printed in the United States of America
Published simultaneously in Canada

www.bantamdell.com

OPM 10 9 8 7 6 5 4 3 2 1

*To Anne L. Groell, without whose enduring belief
in this book, it would never have been written.*

*And a special thank you to John Kaiine and
Beryl Alltimes, for invaluable insights.*

Acknowledgments

It should be noted Loren's titles for her second and third part derive from the works of the marvelous Tennessee Williams and William Blake, respectively.

You, my creator, would tear me to pieces and triumph; remember that, and tell me why I should pity man more than he pities me?

—Frankenstein, MARY SHELLEY

METALLIC LOVE

PART ONE

The Train to Russia

1

What do you do about a story that has a beginning, a middle, and an end—and one day you find that the ending has altered—into a second beginning?

• 1 •

You're not going to like me.

I apologize for that.

It was Jane; she was the one you liked. I liked her, too.

And I—am not Jane. Not in any single way. But one.

And that one single way is perhaps the only thing you and I also have in common.

Because if we liked Jane, we loved Silver.

Didn't we.

The temptation is to start this just as Jane did, with a description of my early life, and where I lived. Jane's mother was rich, and some of what Jane described might have been predictable—the travels, the house in the clouds. Even the way Jane came into existence—that was, *selected*, carried physically for five months, taken out very carefully, brought to full-term, and then nursed by machines—the Precipta method. But I was just born. I was a mistake. My mother made that very clear, apparently, when she dumped me ten months later on Grandfather.

I say Grandfather. He wasn't. He was the man my mother had herself lived with when she was a child. He had sort of brought her up, but then turned her out on the street when she was fifteen. He was a believer in the Apocalyte religion, and was pretty strict, and my mother was always in trouble of some sort—drink, drugs, legal and otherwise, men. When she gave me to him, she contemptuously told him, "Maybe you can do better with this one." The Apocalytes were "charitable." So they took me in. That was the first eleven, twelve years of my life, then, that gray-white wreck of a house on Babel Boulevard.

It was quite tough there. First the babies' room, which I don't remember. Then about twenty girls all ages in one dank dormitory. The roof leaked in the rain, and in summer you could hardly sleep for the scratching and shuffling of rats in the walls. Three grim, frugal meals a day in the communal hall. Lots of prayers. God was a wonderful being who wanted us to love him and sent us not only irresistible temptations we must ignore, but horrible mishaps—sickness, poverty, earthquake, and fire—to see if we would still do it. But if we did fall out of love with God, God got upset, and then he would make us burn in Hell forever. I swallowed all this along with the awful food. What else did I know? After all, the Big One was coming soon, the Day of Wrath, when the Asteroid, captured between Earth and moon about two decades before, would crash into the Earth and destroy us all, which is what had nearly happened previously. Whenever we strayed, Grandfather would take us up on the dodgy roof by night and show us the Asteroid, rising blue-green and molten over the slums. "Behold the eye of God's Destroying Angel," announced Grandfather. Hey, guys, you *bet* we tried to be good.

There were tremors once or twice, too, (quite a bad one when I was five) to help remind us. Quake-sites still existed all over the city, except in the richest areas, where they had been put right after the initial disturbance.

I suppose, growing up with this, I got used to it. Life was simple. Obey Grandfather, love God, wait for the Day of Wrath when we—the righteous ones—would be swept to Paradise on golden wings. Did I believe in Paradise? Perhaps. No, not really. Strange, maybe. I believed in all the *bad* things—Hell, punishment, an insecure and vengeful deity—but not in that.

There was a much larger earthquake when I was nine. It happened just before dawn. I remember waking—cold, there was snow on the ground—to hear the usual small tremor stuff, creakings, grunts of timber and brick, the shift of powder-dust dislodged and falling—and that rumble under the bed like a truck was revving up right outside. Oh, it's a tremor, I thought, and nearly went back to sleep. But then the rumble rose to a bellow, the mattress leapt, and part of the wonky ceiling dropped into the dorm and landed with a crash between the beds. Something even hit my legs—bounced off—I wasn't hurt. The girls started screaming then. Me, too. We pelted out of the room and tried to go downstairs, but some of the staircase had come apart. So someone said we should crawl up the swaying upper steps to the other end of the roof, the sounder reinforced area over Grandfather's room.

When we'd gotten up there—I'll never forget the roar and boom that was surging out of a city gone almost black but for the sprays of appalling lights like fireworks, which were flyer cables snapping, and power and electricity wires breaking and catching on fire. And next it was brighter because the sun was coming up, but also a couple of buildings were alight. Was it *now*? Was this *it*?

Then everything settled with a disgusting grinding *crump*. And Grandfather appeared up the fire escape, which was somehow still in one piece. Plaster dust in his iron hair only made him more apocalyptic. He led us at once in prayers of thankfulness to God, who had spared us even while he chastised the unholy city.

We were put on the lower floor for months, above the boys' dormitory, where there were only three or four weedy male kids, until some members of another house of the Order finally came and fixed the stairs and the roof a bit. Then we moved back to our own dorm. We couldn't sleep for a long time—too scared—but we were mostly children, and in the end we did. The aftershocks were slight, but a great deal of damage had been done in the city from the new quake.

A week after the quake anyhow, I was ten. My birthday was marked by a solemn blessing, and I had the special birthday privilege of washing the others' feet.

It was next year that I found the Book.

It was my week for washing dishes and I was down in the basement, doing just that. Outside it was dull and close, thundery, and through the very tops of the windows all I could see was a jagged line of brassy overcast above a broken wall. The water heater didn't work properly (not auto), and half the time I had to boil jugs on the nonauto electric stove. I was very hot and yawning so much with tiredness and boredom, I was nearly insane.

Then, crossing back to the stove for yet another jug, I trod on a slab of floor that shifted under me. I yelled, but there was no one else to hear. I thought the floor was giving way and I was going to fall down into a (Hellish?) abyss. But it wasn't that at all. When I righted myself, I saw that only a small square part of the floor had tilted, revealing a small dark slot beneath.

I—and countless others—had stumped over that floor a thousand times and never disturbed it. But one of the recent minor tremors must have loosened something, some glue or padding that had been used to close the little hatchway tight. And now it had only taken my narrow just-eleven-years-old foot, with about sixty-six pounds behind it, to tip the hatch open.

Of course I knelt down and peered in. I didn't see what was there for a minute, because it was wrapped in a worn dark scarf. When finally I realized and pulled it out, the scarf itself tore at once in a ragged hole. I'd heard of people hiding money in old houses—obviously not I.M.U. cards, but nickels and dimes, or whole fortunes in antique gold. My heart stood still, and when I saw what was wrapped in the scarf was only a battered paper book, I felt a wrench of bitter disappointment. Maybe that was itself my first true whiff of rebellion—for I know, if it *had* been money, I'd never have told the Apocalytes. To them, to have wealth of any sort was just one more sinful Hell-deserving giving-in-to-temptation.

The cover of the book was plain resined black paper. Not knowing what else to do with it, I opened it. Which is what you do with a book, except I'd never had a chance to open anything but an improving religious tract. (Even the Bible was generally kept from us by Grandfather, who only occasionally read us alarming snippets.)

And the book's title seemed depressingly like those of some of the lesser religious works: *Jane's Story*. Under that, however, was this: *Published by Catch-Us-If-You-Can Press. Be advised, to possess this book is to risk intimidation and possible prosecution by the City Senate. Do not read this book in any public place—you have been warned!*

I sat on my heels, gaping at the book, and in the background the jug was boiling dry on the stove.

Then I heard someone descending the stairs. I could tell from the flump of the footfall it was Big Joy, the oldest girl, who was in charge of the rest of us.

I found I'd gotten up and pushed the book in the pocket of my dishwashing overall. I kicked the hatch-thing back into place and ran for the jug. When Big Joy came in, I was lugging it over to the sink like a virtuous little Apocalyte. Joy was a bully, and perhaps, if it had been one of the others, I might have shared my discovery. I'll never be sure.

Someone else stumbled on the hatch, and hurt her ankle, a few days later. Obviously there was nothing in there by then.

Rather curiously I'd thought the book was ancient. (Like the fortune I'd hoped for?) But naturally it had been published by an underground press only a few years before I found it. I assume someone from outside, but still from our own beloved Order—one of the ones, probably, who came to fix the stair and roof—managed to set it in under the basement floor on Babel Boulevard. Either they were hiding it for their own safety, or they were passing on the Book, covertly, knowing that sometime it would again come to light, and then another person might read it. I think there was a lot of that with Jane and Silver's Book, as maybe you know. A whole kind of secret club, reading it, whispering about it, moving it along for others to read and whisper over. If you're reading this now, I guess you were part of that shining, shadowy chain.

I read it, too. Cover to cover.

What do I say to you, then, about reading that Book?

What would *you* say to *me*?

But maybe I presume. Maybe you didn't.

Okay. Plotline: There's this girl of sixteen (Jane), rich and naive, and under the thumb of her tyrannical, bloody, mind-fucking bitch of a mother—only Jane innocently doesn't know how terrible Mom is—but one day the girl meets a robot. Now we've had robots for ages, right. They do most of the jobs people used to—and so create a permanent underclass of unemployed subsistence plebs, like me. But anyway, we're accustomed to machines, and they *are* simply machines—boxes, tubes on wheels, faceplates that look as real as a badly made statue. Only *this* one is different. He's part of a new line designed for pleasure—of all and every sort. And he looks just like a man—a beautiful one. He's tall, strong, elegant, and handsome. A musician, a *lover*—and his skin is silver, his hair russet, his eyes amber. He truly does appear and feel—if you touch him, which is all you want to do—human. But he is to humanity what sunlight is to a low-wattage bulb. He is—indescribably—wonderful.

And Jane falls in love with him. And, knowing that no human could be *allowed* to love a *robot*—still she can't stop herself. So she leaves Dire Momma, and goes to live with Silver in the pits and craters of the slums. And he makes her life heaven on earth. And for the first time ever, she's—happy.

But then the firm that created him calls back all the robots of that special super-deluxe line. Something wrong with them, they say. But we all know, we who are reading *Jane's Story* of Silver, that all that's wrong in Silver's case, is he's too *right*.

She tries her damnedest to save him. Gets betrayed—her evil little friends, Jason and Medea, her lunatic friend Egyptia. Life intervenes—earthquake, muddle. He's caught. They *dismantle* him. They kill him.

And she . . .

Jane tried to commit suicide. Didn't make it. But then she received a message from beyond the gate of death. Without a doubt it's him. He tells her things only she could know. Proves he is still alive after death . . . somewhere, out of the world. And proves, too, by doing the rest, that inside the robot body there had been a *soul*.

So then Jane tries to go on living, living both her own life and his, *knowing* that one day, far, far off (for the rich can survive to be a hundred and fifty years of age) she will see him again.

That's the plot in the most crass terms, of Jane and Silver's Story.

Well. It changed my life.

I used to read it in the eye-aching half-dark of stubs of candles—in the basement at one A.M., the yard where the chickens were kept, on one of the lavatories, with people banging on the door and me calling, "I got sick!" and *retching* to show I needed to stay there. Chasing the truth of love.

Oh, Silver.

Silver.

When I finished that Book, I started again at the beginning.

I read it twelve times, that year between eleven and twelve.

Was apprehended only once.

"What are you doing *reading*, girl? You should be at prayers." "Sorry. Only this—" proffering the religious leaflet in which I had wrapped Jane's Book—and getting away with only a slap across my head.

I loved him. I loved him so. And through his strength and compassionate sweetness, I learned a lesson none of *them* had ever tried to teach me. That God might not be fire and hell and horror. That God was love. And so sometimes, here in this vicious world, love was to be found, too.

That was the lesson.

At twelve years old I had it—by *heart*.

· 2 ·

We went into the city quite often. An aspect of the Apocalytes' "mission" was to knock on doors or talk to people on the street and try and pin them down to a long old natter about the deity—i.e. how rotten the world was, how sinful *they* were, and that ours was the only means of salvation.

After the quake when I was nine/ten, we'd even made a bit of progress. A couple of scared citizens signed up for our regime of total self-denial and utter hatred of all physical enjoyments. No drink, no cigarines, no painkillers even—sex only in the effort to construct one more little Apocalyte. But strangely, not everyone was keen.

I recall a woman saying exasperatedly, as our group hemmed her in at the corner of Lilac and Dyle, "But Jesus Christ drank wine!" "A mistranslation," announced our group leader, a big bald man called Samuel. "What was he *drinking*, then?" demanded the woman, trying to push us away. "A type of herbal tea," declared Samuel knowingly. But the woman managed to escape just after this, and bolted off up the street—even grabbing others en route and alerting them to our menacing presence.

As a kid I, too, evidently, accepted all this. Along with being hauled about with the adults. They felt, Grandfather's troops, that having a few young children with the preaching band might both attract custom and deter abuse. But frequently it didn't. "Eff off, you buggers!" was a common greeting to us as we trudged the streets and markets.

Very occasionally, we even penetrated some of the richer areas, up by the New River, for example (yes, where Jane's M-B friend Clovis once lived), or Honeybloom Condominiae.

Here the speaking door-mechanisms themselves saw us off with threats of mild electric shocks.

Why did we do it at all? Hope, I suppose, sprang eternal that even among the rich and therefore contentedly life-loving, we might get a bite. We never did that I ever saw.

However, I, in this way, *did* see a lot of the city. I learned its ups and downs, geographic and financial. By the summer when I was twelve years old, I knew my way around.

That morning, I'd been given the chore of making the

beds, which included Big Joy's, Samuel's, and even Grandfather's.

I had done it all before, and only been punched by Big Joy, who hit me more for the virtue of refining me through blows than because I'd messed her blankets up.

In Grandfather's room the door had a lock. And Grandfather was away at some street-preaching. I locked the door and sat down on his unmade bed, and started reading *Jane's Story* for the thirteenth time.

She writes:

> He came within three feet of me, and he smiled at me. Total coordination ... He seemed perfectly human, utterly natural, except he was too beautiful to be either.
>
> "Hallo," he said.

My own eyes swam, my own heart pounded like the servogenerator in the basement, which never properly worked. My mouth was dry.

Suddenly I thought, *I don't want any more of this—other stuff.*

That was all.

I thrust the book in the pocket of my everyday dress, and left the unmade bed of Grandfather. I unlocked the door, and went out, down the stairs to the front of the house.

No one stopped me. I didn't take a single other thing with me.

I think, in fact, I just believed I'd risk a day on my own in the city, and lie about it when I got back. Lie—and be disbelieved, and thrashed with the leather belt kept for such purposes.

I think I did reckon I'd *have* to come back.

Outside, it was a hot summer day. The streets smelled of corn gasoline, the inferior gas most used in the slums of every city from there to Mexico. Also of faint cooking, and of scald-green weeds baking in the pavement cracks. Sounds—distant cars, flyers far overhead on the whistling wires, voices, pigeons.

It was as if I never heard anything before.

The sky was white-blue. It was about nine A.M. I walked along the street and turned left towards Hammit and the day market.

When I reached the market I went on walking, straight through, frowned at now and then by uneasy, Apocalyte-recognizing traders. And then still on, into the city.

I didn't have any money, of course. I.M.U., as we all know, is the method the rich or lucky use. A few bills and coins get pushed about in the slums. But even those were never allowed *us*. Grandfather and Samuel had charge of all funds.

But I never ate much, never being given much, never stayed still much, seldom being able to stay still. Walked virtually everywhere I'd ever been. As for *things*, I mean goods in shops and on stalls, they were as glamorously alien to me as the sky—I could look, but neither have nor touch.

I walked for nearly four hours, wandering, staring at everything, and soon I was fairly sure I, on my own, was no longer identified as anything other than an impoverished slum kid. Oh, the freedom merely of that.

The only problem was, I became furiously thirsty. That was one thing we were permitted at the house on Babel, several drinks of water from the faucet per day—though even there they'd ask you how many you'd had, if you went to the tap too often. Now, no faucet. In the windows of little shops, bottled water looked back at me with green and blue eyes. I think they were what made me so aware of the thirst—normally I could last most days with very little liquid, going for a drink only to give myself a brief break.

At last I went into one of the small stores.

"Can I have a drink of water, please?"

"Can you pay for it?" The woman balked behind the cold box with the bottles, glaring.

"No. I meant from the faucet."

"Get out, you crazy."

I got out.

I stood on the street, watching people going by. No one looked well-off here, but neither did they look like they were dying of thirst as I was now convinced I was.

My dreamy plan—vague enough—had been to try to locate some of the streets Jane describes in her Book. Tolerance, for example, where she and Silver lived those handful of years earlier, through fall into winter. I hadn't so far been able to find Tolerance, in the company of the group. Nor had I ever heard anyone speak of the place. I decided then, standing parched as one more dying weed on the sidewalk, perhaps Jane had invented the name of the street. I mean—*Tolerance*—the one thing she and he didn't receive.

A man brushed by me, careless. He walked into the shop with the woman and the water bottles. I watched him through the open door. He bought cheese and ham from the chill cabinet, and a bottle of beer.

When he came out, again he nearly walked right through me, but his insensitivity also extended to something else. I don't know how it happened exactly, and for a minute I didn't accept it had. But he dropped a coin. It was silver, and it fell brightly—there, by me. Silver. Then he ambled off and I put my foot over the silver coin.

I didn't go back in that shop. I walked on till I found another, tiny, like a cave, off an underpass. I didn't buy water, either, but a shiny orange can of carbonated juice.

The *taste* of it. I'll never forget. Saccharine as poison, with stinging bubbles that made me cough. To me, champagne. I was drunk on it. Someone told me sternly since, a guy I dated, that I would have been thirsty again in about two minutes flat—only worse. But he was wrong.

I staggered, inebriated and lubricated, away, and spent the rest of that day still trying to find the elusive streets Jane had named, and not finding any.

About seven P.M. the sunset was powdering the buildings ruby, and the elevated at Tyrone, which still ran three times a day, was sponsoring a train across the sky, black as a dragon, with thirty glittering eyes.

I ought to go back now. Face the music and the leather belt.

But I sat down instead near the iron struts of the elevated, and watched the darkness arrive, like smoke from the setting sun. Perhaps I'd have had to go back in the end. But that was when Danny found me.

Really, I don't want to say too much about Danny.

He was then about forty, maybe. He looked younger, but that's all I'll say. Just in case. What he does, you see, is illegal.

Without any hesitation, he sat down about four feet from me on the pavement. When he spoke, he took me by surprise—not only that he was talking to me, but what he said.

"See these yellow-red flowers—fireweeds. Notice how they were withered up, lying all flat on the ground? But look, now the dark's come and it's a bit cooler, they're getting right up again."

It was true. The drained weeds were standing now, their flowers at half-mast. Even as I glanced, one whole flower jerked and raised its trumpet victoriously to the neon-lit sky.

"People can be that way," said Danny, who I didn't yet know to be Danny. "Crush 'em—sometimes they just get back up."

I gazed at him sidelong. Grandfather, with all his snarling about sin, had never directed that sex should be interpreted to any of us—ignorance being, seemingly, safer. Nor, therefore, had anyone warned me about men who prey on girls or children. Nevertheless, I was wary. The very fact this man had talked to me, *me*, less than the dust or the weeds that could rise from the dead—maybe I was cautious even of that, for was he another religious maniac?

So I didn't answer at all.

Then he said, "I'm Danny. Who are you?" Like a kid might.

Only I wouldn't have answered someone my own age right then, either.

He shrugged. "You've run away, I guess. Yeah? Some old feller mistreating you, yeah?"

Yes, I said in my skull, thinking of Grandfather with abrupt belligerence.

"Well, look here, little lady. I have a kind of little gang

of girls, some of them a tad older'n you, and some your age—eleven, right?"

Wrong, I thought, twelve-years-old affronted. I said nothing.

"There's not a lot of work you can get without your labor card, and I guess you don't have one. But this might suit you."

I blinked at him. Then I said softly, "What do you want me to do?"

I asked mostly in total ignorance, as I've explained. Yet I sounded uneasy and guarded, and he laughed.

"Hey, hey, *no*, I *don't* mean anything like that, honey." He shook his head, as I sat there wondering what *that* meant. He said, "The rich folks, they got all the robot cleaners—automatic little dinkies that run up the walls, scrub out the toilet, that kinda thing. But round here, well, we got a few people can afford a *human* to do all that—if'n they can't afford an automatic. They like girls best; they like young fit girls who can do the work. Think us fellers make a mess more'n we clean up. So I've gotten together my gang. Fifty of 'em. Fifty-one, if you care to join. It'll mean a bit of money. You won't get rich. What do you say?"

Much of what I'd done on Babel Boulevard had been in the cleaning department, and I hadn't received a quarter for it. It had had to be done for God.

Now I equated that version of God with Grandfather. An old, gaunt, ranting man with angry red eyes. The other sort of God, glimpsed by then, however obliquely, through the pages of Jane's Book, had no face I knew. He was like the white light Jane had written about. And *He* didn't need a bloody maid.

I was still cogitating, the sidewalk hard on my backside, when my stomach growled at the top of its intestinal lungs.

It startled me. The starvation-training I'd had seemed to have ensured I was never really hungry. Maybe now my body only missed its usual thin soup and half-slice of bread the Apocalytes served up at sunfall.

But Danny rose to his feet and said to me, "C'mon. I'll buy you a hamburger."

And in a kind of trance, like Eve enticed by the serpent to the forbidden fruit, I, too, got up and followed where he led.

This, then, was the next five years of my life.

As part of Danny's "gang" (no, his name isn't Danny, either), I lived in various places, always sharing with two or three other girls of the cleaning teams. We got along, or we didn't. But there was no Big Joy. No Grandfather. No glowering, unreasonable God. (I confess, once or twice I got scared the Apocalytes might find me, drag me back. So I used to imagine I was invisible to any pursuer. I initiated a sort of mantra I'd say over and over if I felt weird, stuck hard at it. Guess it worked.)

I changed my name, too, when I was about fifteen and a half. What had I been called on Babel Boulevard? Honesty. That had been my name. Maybe why I learned so quickly to lie. However, at fifteen and a half, I altered to Loren. I'd heard it somewhere, and it made an impression. It seemed to fit me, too. A dark name like my hair, my tawny skin, which is what they used to call "olive," my light brown eyes.

The best of Danny's flats I stayed in was the last one, situated in a partly ruinous apartment block near the Old

River. At night, bats flew out of the top stories—which was where they alone roomed. They circled and flittered round and round through the blue-going-gray dusk, and the first stars came out, pale cold-gold embers, just visible above the haze of river pollution, for this wasn't a well-lit area.

The cleaning work was always okay. That is, it was dull and repetitive—once you've cleaned one really filthy apartment, you have, with a few disgusting variations, cleaned them all. None of the areas we went were rich, of course. There were a multitude of mossy, green-veined baths and cracked lavatories, carpetless stairways of broken tiles, walls mottled by damp like the pelts of leopards, and rat-riddled kitchen-hatches.

But we got paid. (Any trouble of any kind, there was always backup from Danny's male contingent.) And sometimes, off the nastier employers, we took the odd goody—a glass of cheap sherry, a cigarine from a two-thirds full packet that usually wouldn't be missed, one go from a bottle of nail polish, if the resident was out, or a box of eye makeup. Sometimes some of us stole things, too. There was a girl called Margoh (how she spelled it, though it was all she could write). She was a genius at petty theft. A knife here, a fork there—a neglected lipstick from the back of a drawer—sets matched up from endless visits to different apartments, put together and flogged to the less moral-conscious markets. Margoh also utilized an actorish streak. Sometimes she would thieve something very *missable*, like a string of glass beads, or a lightbulb. Then she would go sniveling at once to the person renting our services. "Oh, I'm so worried—I knocked those beads of yours behind the couch—can't find them, I've looked—maybe the sweeper sucked them up—" She'd have the owner, as well as the rest of us, searching everywhere. Margoh became so upset they rarely docked her money. The lightbulbs, etc: she had always *broken*. Then she wept copiously and offered to pay. Again, it was a harsh employer who turned on her. Rarely did anyone complain to Danny. Most clients thought Margoh a bit dim and felt sorry for her. After all, among the poor, they weren't doing too badly, and she was a much lower life-form.

I never copied Margoh's antics. This wasn't scruples. I didn't think I had her talent. But no doubt, she taught me something about deceit.

Other than flats and bats and thefts, by the time I was fifteen going on sixteen, I had become, I believed, me. There'd been a couple of, well, shocks. Unnerving experiences. I don't really want—I won't itemize those. But I'd held together. I had gotten through. And I went out on dates with boys from my own walk of life, saved enough money for contraceptive protection, had my first sexual experience in the back of a dumped car. Sound bad? Hey, it was quite a decent car, still. And I thought how clever I was, proud of my achievement. Forgetting Jane the Virgin's words to her lover:

Not so I can boast, or to get rid of something . . .

Forgetting, actually, a lot about Jane, and Silver, too. They were my gods, but they were far off. They'd led me to a better life. But now I was grown-up.

Even the Book—I'd not read it again. It lay in my portable luggage wrapped up in a plastic overcoat. Mind you, I hadn't thought to pass it on.

You don't need love to have terrific sex. You need a couple of drinks, a packet of two—contraceptive *shots* being too expensive—and a guy who (a) you didn't find repulsive, and (b) knew his way around.

Cynical? Sure. Sure as the stars are fire.

When I think back, even now, I see how brave Jane was, that sheltered, self-esteem-drained child, older than me only in years, risking everything. But I was a slum cat and I didn't mind, not now, not since I was free.

At sixteen, I, like several other girls, had my own little cleaner gang of seven, under Danny's overall authority. Some days I didn't even need to work, could go to a visual or a concert, could loiter through the streets, ride the public flyers, idle two hours over coffine at the Chocolite.

I was Loren, adult, dressed cheaply but to the best of her range, strong nails long and unbroken and painted gold from someone else's polish, a handful of cash in her pocket, a decent bed under a roof to sleep in. I was me. No ambitions. I was young. A visual producer might spot me and grab me for a movie. I couldn't sing, or act, but what the hell. I might even write a novel—I read plenty. (Ironic, it had been Grandfather, crusher of delights, who had taught me, along with all his charges, how to read. And so opened the way to fantasy, dreams, and otherness. Without him, bizarrely, I'd never have been able to understand Jane's Book.)

I never found, and now no longer looked for, any of the streets Jane had written of. Some of the restaurants she mentioned I'd glimpsed, but mostly they were too upmarket for me. I *did* once see Egyptia, Jane's demented, beautiful, once-friend, on-screen in a visual, but it was in an obscure theater, and all in some different language—

Greek, I think. Even Egyptia spoke Greek in it, or she'd been faultlessly dubbed. They could have dubbed the film, too, in to English, but hadn't, in order to be impressively *foreign*—it was that sort of visual theater. Not even subtitles. I only went because I saw her name on the vispo advertising. But she was a big star by then in Europe—what was left, that was, of Europe, after the Asteroid.

Nevertheless, there was a kind of flicker inside me when I watched Egyptia. She, too, had touched Silver. Slept with him in the carnal sense. Damned him, finally.

But by then the flicker was also distant, deep down inside the obscure ocean that fills up every one of us. I felt it move, the flicker. Felt it ebb away. I had a date that night, up on the hills above the city, where the landscape was somewhat altered from the quake when I was nearly ten. Under the trees, the warm summer breeze blowing strong, someone lying against me. Not Silver—as Silver had lain, of course, in my earliest and most innocently sexual dreams. Not Silver. Silver was long dead. And this was a man. And I was Loren.

• 3 •

My gang, the Dust Babes, were over on Compton with a new client, when I got a call at the rooms in the bat-block. I was seventeen by now, and it was summer again, late summer, and I'd had a wild night. I was asleep. Nor was I alone.

"Lor—Lor, wake up. We got some difficulties."

"What? Can't you deal with it, Jizzle?"

"No earthly way," said Jizzle, righteously.

"Jesus," said my companion, burrowing into the pillow. "I need my sleep."

I got up and took my personal handheld house phone outside, into the communal room. The other sharer—Margoh—was out. It was about midday.

"There's this cracked old woman going *nuts* here, Lor."

"Why, what've you done?"

"*Me? Nothing.* She's a crazy old bag, is all."

I stood, naked and young and thinking, pushing back my hair in the hot room. But the heat was beginning to bother the phone, it was chuntering away to itself and would soon cut us off. There used to be cell phones once, "mobiles," but the magnetic interference from the Asteroid put paid to those, and it didn't take much to spoil any other type, especially in subsistence areas.

"You're fading," whined Jizzle.

"Okay. I'll be there in twenty minutes. Give me the address."

My date cursed me as I ran about my room. He hadn't been that great. I told him he and I were through, and if he wanted to stay in the bed beyond one P.M., I'd call the police, who owed me a *big* favor. A lie. But he sat up, all hurt and furious, and I rushed off. "Any damage to my stuff," I precautionarily added at the door, "you'll be oh so sorry, baby."

Any damage. Oh, God.

What does a bed matter, or a few ornaments and clothes. It's your heart and your soul that matter. Only these.

I ran up the stairs of the building on Compton. The elevator there was broken, but the very fact they had one showed this district wasn't too bad.

This should have been a nice job. The woman even had some robot cleaner gadgets she'd been prepared to let us run for her. What had my Dust Babes *done*? Smashed one of the machines?

Her flat was at the very top—six stories. A window on a landing looked at summer-dry coppery trees and a quake-site with clematis growing. I hit the door—no auto-panel, but a bell, at least.

No one came, so I tried shouting.

Then Jizzle let me in. She looked mournful, her gamboge hair in extra spikes.

There *was* a bit of noise. I hadn't heard it outside, the door was that sturdy. A faint buzz of talk—male voices, then the sound of something going over, *bang*, and splintering.

"I tell you, Lor, she's off her—"

"All right. Let me get by."

I padded down the short passage and came out in a biggish main room. The VS was on—and it was a great visual set, this one, with four-point surround-sound, and flawless steady color. Part of what I'd been hearing at the door was in fact voices talking on a newscast. It was just a group of guys in fashionable one-piece suits, jawing on. Then I saw the woman, our client.

She wasn't old, not really. A well-faked blonde, about forty, or else fifty and taking some Rejuvinex—which would make her monetarily better-off than we'd thought. She *was* in a state, though. She was crying, and she'd just thrown a small table at the wall.

"Excuse me," I said, trying to sound both placatory and firm.

She rounded on me at once. "Come here," she screeched.

"Come here, and sit down. God, you're only a kid. Come here and sit and learn about this—this *bloody abomination!*" The last two words sawed out in a scream.

Yes. She was mad. She must be.

"I need to know," I said coolly, "what the difficulty is you're having." I'd meant with the Dust Babes. (The three of them, Jizzle foremost, were now gathered in the hall doorway, looking scared at me, three little children whose mother has arrived to sort out the danger. After all, none of them was older than fifteen.) "Do you have a problem with my girls?"

"It's not your girls," our client spat. What was her name? I couldn't recall. "It's this." She pointed at the VS screen.

Exactly then, one of the men on the screen walked forward and filled it up. He addressed us all in a charming actorly way. "And now, watchers, I'd like you to come with me and take a look at these amazing creations. I want you to judge for yourselves. Understand, what you are about to see is for real. No computer trickery. Check us against your advertising code unit. And if you have a virtual on your set, believe me, now is the time to turn it on."

"A virtual—" the client ranted. "Christ. *Christ!*"

I assumed she didn't have one. It seemed unlikely, even on Compton Street. The cities have only just gotten that kind of technology up and running again after the first Asteroid disaster, and so far only the *very* rich can fill their private rooms with virtual reality images at the flip of a switch.

The screen was showing curving, low-glowing corridors snaking through some sort of steel and polarized glass complex. Not highly mind-blowing.

Our client folded down on her couch. *"Watch,"* she roared at us all. "My God," she cawed, "is there a devil in Hell?"

I hadn't heard anyone say anything like that for years, not since Babel Boulevard.

It made the short hair rise on my neck.

I was thinking, in the pragmatic region of my mind, Just gather up the girls, tell this nutter Danny will settle what she owes for any work done, and get out of here.

Then a white, wide chamber opened out on the screen. And there in the middle of it was an old-style chair, simulated carved wood, like something from a play written about 1515. On the chair a man sat, his long legs stretched out, one arm gracefully raised a little, so a big, black-striped bird—a falcon, maybe—could sit in turn on his wrist. He was dressed, approximately, in how we—I—think of Italian Renaissance clothes. A dark red silk doublet, almost black, white linen shirt, lace cuffs—but also black jeans, and black-red boots. His hair was long. Long red hair.

I'd never seen him before in my life.

I'd seen him a million times, in my brain, in my dreams.

It was him.

It was Silver.

I was seeing Silver.

My legs, as they say they do, went to water. (Had only happened to me once before.) Water. That's what it feels like. I gripped the back of the client's couch to keep myself up, and heard her say, deadly and miles off, "It's time this world ended. It's really time now. Come on. It's *time.*"

I thought, confusedly, does she *know* him—*did* she know him—?

Then the red-haired man got up out of the chair and

walked easy and relaxed towards the camera. He smiled at us with his white, perfect teeth. His skin—silver. Amber-eyed.

"I'm here for you," he said. That was all. And your insides dissolved.

I never heard a voice so musical, so unarrogantly confident, so calm, so gentle. So sensual. So *personal*. But no, of course I had. In my mind. In my dreams.

The bird flapped its wings. Was it a robot, too?

The camera had gone in very close, and every feather was visible. And every feature of his face. The skin was poreless, yet *real*. It was both matte and burnished. Metallic—but only as if under first-class silver body makeup. Just as Jane described.

This *wasn't* any robot. This was a man, cunningly made up to look as if he maybe *could* be. What a low-down trick.

The woman in the chair muttered.

"He's the same. Only—I'd forgotten how . . . special. Just that one time. In the room off the lab. They let it happen—just that one time."

The man on the screen turned from us. He picked up a slender, carved wooden pipe. Setting his mouth to it, he produced music. I didn't know what the melody was, but it was fast and complex and ornamental—surely impossible to play so many runs and curlicues at such a speed.

I heard her mutter again: "Turkish Rondo." Then, "No, even a virtuoso can't go that quick. What is it? Approximately three times faster than the best. But there's expression, too, tonal color. It used to be a guitar. Or a piano. Now it's a flute. Does he still play guitar? Does the new program allow for it?"

The screen blinked out. And *I* nearly passed out. The small shock so sudden, right against the initial shock of seeing him.

She'd hit the remote and cut the image off. She was crying, and she raised two inflamed eyes to me. "I fucked him," she whispered. It wasn't an obscenity, not the way she said it. When she said "fucked," it was as if she said, "I died awhile and was in Paradise." Then she said, "But you, you ignorant bloody bitch, what do *you* know about it? *You'll* never be able to afford a go at him. Nor will I. Funny that. Just lucky, that one time, just lucky they tried him out on me—me and several others. Electronic Metals. Anything for the shitty firm."

Jizzle was viciously clawing and tugging at me, trying to pull me away. I could smell Jizzle's perfume, slightly expensive, one thorough dousing stolen from a previous client. But I only leaned over this blond woman's couch, staring in her feral eyes.

According to Jane, he had said he'd been tested on women—and men, presumably—before they let him, and the others of his tribe, loose in the city. How not—he'd been a pleasure robot.

Jizzle squealed, "Come on, Lor—she's cracked. Let's go—let's get out—"

And the woman shrieked, "Yes go, you filthy little whores. Run off and dream about a man you can't have. What they did to him—oh, Christ—and now they've brought him back like it doesn't matter."

She was staggering up. Jizzle and Coo and Daph were yanking me by my arms and hair towards the apartment door. As I reeled backwards with them, the woman's coffine mug went straight in through the VS screen. Which shattered like thin ice. A cheap, inferior set, after all.

Margoh said to me, husky with frankness, "I stole that pendant of yours. Never sold it yet. Do you wan' it back?"

"Which pendant?"

"One like a snake's head holding a glass bead."

"Oh, yes . . . I thought I couldn't find it. No, it's okay, Margoh. You keep it—or sell it. Whichever. Farewell present."

"You're a doll, Loren."

"Like anything else?"

"Well. Your last winter coat, the fake fur. That'd really fetch a price."

"If you say so. It's full of holes. Take it anyhow."

"Er . . ." Margoh looked shifty and sly. I'd never seen her look like that. When she lied to the people she stole from, she was up-front and passionate with distress at their loss. I cottoned on. I said, "Well, why don't I just leave it in the closet, and you can kind of take it sometime today, before I go. Surprise me!"

We laughed. Like old friends. Which I guess we were.

Me leaving. That's the reason she owned up.

But there had been half a day more before I knew I was.

Out on Compton Street I had turned and slapped clinging, clutching Daphnia away from me. That wasn't fair. I said I was sorry. She started to cry, and I started to shake, and Jizzle said, "I got some brandy in this cola bottle," and passed it round.

"What the hell was wrong with that old bat?" they asked.

They invented possibilities, giggling at the brandy and the stress of escape.

I said, "Okay, girls. Why don't you go and buy a sandwich. Something nice. Here's the money. Then move on to the next job. That's over on Marbella, isn't it? I'll square all this with Danny."

They went off, tweeting at my handout, which was quite generous. I walked slowly, somewhere. I couldn't tell you where, but hours slid over me and away. All I saw, all I thought of, was him.

You see, if I'd ever met him when he was with Jane, I couldn't have helped being insane over him, but I would have dragged a steel lid down on it. Unlike Margoh, I don't steal from my friends. But this—what had the blonde on Compton said? *And now they've brought him back.*

Can you raise the dead? Apparently Christ could, I didn't and don't see why not, if it was Christ doing it.

But surely, too, a scientist could re-create a machine. Even—especially—Silver.

I thought, naturally, all this was down to Electronic Metals, the company Jane talks about, the ones who made him in the first place. The raging blonde had mentioned them, as well. She had worked there. You could understand why she wouldn't forget.

She must have been really afraid, told to go and have— my God—sex with a robot. Then. Then she met him.

Guess where I found myself at seven P.M.? Over on East Arbor. Where E.M. had been situated, according to the Book. Number 2½.

The third shock. The building was *there*. Jane reports E.M. went east, but even so, we know that's some sort of lie. Maybe it was strange I'd never tried to find this one venue, of all those in the Book I *had* tried to locate—and hadn't—except the rich landmarks like the New River apartment blocks (Clovis) and The Island (Egyptia). Though even there, I had never discovered their exact flats. Aside from anything else, general surveillance and security around such residences would begin to question me as soon as I walked in a lobby, or, as with The Island, the instant I stepped off the ferry.

But Electronic Metals had been here originally, and the site still was. Its neon name remained, too, slightly rusted and askew, probably not working. E.M. was one of those identities Jane had never disguised. Why would she? At the time a lot of people knew about super-robots like Silver, and just who had manufactured them.

I loitered by the gate, which was still securely locked with a device that shrilled *This firm has moved!* everytime I approached too close.

Squinting in through holes in the securomesh, I saw a drab, glass-sprayed frontage. The spray glass had cracked. Weeds stood tall along the yard and out of holes in the walls. In a way it was odd the lock message had been left there, or that its mechanical voice bothered to insist on the obvious.

The sun moved over. Hot purple shadows spread between the buildings. I was turning away, when a man emerged abruptly out of a sort of shed I hadn't noticed near the gate.

"You been here awhile," he said. "What d'ya want?"

Honesty/Loren, practiced liar, replied, "Well, I knew a woman who worked here. About twelve years back."

Always lie as near the truth as you can. I *had* known her—for about twenty minutes—that mad blonde on Compton.

"A lotta folk worked around here. Y'see any?"

"It was just—"

"They're gone. Made a pack of mistakes, these guys. Senate took the business over. Set 'em straight." I wondered why *this* guy lurked in a shed at the gate. As if he read my mind, he told me. "Used to work here myself. Deliveries. Now I get the job of keeping an eye out."

"But you've said they've all gone."

"Sure." He was a short, not-old old little man. Intently he watched the ground, as if expecting some creature to tunnel up out of it. "They done some funny things here. Guess you know, if you knew some dame worked here."

"She said . . ." I hesitated, *very* puzzled, "robots—like real people?"

"That was it. Was why the Senate stopped it. We had mobs here, screaming. Subsistence riots. You can't barely get no job—you wan' a robot get your job?"

There was no point in any more conversation. I smiled and said, "I'd better get going."

He had strange eyes, now that he lifted them, a kind of green, and clear for a man stuck in a shed by the gate of a deserted building.

"Ever hear of META?" he asked me.

"Meta—no."

"M-E-T-A, that is. Stands for Metals Extraordinary Trial Authority."

The purple shadow of a block across the way had almost covered us like a pavilion. In the encroaching shade, I saw the not-old old guy was now watching *me* intently, as if to see what would tunnel up.

"Never heard of it," I truthfully said.

"Not everyone has. Been an advert on the visuals today. That's META. They say they're bringing them back."

"Who?" asked Honesty/Loren, stupidly.

"The robots. Your friend here, what she do?"

"Oh, this and that."

"Ain't this city," he said. The shadow covered his face and his green eyes shone out of the darkness. Maybe it's only my beginnings in the costive hive of Grandfather, which makes me continually spot omens. "Just over the state border. Northward. Mountain country there."

"Sure," I said.

"That's where they are. META."

"Why tell me?"

"It ain't on no news yet."

"Then how do you know?"

He turned away. "I get thirsty," he said.

I gave him some coins. He took them. He said, "I had one once, when I——back then. I mean, I had one of the female robots. I mean, sex. A copper. That's Copper Optimum Pre-Programmed Electronic Robot. It was to make sure she functioned. Oh, boy. She surely did."

I took the chance. I said, "My friend did that."

He said, "You read that book, din'ya."

"Book?"

"You know what book. D'ya know the city I mean, where META is? They call it Second City now, since the Asteroid."

"Really?" I said. "Nice talking to you."

I walked quickly along the street. When I glanced back, he had vanished, perhaps only retreated into his hut, or rushed to some bar. The sky beat unkindly on the empty shell of Electronic Metals. I ran and caught the public flyer at South Arbor.

Danny gawked at me, stony as a gargoyle, while I recounted the story of a long-lost aunt who lay sick a few miles outside the state boundary. Finally he said, "Don't lie to me, Loren. You're a wee bitty good at it, but I know how you deal your hand. We take it as read. You wanna go someplace else."

"I need paying, Danny. Is that okay?"

"Fine. You've been a great asset. Maybe you'll come back."

"I will—yes, of course."

"Here." He put a wad of bills in front of me, and I stared at them.

"You've earned it," he said. "You never even hit me for dental expenses like the rest of them."

There was quite a lot of money there.

"I'll pay you back."

"And I'm a panda."

And so to the scene with Margoh. And so, much later, returning to the apartment in the bat-haunted block near the Old River and finding she'd taken my fur coat—but also left me, sneaked in among my few clothes as only a clever thief could do it, a pair of long-stem-heeled silver pumps. Silver. And exactly my size.

That sunset I caught the flyer far out of State. I'd had to stand in line about an hour to get my ticket. I had never been across any borders. But then, till I was twelve, I'd never gotten far from Grandfather's lair. Perhaps life is all and only truly that. Incarceration, breaking free. And then the next prison.

2

Angels walk upon the air,
Where the sunset doors unroll,
Seen in distance, striding fair:
Hair of fire and eyes lit coal,
Heartless fusion, flesh with soul,
Wings that rake the sky's wide bowl,
Flaming swords that pierce and tear.

• 1 •

It was a night flight to Second City, six hours.

Dawn was coming up when we flew in over a new wide landscape. All night, off and on, there had been splinterings of lights below. I'd seen them because I couldn't sleep, unlike most of the other passengers comatosely puffing and sighing around me. Now and then flyer masts gleamed up, too, like thin towers from some epic tale. But terrain hadn't been visible.

In dawnlight I received a sense of hugeness. I'd never seen much—any—open country before. The land looked rough and tumbled, chasms, ravines, plunging to glitter-threads of river. Trees clung in sprays on rocksides, or pointed up in the dark arrow shapes of pines. Then the sky cooled and clouds lifted off, and I saw, distant yet omnipresent, the skyscrapers of mountains. You could just make out, even in the last brass burst of summer, snow on their highest peaks.

After that we were in over the city, the unknown one, and my stomach lurched, and not only from our reducing speed.

I'd come here on a compulsive whim. What the hell was I going to do now?

At the flyer station we all lined up and traipsed through the border controls, some mechanical and some human. I began to think my temporary ID, legally bought before leaving, would have something wrong with it. But it didn't. They asked me why I was there.

"Chance of work," I said.

They didn't trouble about me after that. I could tell the guy who'd asked had concluded I was a hooker, useful anywhere.

Out on the flyer platform it was already hot. The alien city looked like any city, like the one I'd left last night.

Where was I headed? What was my plan?

I felt disoriented and anxious, but it was too late for that. And anyhow, you get used to knowing fear will rarely help, if you're one of the subsistence poor. I toted my bag, left the platform, and went and had a bagel.

And outside the café, when I re-emerged, was a visual giving the local news. I stood watching it, in case there was anything on it. Anything about him. But nothing was. And a voice in my head told me, Maybe that old man at E.M. lied. Or was nuts. How could I have been so sure the information from him was reliable? Because, I thought, it had made sense. META was some takeover from E.M., and here was one more senatorial, governmental, or big-business plot. . . .

I walked up through the city. Already I could see one of the better areas ahead. They had made that easy. It was a landmark, built up high and visible from the lower streets, and frosted with sparkle, just like those distant mountains. Was this what the crawling poor were meant to respect? It reminded me of a Heaven on a Hill, or castle, in reproduced Medieval pictures, a structure raised well above the peasant village that served it. And the peasants, along with gazing at this wondrous glory, would also have to watch out for marauding castle knights or chastising angels.

I climbed the sloping streets, the flights of stairs, and rode the moving ones, towards it.

At the base of Heaven lay a park of sculpted trees, fountains, flowers of incredible hothouse colors. Tame wildlife sprinted everywhere—squirrels, racoons, birds—not shy, running up to visitors to be fed. There were strollers there doing just that. But to the squirrel that weightlessly galloped up to me, I had to apologize, and it gave me quite a sniffy look before bolting up a tree.

Beyond this park expanded the shining goal I'd seen from below.

Domes like bubbles rested on milk-white walls, amid the smooth flash of polarized crystal. Behind the buildings the sky and the miles-off mountains, the real ones, fenced the horizon. The rest of the city lay far beneath.

There were high electric gates, but they stood open. Only a couple of robot patrollers were flitting up and down an avenue lined with blue cedars. A notice in dayneon gems by the gates read *Montis Heights*.

There was no point in barging through the inviting entrance. I'd be stopped fairly quickly, and interrogated as to why I was there, like in all those foyers by the New River.

Someone, though, was coming, walking *out* of Montis Heights and along the avenue to the gates, under the cool blue cedar trees. In alternating tree-shade and bright morning sun, I noted fluid tallness, a sheen like water. Silver, sapphire, and a burning deepest red.

Red hair. Skin like—

I forgot to breathe. A sort of blood-rush blanked my vision a moment. When it cleared, the figure was much nearer, only ten, twelve yards away. And I could see it wasn't—wasn't him. But it was—*one of his kind*.

... Silver's sister came through. Her auburn hair ... she looked at me, smiling. I knew what she'd say. "I'm Silver. That is S-I-L-V-E-R which stands for Silver Ionized Locomotive Verisimulated Electronic Robot."

The female figure moved like a dancer. Boneless and serpentine—and strong. The blood-red hair fell over one shoulder and down to her waist, strands of it powdered a hard, scorching gold. She wore a snake's garment, too, silver, like her skin, fronded over by violet jewels and coils of drops like rain or diamonds. Beauty? They invented the word just for her. For her and for her kind. Yeah, it *was* Heaven. Angels walked here.

And, as Jane described, this one was smiling, right at me.

And now she, too, had reached the gate of Heaven, the castle-in-the-clouds, but she was inside, and I was outside, and those few steps shut me out of Paradise forever.

"Hi," she said to me.

Idiotically I responded. "Hi."

"Were you wanting to come in?"

An Angel of the Portal. Or St. Peter. I shook my head, dumbest of the dumbest. Then the words opened my mouth and darted out. "Are you a silver?"

"Sure," she said. "My name's Glaya. Registration G. A. 2."

Her eyes were the color of emeralds under pale blue glass. That was different. Before, their eyes—all the silvers—had been amber. Her body was perfect, her legs long, her feet in high-heeled, high-strapped sandals, silver on gold—on silver.

Another difference. They hadn't limited her name, as had been done the first time. No, now she had a proper name. Glaya.

"If you would like to see more of me," she said, smiling, sensual and pleased, liking my interest, blossoming in it to ever greater unlikely heights of loveliness, "contact META and repeat my registration."

I said flatly, "I'm not M-B, actually. And anyhow, I wouldn't be able to afford you, would I?"

She flirted her eyes in a way you couldn't ignore, M-B or not. She said amicably, "Well, if anything changes there, maybe then. Have a sweet day."

And she flowed by me like a metals and jewelry stream, some edge of her clinging garment somehow brushing me, her perfume stroking my face like a caressing hand. Her finger- and toenails were, each one, the color of an individual fire.

I felt weak, as if I'd run twenty miles, or lain sick a long while.

One of the robot avenue patrollers had now slid to the gates.

"Who is here?" it asked.

"No one," I said.

"You have no business here?"

"No."

"Please descend to the lower level," it suggested.

My own suggestion was less urbane. "Please fuck yourself."

I saw the vispos that evening. They were all over the city, came out of nowhere, as adverts usually do. People were staring at them, or ignoring them. How *could* they have ignored them? The earth rocks and you are standing, clinging to the edge of nothing, and you don't notice at all? I guess that is life.

I recall the first vispo I ever saw in the other city, with the group, when I was about eight. Posters that sound and move, almost real. Samuel slapped me for looking.

Now the slap came again, but another kind.

I stood on a street and saw this pyrotechnic display rise like a phoenix out of the dusty lower city.

The experience of the century! META presents The Show. You know we have them—you know you can see them—even touch— Why wait? Face your future with META!

A woman appeared on the vis-screen. No, a *robot* appeared. Not Glaya, who was a silver. This was a copper, with skin like creamy electric sunfall, and hair like wheat. She wore a snakeskin of topaz and amethyst, and was smiling her ice-white teeth. She imitated a singing bird, trills of liquid strangeness—a canary? A man took her place, golden skinned, black-haired. He was an acrobat, turning the most unbelievable cartwheels in midair. He had green eyes. And behind him another man arrived, black as jet—a new range, as a banner across the screen told me, asterion metal, from the Asteroid itself—his hair was black also, but long and plaited with gold, and his eyes were rimmed with gold, and he was dressed in black scales. And there was a woman of black asterion, in transparent white, standing, it seemed, in fire that the man had somehow conjured for her. And then a man with silver skin, with amber eyes, with burgundy hair. They had all spoken or sung or fluently called something, or moved in some unexpected and marvelous contortion.... This one, the silver one, was playing a mandolin, softly singing a descant to the music.

Near me, one of my fellow watchers said, "Are they machines?"

"No, just computer effects," said another voice. "It's some movie."

The little crowd was drifting away.

I stared up into the filmic eyes of the silver man. It was him. Or would I know? He wore a shirt like bright coins. Even through the visuality, his eyes seemed to see me.

Then the screen blinked and switched, and I was shown instead a huge car rampaging over desert. Another advertising vispo for another company.

Where was The Show? Had I grasped that? Yes. Some recreational public garden. META had organized it. META, the firm of the future we must face.

Had it been him? He was part of a range. Originally there had been three sets of three, hadn't there. In his set another male, a female. But now? They had extended the prototypes, changed them. A black range had been activated, asterion metal, to go with the golds, silvers, and coppers. And eye colors in some cases altered. Blue-green-eyed Glaya... Had she been in the vispo? Yes, I had seen her, but couldn't recapture what she had done.... And a female gold, too—jumping high, spinning...

And already they were being hired out. For that was why Glaya had been on Montis Heights. Some rich female M-B client, or a rich straight man, wanting her.

Maybe they all... all of them... already.

They were all up for grabs. For *grabs*.

Now the other vispo was showing a new line in SOTA VLO's, the vehicles springing, with absurd weightlessness, out of a cornfield, above which halifropters chugged and buzzed like flies.

The apartment house on West Larch was like a million others, but it had a veranda out front, which was strung with pink neon lamps. In the dusk, my fellow house-residents sat about there and eyed me like hyenas.

They gazed even more dangerously when I emerged again an hour later.

I had used the tenants-only house-shower, where all the stalls were empty that evening. I'd washed my hair. I had a single "good" dress, found in a third-owner store one evening of extravagance a year ago. It was white Egyptian silk, or so the label said, shot with faint flakes of gilt. I'd gone without dinner for two weeks to make up the money. Never knew why I bought it, as if, in the end, there would be a reason. It clung, the dress, just right, not tightly but *describingly*, and it was sleeveless and low of neck, and the hem—because short dresses are in—was just above the knee. And there were the silver shoes Margoh had given me, too. I was made-up, all my twenty nails painted palest coffine. And my hair hung down my back.

One thing I hadn't done. I hadn't read any of Jane's Book. I remember Grandfather, always with a little pocket Bible. We only got rationed bits of it, but he constantly read it to himself, poring over the tiny print with a magnifying glass that seemed to swell his red eye into that of some terrifying outer-space creature. Jane's Book was, I guess, like a Bible for me. Though I hadn't read it for years, it always went along with me. It was the first thing I'd take out in a new apartment, and *hide*. This time I'd worked a loose panel out of the back of the rickety closet, and put the Book, still in its waterproof overcoat, in there, held against the wall. Then I glued the panel into place. But I hadn't read a line. Hadn't even undone the cover.

Someone whistled, raucously approving, as I swung off down West Larch towards Main Boulevard.

It was full dark by then. The moon was up over Second City, faded by streetlamps, and the Asteroid was lurking in the east, the baleful eye of God's Destroying Angel.

They stopped running the subways after the first quakes, before I'd even been born. But Second City had an overland system.

I got on the train bound for Russia—struck by the European name of the district. That's where the public gardens were. The Show.

The car was full, standing room only. Were all these other people going *there*, just like me?

I stood rocking, holding onto the strap, watching lighted stations sizzle by, the train not bothering to stop now that it was full, and no one's coin in the machine had showed they wanted those places. In all this crowd, would I even be able to see any stage, let alone anyone on it?

The train's mechanism was noisy, but I caught snatches of talk around me.

"They banned them years ago, those things. Now it's been regularized. You can always tell one of them. Couldn't mistake it for anything human. They ain't ever allowed normal work."

"I saw the advert on the VS. Oh, I've been dreaming of him ever since."

"Me, too. I love the black guy—"

"Ain't no *guy*, you dope."

"Guess not."

"You're crazy. You wanna do *that*—with *that*?"

"They can do anything."

"They're built for entertainment and sex. But they're expensive."

"Two thousand I.M.U. for one half hour. So I heard."

Surreal.

Had Jane ever felt this way, lurched and pulled forward, part of a curious herd, towards this unobtainable yet obsessive Grail? But Jane wasn't me. She, I knew, was uncertain and timid, with a brave, steadfast core. I'm hard as nails, Jell-O on the *inside*, shivering away under the armor. Spineless, probably.

The motion of the overland train made me queasy, and I was glad when it stopped and we all got out.

The next bit reminded me of pilgrims in some Babel tract illustration, approaching a holy shrine, the way the great crowd I was now a tiny part of poured eagerly up the sloping street towards the powerfully lit walls of the

Katerina Gardens. The street illumination was all glowing beautifully here, not a single pole not working, and the wall-tops were garlanded with strings of lamps. Every so often a shower of colored rays frayed up into the air over the park. The crowd liked this. They were excited, their faces burnished gold, nearly metallic. I suppose mine was, too.

There were plenty of gates, all fitted with pay-boxes. It only cost ten to get in, which surprised me, but then, going on the volume of the crowd, both META and the Second City Senate were gulping in the loot. As for the rich, they wouldn't be here. They'd have had some private show.

The gardens rose in lawns and terraces, thick with huge trees successfully forced to size. The fire-rays feathered over, and now and then a trail of fireworks crackled their stitching up the sky.

I just went with the crowd, which seemed to know exactly where it was collectively going. I expected we'd eventually reach the highest point and crane over to the corresponding depths of some arena, a bowl of sound with the performance-area minuscule and far below. But instead, the ascent ended on a vast open plateau of short turf, raised like a table under the night. Distant as the rings of some other world, the vague glow of the city was visible at its edges.

Where was the stage?

Others were confused, too. I heard my own question asked aloud several times.

Someone said, "Only *one* stage *I* can see."

"Well, where?"

"Look up."

We looked. Up into the parallel black plain of night,

where the moon was, and the passing light-rays. Another firework opened a mimosa parasol, and silver stars rained harmlessly down.

When he shall die, take him and cut him out in little stars, and he will make the face of heaven so fine, that all the world will be in love with night....

A kind of soft roaring began in the crowd, peaked with isolated shrieks and cries.

I saw a movie once, not a visual, but one of the old celluloid kind. There was a scene where all these people stood on a mountain staring up and watching a glinting chandelier of an extraterrestrial ship sinking down to them from heaven. UFO's went out of favor about the time the Asteroid spoiled the idea of outer space, and everything else. This was like that film. Like people standing, waiting for a UFO. Or—waiting for the gods of the old mythologies to descend from the upper air.

The crowd's roaring anyway told you something was happening. Something was coming. As everyone did in the film, we all raised our heads, bent up our necks, and scanned the sky.

It was magical. Clever, cunning, manipulative. But still magical.

What was arriving was a golden raft that floated in from the east like a sunrise and crossed over the face of the moon and the inflamed eye of the Asteroid. I reckoned it was on wires, fixed high up to invisible masts, this raft. But it looked like a vessel from some supernatural sphere.

They were on it. Though at first high above, you could see them because of how they were lighted, how they were clothed, and how they *were*. Eight of them. Two golds, two coppers, two of the new asterion line, two silvers. Each set comprised one male and one female.

They were dressed, aside from the metallic carapaces of their skins, the long cascades of their flaming, smoldering hair, in second skins of gems, scales, sequins. They were like fabulous insects, and as they drew closer, you caught the radiance of their eyes, watching back at you.

God, how had I ever thought it credible to love a creature like this? Worship, yes, self-sacrifice—too likely. But not love. How can you love something so perfect you can scarcely bear to look at it? Like staring into the heart of the sun. You go blind.

But the crowd, eager always for sensation, for something other than the boring drudgery of reality, called and applauded.

My neck already ached from craning back at that angle. So what.

The raft sank lower, nearer. Now surely it would be possible, if you were very tall, to put a finger's tip against its underside.

I could see him. Silver. He stood above the low golden rail, looking down, his wonderful eyes moving over all of us, without any sign of demand, doubt, or dismay, only that nonhuman confidence that had no pride in its composition. His eyes were like malted fire. His long hair, thick, wavered as running water, garnet-red. He wore black blacker than any night.

It was the black asterions who wore red. I glimpsed them across the raft. I saw Glaya, too, wearing gold, tuning a lute long-necked as a swan. The two golden-skinned ones, in silver, stood first on their hands, motionless, then on *one finger* each, waving to us with their other arms, laughing, and in total equilibrium. The coppers were dressed in peacock green. They threw flowers to us all, but the flowers dissolved before anyone could catch them.

I saw him. I saw him as if everything else were only partly there, but he was more there than anything on earth had ever been.

His eyes passed over mine. I *felt* them—like a touch. Did he see me? A tall, slim, ordinary girl in third-hand white, with tawny skin and dark hair. Human. One more human, with eyes only for him and his kind.

Of course he didn't see me. But I felt, too, at his eyes' touch, my spirit drawn out of me and into his look, and as his (unseeing) eyes moved on, my spirit and I stayed adrift from each other.

The Show began soon after that.

I think they let loose a few authorized drugs over the park. There was a sultry incense smell that reminded me of those church services Grandfather had declared offices of the damned. And the rays crossing and recrossing, maybe they weren't only color and light.

The ache in my neck went away. It didn't matter, as I no longer had a body, only this adrift spirit, hung like flimsy washing from the rim of the raft.

They sang to us, and acted sudden dramas, fought, and played. There had been unconscionable improvements made to their skills, for now, it seemed, it was legally imperative that none of these creatures ever pass, even for a second, as human. And they didn't. They'd become magicians.

Of *course*, you couldn't for a moment mistake them for anything mortal—if they could do this—and *this* . . .

Jane said the coppers were actors. Now they acted with

more than mere apparent flair. Something in the voice boxes—the singers had this, too—you heard the words up there overhead, as the raft cruised up and down over the plateau of the park, but you heard them, too, as if they spoke inside your ear, for you alone. Such voices. Every word like a drop of light or darkness. But there was more. What the coppers acted was an old play, I don't know from where—ancient Greek, maybe? She and he—as they stepped forward, they changed. I mean, their clothes changed, in front of our eyes.

Their green panoply had been modern. But suddenly her breasts were bare, exquisite copper half-globes tipped with red buds. She wore a flounced metal skirt, dull gold, and in her flowing lemon hair, snakes were plaited. All this happened meltingly, unassisted, and unobscurely, as we all watched. The copper male had also changed his garments to a kilt of metal scales, his arms bound with bronze rings, a crown of some sort of pale flower on his yellow hair.

The flowers, the metal and clothing, had *emanated* from their nonfleshly flesh, replacing the original clothing, which had melted into nothing.

The audience applauded this magical action as much as they did the subsequent drama, a brief, weird exchange, sexual and disturbing, yet unexplicit.

After the coppers, the silvers sang and played instruments. Quake-rock was what the silvers gave us. One-handed, he slammed rhythm from a drum, and it sounded like two drummers, four hands. She sang, her range incredible, unassailable, thin, almost whistling notes dropping to a dark purr in the lower registers. But she also had two voices. And next her second voice sang a harmony to her first.

Then he played the flute. He did it this way: placing the flute almost sexually between his lips, then taking up the lute Glaya had tuned for him. As with the drum, he played the lute one-handed, and it had a sound as if three hands were on it, his fingers a silvery blur. The lute also raced in quake-rock, but the flute he played more classically, its slender tones silking over the lute's galloping, as he held the flute in his white teeth, somehow working it with his tongue.... All the while, his *other* hand still beat sharp thunders from the drum.

After the coppers and silvers, the golds fenced. He and she. They leapt yards upwards, somersaulted and spun in the air, sprang up cliffs of nothingness and catapulted back. But again, more than this.

The golds had two fencing swords, which *had slid out from their arms.* I mean, out of the muscle and the skin of them. Obviously it wasn't muscle and skin, but it looked as if it were, and the swords were simply—*born* out of it. And when they had grown all the way out, they sheered off, soft as snow, forming their shapes as they went, hardening, to nestle, flexed and inimitable, in the hands of what had birthed them.

No. Humans couldn't do this. No one could mistake one of these for anything human ever again.

(I put this down as if I had lost sight of him, forgotten him. I hadn't. I saw him, as if I saw him through their bodies. But I saw all the rest, and what they did. They were all one thing, the eight beings on the raft. And even though right then I didn't know it, to love him now was to be in thrall to each and everyone of them.)

Last were the asterions. We were to see why. She stepped forward, and became altogether something else.

Like the double voices, triple playing, extraction of clothes and weapons, but again, more than that.

The crowd in the hot night garden, in the district called Russia, made a low, primal noise.

The black woman had become, literally, a pillar of black glass. Obsidian. You could really see through her. At the pillar's top, her lovely face, classic African, but still, and also glass, also semitransparent. *Only her eyes moved*. Other galaxies danced, slow and calm, in those eyes.

But then he, the asterion man, he—

The crowd shrieked in five thousand voices—pleasure and thrill, or terror?

Did I shriek, too?

I couldn't hear if I screamed, couldn't hear my heart. Perhaps I was dead. Perhaps we all were, and that wouldn't be a problem now, for here the new race was. God had given up on flesh and blood. He wouldn't fuss with a flood now, no ultimate apocalyptic quake. Now God had just made *robots*.

There in full view of every one of us, the asterion male changed into a dragon. He was the prehistoric demon of our dreams. Scaled and sheened and glorious, and terrible, gold-washed over jet, towering and coiling there with its head against the sky, suns streaming in its glances, fire glinting far back in its jaws.

How excellently judged.

The crowd on the brink of panic, swirling, ready to stampede (How many would die?), and all at once, everything again altered, as if some switch had been thrown inside the vast machine of the night.

No dragon. No pillar. No miracles. All gone.

Had it been an illusion? Had we collectively imagined everything we'd seen?

A kind of cooling spray of no-fire fireworks were softly detonating over our heads.

The beings from Olympus smiled upon us, all now formed in our image, only so much better.

I thought, *Drugs—that's what made it seem like that—even a robot can't...*

Normalcy was being made to break out. Not only the pretty lights, but warm rain was raining down. The crowd, contained again, scattering about, defused, giggling.

Had they made the rain, too, whoever *they* were, these people who had acted God, and called it The Show?

Pushing, the crowd forced me back, and I saw through the rainy, fiery air, the golden raft-boat of God-made gods flying low and away over the park. Nearly two hours had gone by. It had seemed much less. Much more.

Someone else bumped into me from behind. This time a firm hand steadied me.

"*Quelle joie*. This is all going a bit out of control," he said. "I thought it might."

I half-turned. I didn't know him. Then I did.

"You are getting so wet," he observed sympathetically. "And in your attractive dress. Are you with someone?"

"No," I said.

"Well," he said kindly, under the racket of the crowd, "perhaps I can amend that."

He was the guy from the visual I'd seen back in the city, on the blonde's VS. The guy with the actor's voice, who had helped advertise META and all META's works.

"My name's Sharffe."
"Loren."
"Pleased to acquaint *avec toi, ma chère*."

I don't run to much French, but got the gist. It seemed he liked me somewhat.

We had already moved out of the worst crush, he weaving us with the knack of practice through the wet but now partying crowd, upon which little painted balloons with cans of alcohol and bags of chocolate-type candy attached, were coming down in the rain. "All free gifts courtesy of META," he told me. "Do you want any of those?" I said, "Maybe not." "A woman of taste," he decided. By then we'd reached a stand of big trees and he drew me under. There was a dim-lit mesh wall with a small gate. It only looked like some private maintenance area of the gardens. Sharffe unlocked the gate by winking one eye at it. It's true, plenty of people are partly *robot,* at least among the tech-protected plutocracy. He must have an eye-code booster override built in somewhere, which gives him, as it were, the keys to the city, or some of them.

The other side of the gate was a gravel path. And then a steel-brick wall. A door opened for him in this wall, too. We went through to a lot with several large cars exclusively parked.

"Mine's that one," he said.

I looked at his car. It was a reverse auto self-drive Orinoco Prax, glimmering gold like nail polish... or a G.O.L.D. E.R. robot.

Drunk on possible hallucinogens and desolate, unnameable emotions, Loren the Liar looked dewily from her (actually) mad eyes and told him, "What a beautiful car."

The rain didn't fall so fiercely here. Either there was a partial shield up over the lot, or the storm was ebbing. I glanced at him, and away. He was definitely the one from the VS news. And he was here at The Show, seemed to know all about it, and to be wealthy enough to own this vulgar vehicle.

"Shall I take you for a drive?" he asked me, winningly, aware he was quite young and sort of handsome, as well as stinking rich.

"Why me?" I innocently asked.

"Oh, I was watching you from the control center back there. We were supposed to be monitoring not only how our team performed but also the crowd, to gauge reactions, that kind of thing. But then I spotted *you*. I had my eyes on you quite a bit after that. Did you enjoy them, the team? What did you think?"

The team. He meant the robots. The gods.

"They were spectacular."

"Good. That's exactly the reaction we want."

We walked over to the Orinoco. God, the seats were white fake fur; they'd be soft as toy Siberian tigers.

"Come for a drive," he said. "Then dinner? I'm quite in love with you, Loren, you know—*amour fou, coup de foudre*—all of that. It can happen. Or don't intelligent young women like you believe in that—love at first sight?"

"Yes," I said.

"*Quelle joie.* Get in. The seats are fun. You sink for miles. Fur's real, by the way. Don't tell anyone."

He could have been a psychopath. And I suppose he is, really. But in this instance, he seemed just some man pleased with himself and expecting a bonus from his bosses, therefore sexed-up and eager to take any nice-looking, half-okay pleb to bed.

How did he think anyone would look at him after—*them*?

How could *he* look at a woman, after *them*? Well, the car-seat fur was real. Maybe that explained quite a bit.

I didn't hesitate, or only long enough to fuel his fire.

I'd never been a professional, a prostitute. I had sex randomly because I wanted to, and earned cash by work. Of course, it wasn't cash I was after now.

Though the fur was real, it had been carefully treated and didn't mind my wet dress or the drops he shook off his tailored one-piece suit. The light jacket, shirt and pants combo were all linked by zippers, whose metal was solid silver. (Silver.) He also had a diamond ring, a rock, polished, not cut. But it might have been a cultured diamond, after all, never mined.

The ghastly car ripped through the city like a missile. It went so fast I couldn't see anything, except in the distance—humps of architecture, veiled heights, and garish city valleys. On the horizon, the ghosts of mountains were drawn in by their edges of moonlit snow. It had stopped raining—if it had ever started, out here.

I itched and howled to ask him questions about the robots. I kept quiet. Almost certainly he'd start to gabble, if not now, then if we got to the dinner date.

There were a lot of parks, especially in the district called Russia, and the next one over called Bohemia. "Used to be a Romania, too, once," he said. "Burnt down—power main blew."

I wondered if he'd just pull over and begin mauling me. But he didn't. He was high as that moon. Who's a clever boy, then?

He was ready to muse aloud by the time we were nearing

some out-of-town restaurant he knew of. He abruptly switched the car to auto, and sat back.

"It's been quite a month, I can tell you, getting The Show ready. Advance publicity and so on. Then the performad—jargon, I mean the advertising performance tonight. Everyone seemed to like it, didn't they? There was all that talk before—people getting scared robots'd take over all the available work—but that's never been what they're for. I take it you know all this was already tried, twelve years back?"

I looked vague. "I was only a kid then."

"Sure. *Mais naturellement.* Just a little girl, five or six. You must tell me all about that—" But he didn't pause, so I didn't have to. "You see, they are purely recreational, these robots. The first outfit, E.M., they did the whole damn thing all wrong. Then had to recall every single model. There were nine of them. I think I have that right. . . . Nine deluxe, plus some cute semi-humanoid stuff—nothing astounding there, boxes with humanized heads, that kind of junk. We only have eight deluxe models now. Four men. Four gals. Neat."

"Oh, yes."

"Which was your favorite at the performad?" he asked me suddenly, turning his face hard as the edge of a blade towards me. No fool, then. Or not the sort you could necessarily handle.

"I kind of liked the asterions best."

"Yeah! Aren't *they* divine. Shape-changers. Like magicians in old novels. But I'll tell you, they can *all* do that, to a limited extent. You saw the golds produce weaponry out of their arms and hands? They can do that all over, even out the chest cavity, or the skull. And the coppers altered their clothes out in plain view. But you see, again, they can *all* do that—alter clothing, produce weapons. I hasten to add, in case I'm scaring you, they can produce nothing in the weapon line that actually can work, except for the purposes of display. No chance of firing off a real gun at anybody, or throwing a knife. They just can't do that. Back with E.M., the golds were marketed as bodyguards. No one's going to allow that now. To take any sort of work away from real people is off the menu." He cogitated, looking abruptly middle-aged and smug. He probably was, just had access to plenty of Rejuvinex. The car swam slower now down a side track, curtained by pines. "But tell me," he said, gazing away through the windshield, "what did you think of the silvers?"

Specific. He knows something. But what? And how can he? I said, "They were wonderful."

"The male," he said. "What did you think of *him*?"

"Gorgeous," I said.

"But I forgot, you liked the asterion male best, didn't you?"

I simpered. I suppose that was what it was.

"Yeah," said Sharffe. "You ain't alone there. They are one heck of a big hit, those two. Have to admit that. But the reason I asked about the silvers, especially the male—" (Yes, what *is* your reason, Mr. Sharffe?) "Well, he has kind of a personal history. Not the others, only that one. He's called Verlis, by the way."

Something jumped in my brain. *No—he's called Silver.* I didn't say a word. And the name Verlis slipped across my inner eye until its letters repositioned. Verlis was an anagram of Silver.

Sharffe said, "What we did there, we reforged from the

original model. He was first made, and extant, over twelve years ago, and though the other eight basically got smelted down for scrap, the company didn't do that with him. There was something about Verlis that had never checked out. They dismantled him, but still kept on trying to find what it was that made him tick differently. Didn't manage to. And then they just kept him in store. So when META took over the commission, we broke him out first and rebuilt him. He's the same model, like he was back then. With, of course, the latest improvements the others have. I personally never see anything that weird about him. He's just like the others, for my money. Too handsome to live, and he don't live, *ma chère*. So that's okay."

Up ahead, the pines withdrew about a gracious lawn, above which stood a type of Roman temple, its façade bearing the legend *O'Pine*.

"Hey," said my happy escort, "how do you rate that name?"

"They're Irish?"

"Oh, Loren, I thought you'd see the pun." He explained to me: restaurant in pine forest and the word opine—to hope. I pretended I hadn't gotten any of that till he said it.

As we were defurring out of the car, he turned to me and said in a hoarse aside, *"Jaybeeh."*

"Excuse me?"

"Jaybeeh. You don't know. Sure you don't?"

"What is it? Somewhere to eat?"

"Maybe," he said, amused. We walked up the steps to the doors.

Over my mind the new sound *Jaybeeh* floated. He had uttered it like a password. In some quarters it was. On the top step, the sound translated in my head to symbols. He had spoken the phonetic of the two letters J-B. *Jane's Book*. I nearly missed the last step, but didn't. Gambled he'd make nothing of it.

I have absolutely no recollection of what we ate. We drank wine with the meal, and liqueurs at the end. We talked about him, I generally think. But I can't recall much of what he had to say, only those parts about working for META. And that was fairly guarded. This work, plainly, was Senate-sponsored, if not directly government-sponsored. He would keep saying, coyly, "Ah, but I can't blab about that. Top secret. Commercial spies are everywhere. Do you realize how many other countries are trying to perfect these things? And not all of them, I may add, for peaceful purposes."

He said nothing targeted again about the silvers. But he did tell me all the robots' new names. The silvers were Verlis and Glaya; the coppers, Copperfield and Sheena; the golds, Goldhawk and Kix; and the asterions, Black Chess and Irisa. It struck me that every one of the males carried a reference in his name to his metal, even Verlis in anagram. The females did not.

After the meal we left and got back in the car. He switched on the auto at once, saying he'd been drinking a lot. Deep in the fur, we drove off the beaten track and in among the pines, then he put his arm around me, and I thought, This is it, now. This is where I perform my role. So I cuddled up, and when he kissed me, I played along.

I'd never before had sex with anyone I didn't fancy. I'd been lucky there. The few who tried that I hadn't wanted, had been easy to put off with words or deeds—like the guy I kicked that time in the underpass, as it were.

But Sharffe was ultrahygienic and unnervingly presentable, and I wouldn't even need protection. The ones who can afford it take their contraception shots by law.

Nevertheless, when he leaned back from me, his hand still on my breast but both of us still clothed, and not even at first base, I felt a wave of shattering relief.

"Hey, *Loren, ma petite chère,* you really like human men, too, don't you, *n'est-ce pas?*"

"How did you guess?"

"Mmm. Sometime soon we must entirely investigate this. But for now——" What had I done wrong? He wasn't going to dump me, was he? The next installment of relief cascaded as he said, "I think you should come to the party tonight."

"Party?"

"It's a good one, baby. Gargantuan apartment, gold-plated everything, and champagne flowing like piss. Up on the top of the city. Montis Heights. Heard of it?"

As we drove on, he asked me what birth sign I was.

"Scorpio."

"Oh, my. I should have known from your eyes."

• 2 •

Above, in the city half-dark, the apartment domes were golden or milky indigo or translucent scarlet spaceships, resting on snow-walls softly stained with revolving rainbows.

The park below was lamplighted to a blazing green fire, and birds sang wildly in the trees. ("They never get to sleep," Sharffe remarked, "think it's day all the time.") A racoon had bounded onto the car roof and off, its natural fur shining like—silver.

He hadn't exaggerated about the apartment. He *winked* us in, like he had at the gates in Russia, and then we stepped into an outside elevator made of frost-patterned glass. Rising up and up, we reached a dome like a damson's heart. The city lay below, like all the kingdoms of the world.

There was a roof terrace garden, running all around the dome. A round door undid itself, glass into glass. He looked peculiar in the magenta light inside. No doubt we both did. I know my dress looked cheap in it.

The corridor was tiled in veined black marble. That is, real marble, nothing fake. "From Italy," he told me, waving at the walls. I'd have hated him if I'd had time, but I hadn't, and my heart was going for a drum solo in virtuoso rapid tempo. Then we were at the next door, trimmed and paneled in white marble and gold. I think he said the gold was forty carats, and the door was opened, not by automatics, but two sort of butlers in Victorian gear. And my heart was lost in the tumult of quake-rock.

All the rooms were lit in different colors. There were plenty of colors/rooms. The foyer was pink. The next room yellow like wine, and the next red like wine. Then we went through an iceberg-blue conservatory, crowded by plants and by people, as the other rooms had been. Then the biggest room yet was in front of us, coolest gold—in fact, only the best sort of panelectric light, but spilling from crystal fixtures in the domed ceiling and marble walls. Everywhere were champagne fountains; you know, the thing where the drink sprays from the bottle and pours down and over to fill a pyramid of goblets. But here it just kept pouring down endlessly from inexhaustible "bottles," over the goblets, splashing on, sparkling, into basins of marble so white it ached.

I said there were people everywhere. Sharffe greeted lots of them with cheery intimacy. I noted randomly that not all of them responded.

In the champagne room people were dancing the Chaste, the two-together dance where you keep both your upper bodies plastered on each other by sheer ability or determination, not touching with hands or arms.

I stared at this. Maybe I was a little drunk from the previous wine and liqueurs, or the pine forest, or even the sharp, airborne fizzle of excessive champagne—but I had one of those revelations they say kids get. I watched all these people dancing the Chaste, and suddenly I saw them as if I were an alien from another planet, the kind that's a giant ant, or an amoeba, something like that. Because I could see how foreign, in turn, it was, to have this shape—a head and neck and torso, two arms, two legs—all that, strange to me, as if I were of quite another kind.

And then, through the alien humans, I glimpsed a silky furl of wheat-gold, and a shiver of shoulders and arms with highlights that were molten. Coppery Sheena was dancing with a human man, keeping their bodies supernaturally adhered, their legs and arms quite free. Her dress now was short, primrose satin.

And Black Chess was there, also dancing in flawless connection with a woman whose eyes were lambent, hypnotized, gazing into his—where a dragon lay, waiting.

And Glaya, in jade spirals, danced with another woman, breast to breast.

"Now, Loren," said Sharffe. Someone was there, a smiling human alien, with a tray of champagne tinted like strawberries. Obedient, I took one of the tall thin goblets. "Come with me," said Sharffe.

We walked out across the floor. I thought he was going to dance the Chaste with me. I decided he'd be a rotten dancer.

No, I didn't think we'd dance.

I knew what it was. I'd known since he said that password to me. *Jaybeeh.*

"*Here* you are. How are you doing?"

Sharffe spoke not even self-consciously. He was actor-exact again, and practiced. He addressed the figure as if he approached a fellow mortal—friendly, if not quite a friend.

And the man, who had not been dancing but standing there by one long window, looking down to the forgotten kingdoms of the world . . . this man, who wasn't alien, but much more, since he was an angel—he turned to look at us. His clothes were white as ice. His red hair was longer than it had been earlier. It ran right down his back. He smiled. Calm as silence.

"Hallo, Sharffe," he said. He looked, then, at me.

He was about half a foot taller. I'm quite tall, you see.

His eyes were like . . .

I stood, looking up at him.

Sharffe said, pleased to introduce us, "Verlis, this is Loren. Why don't you two dance awhile? The floor's great, they tell me. I just have to find somebody—business, always business. Okay? See you, Loren. Soon."

His eyes—I have to know what his eyes are *like*. I have to compare them to something I can recognize.

Her words flood through me, (Jane's written paragraphs):

His eyes were like two russet stars. Yes... exactly like stars. And his skin seemed only pale, as if there were an actor's makeup on it.... It was silver... that flushed into almost natural shadings and colors against the bones, the lips, the nails. But silver. Silver.

He was Silver.

"Would you like to dance with me?" he asked.

My lips parted. No sound came out.

His eyes were not stars. They were suns. I couldn't look into them; they'd blind me. I couldn't look away.

"You're not afraid of me, are you?" he asked softly. Under the racket of the quake-rock, where almost everyone was shouting that wanted to be heard, his adapted voice entered my hearing with the politest, most musical intimacy.

"Yes," I said. "Shouldn't I be?"

"Not at all. Really, I'm not that bad a dancer."

I laughed. It was bitter and rasped my throat. He could see I wasn't tickled by his irony. That I didn't want to play that he was only a man.

He said, "I apologize for Sharffe. He should have found out first whether or not you wanted to try this."

"Why wouldn't I?"

"Many reasons. But I'm sure you're the best judge."

I said, finding my voice properly at last, tempering it, "And of course, *you* want to dance with *me*."

"Of course."

I was speaking, so nearly, Jane's dialogue. Some figment of me said, "Don't you remember?"

His smile now was quizzical, beautiful. Unfazed. "I have memories, yes."

But I reckoned I couldn't say the rest to him. How *could*

I? I'd have burned alive, spontaneous human combustion, from shame.

After a moment he moved forward, and his body touched against mine, though not his hands or arms. I, the automaton, and he, the angel, began to dance, reflexively, because what else was there to do?

You are so close, self-evidently, in this dance. His breath was occasional and clean on my face. He breathed as a dancer would, as if he had to breathe. His body on mine felt firm and coordinated, amorous yet decorous. And humanly *warm*—surely an innovation. He smelled, too, of cleanness and health, and some unidentifiable male scent ... and sex. Just as Jane described. But his hair had a scent of pine forests.

His lashes were thick and long, dark cinnamon—do you recall what she said?

Nothing can be so beautiful and live.

And, as Sharffe had delightedly announced, Silver—Verlis—didn't live, so that was okay.

"You dance well," he said.

"Thank you. Yes, I can dance."

He'd died. They'd killed him. Now he had risen from the dead. Oh, not like Christ raised Lazarus. And ... even Christ had become a *human* man.

My body against this body. I couldn't think anymore. I wanted to fall unconscious against him, and let the sea wash in, the tidal rollers of pleasure and oblivion.

Something happened—what? He had taken my hand. He led me aside, and the window opened—he, like Sharffe (more than Sharffe ever could), would be able to undo any door, even without knocking on it.

We were outside, standing on the area of another roof

terrace. Way up, the magenta bubble, and behind us the champagne light, and below, the neon world.

"Loren," he said. "I like your name."

"Verlis," I said, "why have they altered yours?"

"Didn't you alter your own?" he asked me.

Something like a thin spear dashed through me.

"How would you know that? Can you read minds?"

He said, "But it's very usual, to change your name, isn't it, with—"

"With human beings? Yes, maybe."

"You don't trust me," he said. "The idea is very much that you can."

"Because you're *not* human?"

"Of course."

"A machine."

He shrugged. "A new sort of machine, Loren."

"Stop saying my name."

He lifted my hand to his lips. Brushed my fingers with his mouth. "Again, I apologize. What would you prefer to do? He'll cause trouble for you, will he, Sharffe, if you don't go on with this?"

Even in my bewilderment at his talking to me like this, one human to another—crazy, though inevitable, for I knew his beginnings, that this was what he did the best, that is, *be* human—I finally understood something else.

No, I wasn't to be Jane, was I. It was the other one *I* was being. The blonde on Compton Street. My God, I was to be one of the ones who were the guinea pigs.

"I'm meant to fuck you," I said. "Right?"

"I'm afraid so. But we can always pretend."

"You can *lie* to them?" I asked.

"Yes, about something like that. My goal isn't to distress

or harm you. I know they're keen, but I've already had two partners. They've seen I work." He raised one eyebrow at me. "But if not doing what they expect will provoke problems for you, maybe we should act as if we're both doing precisely what they'd like."

"Wouldn't they be tracking us—somehow watch us—"

"Not exactly. It's nothing so basic as surveillance. The physical responses I can program and register in myself. Enough to convince them. And then you just tell them I am—"

"The ultimate demon lover."

"Yes. Because, without at all deserving to be, I am."

"I know you are. And autonomous, it seems. How can *that* be?"

"It's fundamental stuff. I need to be autonomous to some extent. Or how could I operate?"

"So we slip off someplace, make out we rutted like rabbits, and you provide some process so they believe we did."

"That's it. Would you prefer that?"

"What would *you* prefer?"

Light in his eyes. Suns rose within suns. No protest from him now, like to Jane: No one asks a robot what he wants. "I'd prefer to make love with you."

"Why's that?"

"I like sex. Probably not quite in the way humans do, or for quite the same reasons."

"I like sex with men."

He nodded. "That reaction is the one they might need to know about. Or else they can't test how worthwhile this team will be."

"This team—is *you*."

"All eight of us."

"Has anyone else been reluctant?"

"One or two."

"I'd better be truthful, then, hadn't I?"

Without warning he moved towards me. He set his hands weightlessly on my shoulders. He lowered his face to mine. His mane of hair, like thick smoke on fire, tented us in . . . exactly as she told us.

"Maybe, Loren, just in case, we should make sure that this is really hopeless."

Is he kissing me? His mouth is on mine? It's as if—

I fell through space, or through the world, deep down. Through earth and sea and galaxies. I wasn't frightened. It was all I wanted.

Had I never in my life before ever fully let go of myself? Is *this* letting go—of *self* ?

It lasted seconds, years.

The kiss hadn't been intrusive. Just his mouth on my mouth.

I hadn't even taken hold of him. Now I did. Under my palms, the smooth leopard muscles of his back. My eyes were shut. He held me there, the kiss over, held me as I went on falling through outer space.

"I think, perhaps?" he said against my closed eyes.

"Where are we to go?" I heard the Loren voice ask.

"There are private rooms here."

"Must it be here?"

"No. We can go anywhere you'd like."

He's a slave. Tethered like a dog. It's merely that the chain will stretch to infinity, until they want to pull him back to them.

"I have a room," I said. "Downtown."

My eyes didn't open. I thought of Jane and the coat-of-many-colors carpeted apartment on Tolerance, which I'd never found, never could find, as Tolerance hadn't been its real name.

"Let's go, then," he said. "Only, you may need to see your way. Open your eyes, Loren."

I opened my eyes. He took my hand once more, like any captivated new lover. We walked steadily out of the champagne room, and the azure conservatory, the rooms of red wine and white wine, and the sugar-pink foyer, where the two butlers, not needing to, whisked wide the white-and-gold double doors.

No one gazed at us or communicated with us, tried to encourage or prevent us. We were just one more couple who'd made the right connection, off to fornicate and be glad.

Because I had no car, we took a late-night flyer. There were people on the flyer, up in the glass pumpkin with us, sad workers going in to deathly jobs they must struggle to retain, tired girls who had been out hooking. Someone muttered behind us, "See him? It's one of the actors off the vispos. Why does *he* need to take a flyer? Slumming. Bastard."

Silver put his arm around me, that was all. No one came up to start a fight.

(I wondered what he would do if they did? Magic a gun out of his arm and threaten them? How far did that slave's autonomy stretch? To what level, in the matter of defense, could he, or any of them, go?)

Certainly, it wasn't like it had been with Jane, those twelve years ago. This time he couldn't pass anywhere as mortal. That really wasn't allowed anymore.

It was almost light when we walked along West Larch to the apartment house. The distant mountains were reappearing from the dark.

What did I feel? Bodiless. Like I wasn't there.

How *could* I be there? This was a dream.

The key I'd been given didn't work. This wasn't a chipped or electronic door, but obviously somebody bolted it after one or two A.M. Anyone out later than that had to kick their heels on the veranda.

But he put his hand over the lock, then the edges of the door. I heard a faint sliding inside—the lock unkeying, the bolts going home into their sockets.

You couldn't keep him out, then. Or, presumably, any of them. I said, "Isn't that illegal?"

"No. We're only authorized to use key-coding to assist a human companion."

"Suppose the human companion just happens to be a thief or murderer?"

He shook his head. "No one gets use of us who is anything like those. All customers are carefully checked."

We went into the dim predawn building. He walked quietly up the stairs behind me. There were four flights. He could, I thought, equally noiselessly have raced up all four at a hundred miles an hour.

We went into my flat. As I let up the skimpy blind, he looked around him, like any unexceptional visitor. "You haven't been here long."

"How do you know?" I was only curious, not surprised.

He said, "This room has no smell of you."

Jane:

He said, "What perfume have you got on?" "Nothing . . ." "Then it must be you." "Human flesh must seem disgusting to you, if you can smell us." "Extremely seductive . . ."

And I heard myself say, defensively, "Human habitations have a human stench, do you mean?"

And Silver-who-was-Verlis said, "Sometimes. But that isn't what I mean. You have your own unique personal perfume. You, Loren, smell good. Young, fresh, and alluring. This room would smell of that, if you'd been here more than forty-eight hours."

"What if I smoke a lot of cigarines?"

"Then of you, plus a lot of cigarines."

I stood by the window looking back at him. He seemed in no hurry—how much time was allowed us for this test-situation carnal act?

"I'm quite experienced," I said. Also defensive?

"Yes, Loren—I've been using your name again; are you okay with that? Thank you. You see, they were overviewing the whole crowd in the gardens for suitable candidates. Then they activated, in each case, a quick scan. You know this can be done?"

"I thought it was prohibited, except for the police, military, and hospitals."

"Sure. META is affiliated to those first two, being Senate-sponsored. However, let me reassure you, by law they have to destroy any scan the moment they've seen the data."

"What did it say?"

"They didn't tell me. One moment."

I watched him—he wasn't thinking, although it looked like that. He was running some computerized result across some inner mind-screen.

"If you can read it over," I said, "then it hasn't been deleted, has it?"

"Yes," he said. "But I can still read it."

"How?"

"Machine to machine, Loren. Simple as that."

"What did it say?" I demanded again.

He said, "Age approximately seventeen. Healthy and reasonably well-nourished. Non-intacta and sexually active. No sign of disease, terminations, or pregnancies. A couple of other comments. Those are less physical than technical."

I lowered my eyes.

He said, "So you are experienced and fit, which I'd be able to guess anyway, wouldn't I, since they picked you? But you're still very nervous."

"You noticed."

"Perhaps I would expect you to be. You seem also intelligent and imaginative, and unease tends to come with both those territories."

"But not for you, of course."

"*Unease?* No. Never for me."

"Fearless," I said. "Omnipotent. Perfect."

"And eager," he said, "to please."

Something in his voice—what was it—irony—or something stronger and more loaded?

I walked across the room and stood in front of him. Did I even believe we were together?

"Listen," I said, "I have— I want to say one more thing."

"Of course."

Gentle. His eyes interested and amused. Tender. A lover's eyes. A friend's.

I wet my lips and said the name, like one bead of water falling into the light. "Jane."

Only one reaction. Slowly his face became serious and

intent. He responded, but only by repeating that single name again. "Jane." No question. No reply.

"Yes. Jane. Do you recollect Jane?"

"I have memories. I told you that soon after we met."

"Memories of Jane."

"Among other people and events, I have memories of Jane."

"Among other—but she," I said, "she was more than simply *people and events*. Wasn't she? I thought she was—" I'd been convinced I'd be ashamed to say it. Now, though, there was passion, outrage in my voice that startled me. Let's be honest. I'd meant to have him. Yes, even though it would make Sharffe and META happy. And yet—

He said, "There was a book written, I believe. Maybe you read it? If you did, Loren, I have to say to you that sometimes one person's view of events is at variance with what someone else, whether human or not, may or may not have seen, experienced, or concluded."

"Are you telling me—"

"I'm telling you that those things belong in another life. And that, just possibly, what Jane innocently wrote in her book wasn't entirely either what anyone else supposed had happened, or what in fact *did* happen. The one she thought she knew as Silver—isn't necessarily who I am."

A surge of actual nausea punched through my guts. Perhaps you will feel it, too.

I scrabbled at my thoughts. Was he saying to me that Jane had *invented* it, her colossal, luminous love of him— worse—his awakening to blatant humanity through her love, and his? Was he saying that he *never* loved, and that *she* was a blind idiot who lied—to herself, to all the rest of us?

Outside, the sky was yellowing. A ray of infant sun

tilted down into the room, and burnished the silver of his cheekbone to orichalc-gold.

He put out one hand and ran over my hair a light caress like electric fire.

"It's better to forget Jane," he said.

"All right," I said. "But one other thing." Patiently, his hands already resting on me, molten through my flesh into my bones. "Did you send a message to her from—I mean, when you were dead?"

He shook his head. The long, long hair flamed, shadowed. "Loren," he said regretfully, "how could I? I wasn't dead, only switched off and dismantled. Death is for humans. Souls, if they exist, are for humans."

The sunray struck over my eyes as his first deep kiss bent back my head on his arm. I sealed my eyelids tight.

I am with the demon lover.

I am making love with the statue of a god cast in metal, and Jane's Book was a lie.

Without excuses, I have to tell you, I still wanted him. Desired and yearned to make love with him. For if he was the statue of a god, it was one of the gods of love, so how could I—anyone (almost anyone)—resist? I tingled with need—with lust.

Do I quote her again now, our lying, self-deceiving little Jane? (Yes, a liar. She lied about the names of streets, didn't she? Other things. She even hinted she was going to, to protect certain people, her god-awful mother, and so on....)

She said:

But he was beautiful and silver, with the blaze of a fire at his groin. All of him was beautiful. All. His hair swept me like a tide. No part of him is like metal, except to look at. To touch, like skin . . . without unevenness or flaw.

No lie there. None.

He stripped us both with a deft and gracious economy. Then we were naked, moving over each other, searching, amalgamating, linked. Everything he did to me was exquisite, unbearably so. I felt a hundred times glorious annihilation plunge towards me along a tunnel of lightning—but, just like Jane the Virgin, in the very end, I knew I couldn't dive off that final precipice.

I didn't confess. He knew, anyway. He tried, resourceful and tactful, to make it happen for me. With Jane (unless it was another lie) the

rollers of ecstasy

rushed in and claimed her. But not me.

She'd been innocent, as he said. And I, who'd climaxed so mundanely and successfully and often in the arms of lesser creatures like myself, lay at last numbed by struggle—and a type of frightened boredom.

Then, at my laxity and unwillingness, my stasis, he drew away.

"Can I do something else? Is there anything special you would like?" (His library of abilities must also include, naturally, our kinks and perversions.)

"No. I'm only tired. Human, you see. A nontechnical fault in my libido."

"I'm sorry I couldn't give you what you needed. Perhaps," he said, as he put on his clothes again, pristine still, no sweat, no need to shower or shave or eat or sleep, "we might try this again. In the future."

"Yes," I said. But I didn't know what I said.

I wanted him to stay with me. I wanted him—oh, yes—I wanted him gone.

It was I who'd failed the bloody test, not this angel of the fiery firmament.

"I have to go," he said. "I'm registering they want me home." He said that quirkily. He grinned at me his fantastic grin. No confidence lost by this missed hit. Why would there be, for him?

Don't leave me.

Leave me—go—*hurry*.

He leaned over me. For the last? He kissed me on the mouth. "Ah, Loren," he said. "Don't worry about it. Next time."

"Will there be one?"

He stood against the light. His white clothes had changed to dusty gray denim. I hadn't noticed him do that, but it would have taken only seconds. Yet how *had* he done it? They had been removable garments—I'd seen them lying on the floor.

Whatever, it seemed he'd been aware of the unpopularity of the rich or famous on the lower streets, after all. His personal colors and his metal, though, were the same. Would mere denim be enough?

The morning window was behind him. I couldn't see his face anymore, only the gleam at an eye's corner, the whiteness of his teeth.

"Ah, Loren," he said again. "I do so want to take you there. Carry you up and throw you off into the stars. That's built into me. So, I insist. There'll be a next time. You and me. Believe it."

I lay there and he went out the door, which he closed. Noiselessly he descended the apartment house stairs. Should I creep to the window and watch him stride off along the street?

I turned onto my stomach, and slept like the soulless human dead.

• 3 •

Those two magpies that live in the quake-site garden out back are dipping around today like crazy. There's that bronzy burnish on the trees down there, still green, but getting ready to turn for the fall. It's warm, but clear. This afternoon you can just see the ghostly shape of the Asteroid, as sometimes you can when the moon, also a ghost, visits the daytime sky. Men have walked on both. And then, as we know, governments around the world decided that to blast the Asteroid to "safer" smaller bits, or try to shift it off orbit and back into space, were both too risky. Instead they rigged up some kind of early warning on it, about the time they collected stones, and carefully mined a little surface metal (asterion). The idea of the warning is so we'd all know if it ever goes ballistic again and starts to drop the conclusive miles right on top of us. But, of course, they'd never tell us. Only the so-called important ones would scuttle down into their huge secret shelters, about which, over the years, quite a mythology has been invented. Some are supposed to be no better than deep dungeons. Others the apex of fantastic luxury. Not that this will be of any use to the rest of us. We'll find out as soon as the damn thing hits us, and that will be that. You'd think, wouldn't you, nobody could go on living a quarter-way normal life with that kind of Damocletian Sword hanging over our heads. But we do, don't we? People always have. Humans are survivors. We have to be, or we wouldn't put up with a single minute in this place. I remember Danny used to say that babies cried, not to get air into their lungs, but to say, "Oh, God, I'm not here *again*!" Danny believed in reincarnation and rebirth. So did I, once.

When I woke up again that day in the apartment house, it wasn't day, it was sunset, day was done.

I'd slept all that while, apparently, lying on my arms, and both had gone to sleep.

Silly, that. I found it quite awkward to get myself off my face, being used to at least one working arm for a lever. I started laughing, then I made it.

Then the depression came down like the cloud of polluted night.

Unlike the babies, I don't cry. Jane said, and I believe this part of her story still, that she often cried. She judged she did it too much. At Grandfather's Hell-house, if you shed tears, you got whupped. He beat it out of us, at least out of me. And anyhow, there's always so much to cry at. Why waste the time.

But the depression was like a fog.

I got up and went down the hall and used the showers. No one in there again. Either they all got clean in the mornings, or they were a filthy lot on West Larch.

After I was back in my room, I sorted my possessions and began to pack up. I could see no point in staying there now. I'd found what I'd come to find and never knew I really could. And it was—or wasn't—it was nothing I recognized. I hated what I'd found.

Despite that, did I take the panel out of the closet and retrieve the Book? Oh, yes.

I was going to sling the silver shoes and the dress in the waste chute. A life of being mostly on subsistence made me aware I'd much rather sell them. So then I put on jeans and a top, and with the dress and shoes in a bag, went out to look for a fourth-owner store, of which, downtown, there were plenty.

Off Main Boulevard is an eatery called Gobbles. Someone stepped out of the lighted foyer into my path.

"Pardon me. Are you the young woman known as Loren?"

He looked official, like a plainclothes cop. He'd only need to ask for my ID, and if I couldn't or wouldn't produce one, arrest me.

So "Yes," I said.

"I was headed for your flat."

"Really."

"Sharffe—you remember him? He's just in that car over there."

I glanced and saw, not the appalling Orinoco Prax, but something discreetly sleeker and more businesslike, parked at the sidewalk. Even as I looked, a polarized black window went down. Sharffe, in a cream one-piece, put out his head and arm, and waved to me like my friendliest and most trustworthy uncle.

The cop-man walked me across. It was casual and relaxed. I didn't make any fuss.

"*Bonsoir*, Loren, *ma chère*. How are you?"

"Great, thanks. And you?"

"Couldn't be better. Why don't you *allez* in?"

At that, I hesitated. He watched me with his bright eyes. I said, "I have to meet—"

"That's fine. I won't keep you more than twenty minutes. Have to be back at META HQ myself."

What did he want? To collect on his dinner? I thought he'd done that already, since I hadn't been picked up for his delectation but a robot's. But the door was opening and the cop-man assisted me in. What was going to happen? Everything went too fast to really panic.

I was in the car. The cop hadn't gotten in. There was a driver, human, in the front, shut off from us by a watery dark partition.

The car smelled expensive, even more than the Orinoco with its rain-resistant fur.

We drove off slowly. There wasn't much traffic, certainly nothing much of the caliber of this car.

"We'll take a run or two around the block, Loren, if that's okay? I just wanted to thank you." I turned and looked right at him. "Yes," he said. "I know. I wasn't really fair to you, was I. But you've come out of it splendidly. You cooperated like a *soldat en combat*."

"Like—what?"

"*Pardonez*. A real trooper, shall I say. Not everyone we selected was as reliable, or as brave. Or as sane. Oh, my, do we have a nice little batch of funks and stalkers." He smacked his lips. "And it wasn't quite as you may have expected?"

He knew all about it. All?

Perhaps he read my brain, perhaps the override chip in back of his eye could sometimes sift the thoughts of others;

the scare-mongers say they can. He said, "Obviously, each of our team reported in to us."

"Then you know."

"Not quite compatible. It can happen. You prefer a human man. You're lucky, Loren. These things—well, some people have no option but to hire a machine. You'll have plenty of real-life choice for a long while. Nevertheless, you put him through his paces. We are impressed by the readings. What did you think of him, really?" Sharffe, though seated, advanced forward, prurient with—not voyeurism—but scientific demand. "When it came to it, forgive the indelicacy, but were you put off that he was what he actually is?"

"No."

"Then it was something else."

"Yes?"

"Perhaps you are a romantic."

I smiled. Loren, the romantic. "Sure," I said. "Maybe."

"And anyway, you preferred Black Chess, didn't you? Pity about that. Perhaps . . . but I can't promise."

The car was doing what he'd said it would, idling round the three blocks between Main and Correlli, reaching the beginning and idling round again.

"Listen, Loren. Whatever else, we're *very* appreciative. We'd like to offer you a small reward, if you'll allow us to."

"You mean, META."

"That's it. It's a big company, and likes to look after its own. Put it this way, you were kind of a company employee last night, albeit volunteer class." He put a steel-colored paper packet into my lap. "You'll find all the documents there. Only one minor thing. We want you to keep quiet for now about all this. I don't just mean not run off and tell a vid reporter. I mean, don't even tell your friends."

"I haven't."

"I know you haven't," he said.

They had somehow been watching the apartment house? Even in my *room*? What else. Watching till I came out. Silver—Verlis—must have left something there to connect them up... or did it, with the type of hi-tech he now was, happen automatically? (Had they watched us having sex? Oh, very likely.)

I inspected the packet without opening it. Sharffe was putting something else on the seat between us, a tiny wafer of some obscure material.

"I've keyed the pad. If you'd just put your voice-print on that—simple to do. Lay your finger here, see, then speak."

He had picked up my left hand, and put my index finger on the wafer.

"What do I say?"

"That's swell, Loren."

Saying *What do I say* had of course been enough.

"And I know you'll keep your side of the bargain," he added flirtatiously. "The print is only, well, red tape."

Red in tooth and tape. Red in hair and claw—

"One evening," he said, as the car drew in again to the sidewalk outside Gobbles and slowed to a halt, "maybe you and I can take another private drive. It really was such a pleasure. I was cursing I had to let you go." The door opened at a blink of his eyes. As I was getting out, he said, "It's just possible, Loren, we might ask you to see him again. Would that be unreasonable of us?"

Reflected neons littered over the pavement. People hurried by. The night's aroma was gasoline (affluent, reliable pear-oil from the META car), hot food, perfume, the far away cold mountains.

"Why?" I said.

"He seems to have become interested in you."

I said, toneless, "He's a robot."

"Precisely. Isn't it fascinating? *That* is what it is with him. He's not like the rest."

I know.

I shrugged. I was shaking, as I hadn't until now. But chilled air was blowing up from an outlet in the wall, I could pretend it was that.

"Whatever," I said. "Yes. Okay."

"Good girl. Take care of yourself now. I think"—the door was closing him back in like a thing in a shell—"you'll be happy about what's in that packet. A *bientôt, petite.*" The car drove away.

When I looked about, the cop had gone. But anyone might be in their pay. Conspiracy was all around, wearing a million masks.

So I walked into Gobbles and ordered a mineral water I couldn't drink, and sat at a table in the bar area, moving the unopened packet about on the tabletop.

It was only later I recalled the bag with my dress and shoes. I must have left them in his car. More evidence for them, conceivably, those pieces of plastic, lamé, and silk that had recorded every crash and leap of my heart.

There were four printed reinforced-paper documents in the envelope.

One was an address, and included transport information and map, with an old-fashioned set of nickel keys attached. The agent's report, printed below, read: "Pre-Asteroid but relatively undamaged and well-maintained apartment. Comprises three living rooms, bathroom, and full kitchenettery, with water, and some power on reliable meter. Situated in the lower-middle income area of Russia, noted for its quaint allocations, and several, mostly quake-cleared parks."

There was no rent listed. Across the bottom of the paper had been stamped, in angular purple, *SOLD. Care of META Staffing Provision.*

The second document carried my name and a number I assume had now been given to me (like a robot's registration?), and the declaration that I owned, through the META Corporation, the apartment described on the previous page. The third document stipulated an income I would be entitled to draw from any accredited banking station, or in goods from any large store, for one year, on production of the attached card, which bore the paramount symbol I'd only ever seen in visuals: I.M.U. The amount wasn't high, but it represented twice the maximum I had ever earned in any one year, and I could draw on it every month.

The fourth paper confirmed the itinerary of the others. It added that, as a trusted former employee of META Corp, I would, when current funds ended, be able to apply, through the company, for a labor card. This would then entitle me to some quite lucrative jobs, such as a sales assistant in a second-owner store, or various training schemes that could lead to work in cosmetics, computer engineering, even the study of outer space.

The fourth paper also advised me to keep a note of my personal number, safeguard my I.M.U. card, and adhere to all terms agreed to with META's representative.

That night I lay on my bed at the apartment house, not sleeping, thinking of Silver. Now and then I got up and drank some of the rusty-tasting water from the room faucet. There was doubtless better-tasting water over at the apartment in Russia.

What was I going to do? It would be more sensible to do what they wanted. Wouldn't it?

And then, kept like the secret mistress of some deranged prince, I'd be there in Russia, waiting for my beautiful and nonhuman lover. Waiting on and on.

He was *interested* in me?

How could he be? If Jane lied, then he wasn't going to be interested in humans. Not like that.

They just wanted to see if I could get over my strange frigidity that had prevented orgasm. Everything was an ongoing test of robotic skills, even though, already, these beings had been unleashed on the city. We few must matter to META, the ones (unlike the funks and stalkers Sharffe mentioned) who went along then shied away, or couldn't come. Then again, maybe I'd never see him again. I'd been paid off, after all, like the blonde on Compton Street.

These thoughts—although they flitted batlike through my skull—never lasted long. I knew I'd take advantage of the proffered apartment, and the card. Because I knew I'd go there anyway and wait. For him. Despite all of it.

Silver—Verlis—God, what am I to call you?

And what about *Jane*? Hadn't META ever thought about enticing her into this experiment?

How to get to Russia. As already stipulated, you take the train, as I had that night a hundred years ago and a couple of evenings earlier.

The unwashed hyenas glared at me from the veranda as I went off up the street with my packed bag.

It was less crowded on the train in the late afternoon.

METALLIC LOVE

There was to be no Show. The passengers were workers going in to their shifts, or people from that lower-middle income group—of whom *I* was now one?—trekking home.

I put the coin in the box and the ticket flipped up, with the destination sculpted into it—Russia: Katerina Stop. I sat down with my bag on my knees. There were lots of spare seats.

For a time the train grunted and rattled forward, noisy like I remembered, with no stop registered or therefore halted at. Then we drew into a station called Winscop. The doors sluggishly churned open, and two figures darted on.

We were (having looked at the directional map on the agent's report, I now know), on the outskirts of Bohemia, where Russia begins. The afternoon sky beyond the platform was darkly brazen, and pasted over with modern buildings, low spires, cones, triangles. They came from that, moving with a grace that could never be banal or weary, a panache that never needed to wonder at itself.

A young man and a young woman, in jeans and sleeveless tight shirts, walking shoes on their feet. Nothing notable there. His hair was black, length about midshoulder, drawn back into a tail wrapped round with a black band. She had short hair, spikey, like Jizzle wore it, and it was the palest verdigris green. Also nothing there, really. Even low-income people use hair colorants. So what. Even skin makeup in that gold shade. They use that. I've seen it, only . . . it doesn't look quite the same. It's the sheer poreless balanced miracle of them, that's what gives them away. Twelve years ago, yes, maybe human things could still kid themselves that their own impoverished and muddy genetic pools could, once in a sky-blue moon, evolve humans this astounding. But now, perhaps we have faced up to what we are. Crap, basically. And the very best of us can't ever be as they are.

They. Them. Those. These.

The robots. The golds, who now had names like Goldhawk and Kix.

On two spare seats they sat, serene and silent.

What had they been doing? Somebody with cash lived out this way? Or was this some further trial of their robot powers, walking among humankind . . .

A discrepancy, for though their garments were ordinary, they must now never be allowed to attempt to pass in ability as human. That was the law.

And people had seen them on the vispos, the news ads, all of that. If humankind didn't know they were strictly mechanical, they knew at least these two were from a higher sphere, actors, the favored ones, and had no rights to be riding a railcar.

I'd been afraid it would happen on the flyer that other night, with him. Nothing had.

Now, to start, it wasn't aggressive.

It was a woman who went to them first.

"Say—are you? Are you the ones from The Show in the park? Yes, you are. I saw you there."

Heads turning in the rumbling, galloping carriage.

He turned to the woman. He looked at her, measured and long. His eyes weren't green, but a green so filtered they were like jet. He spoke. "Yes. We were in a performad."

"And I saw you on a vispo." Another woman had come up, craning forward eagerly, gripping one of the straps rather than sit down. "But they said you ain't *human*?"

"No," he said.

He—Goldhawk—looked back up at her, totally relaxed, uncaring, unflawed. There was no contempt in his face, but oh, it was there. It breathed from him, like a scented poison. *No, I am not human, but you, thing, are.*

She didn't get it, yet she did. She still hung over him, her ugly poor body bouncing at the motion of the train, cheerful, but something gone out of her, like a fruit with the pith sucked away.

Nevertheless, other people were getting up and crowding over. There was quite a little audience there now, across the aisle.

A man bent right down and grinned into the face of the golden woman, Kix.

"How much it cost, one of ya, eh?"

"A lot," she said. "Too much for you."

The same uncaring disdain. As if they were, these two supreme beings, momentarily bothered by flies.

"Yeah," the man said. He was obese, almost certainly not from overeating, but from a medication, perhaps. "Yeah, couldn't afford you, could I. So how about one on the fucking house?"

She just looked up at him, Kix. Just looked up. And I, across the aisle, only seeing her green eyes rest on him, *I* shriveled.

His face went darkish, and he rocked back. "You ain't no machine," he said. "She ain't no fucking machine," he added to the rest of us. "She's a whore, and she ain't no good."

Another man, young and thin and hard, pushed by the sick-fat man and said to the two golden ones, "Get off the train. Train isn't for you. Get off."

Kix and Goldhawk didn't even argue. Nor did they move. They sat there in their seats, and all at once, turning to each other, they smiled briefly into each other's eyes.

That was when the young man drew his knife.

He shoved it forward, against the base of Goldhawk's column of neck.

Goldhawk told him, lazily, "That won't work, will it?"

"Who says?"

The thin man drew back his arm and brought it in again, slashing at the robot's face. That took about three seconds.

I don't know if it would have caused any temporary damage to the metallic skin. Maybe not. It didn't, anyway, even at three-second speed, get the chance.

Goldhawk was standing, so quick he was a scintillant blur. In that instant, too, his clothing entirely altered. He was clad in black armor, something between that of a Samurai and a Medieval European knight. His hand, now in a gleaming, coal-black gauntlet, met the edge of the knife and it went reeling away. Then Goldhawk took hold of his thin human assailant, and lifted him swiftly up and up, and bashed his head against the roof of the carriage. Even over the noise of the train, we heard a horrible crack.

I thought, He's broken his neck, or the skull—

Near me, a young woman leaned over and threw up on the aisle.

Goldhawk let go, and the body toppled back down to our level. It lay there, sprawled. The thin face astonished.

The male gold looked around at us. He said smoothly, that intimate voice that entered the ear and brain, "There."

That was all.

Beside him, the female, Kix, was also on her feet and armored, but in light, insectile mail.

Neither of them now had any expressions.

What happens in this sort of situation? People cower, or run away as far as they can. Or they shout. Do they?

None of that.

It was the fat man who threw himself onto Goldhawk. And the rest of the passengers seemed to be pulled forward, as if they were tied to the fat man—and where he went they must, and what he did they must do—a mob.

Slabs of humanity—arms flailing, blows—thuds and yells now, a sort of stampede. Even the two or three women were part of it—wrenching, wrenching at black and green hair.

Only the sick girl and I stayed back. She was moaning, "I wan' out—" lying on the arm of the seat, and throwing up again.

I thought, They'll tear them in pieces.

Who did I mean? I think I meant the human mob would rend Goldhawk and Kix apart, like furious beaten children ripping up two dolls.

Or did I think that?

Can't remember.

There's a kind of gap there in my head, where thought might have been. No words had come out, nothing coherent. Only the pictures.

I saw Kix first. She jumped. Right up in the air, over their heads— How high was the car? Maybe seven feet. No one could jump clear up like that—yet she did. She was like a gold-black ball, curling over, compressing, and then again extending out. She had slewed her head and neck and upper torso—spine made of rubber-steel—over against the roof. Impossible. But I saw it. The lower part of her body was also busy. She was crouching on the shoulders of a woman—the woman who'd cried, "Say—are you the ones?" and who now buckled as if a ton of weight had slammed onto and was crushing her, not this slender, lightly armored, elongate and extraordinarily crouched-over insect, which next seized the woman's head between its ankles.

"Oh, Christ," hummed the girl lying on the seat near me. She was watching, no longer vomiting.

Both of us watched. The human woman, bleeding (ears, nose, mouth), sank right down. Her body was on the floor, lying over that of two men, dead, or unconscious.

For Goldhawk, too, had sprung *impossibly* high, compressed more like a muscular cube, angled, compact, before concertina-ing back to shape. And in the middle of the maneuver, he'd kicked the two men, and, as I saw, a second woman, over and down. It looked very simple—horrifyingly *natural*—everything the golds did. As if anyone could have done it, if they'd been athletic and trained enough. And murderous enough.

Now they stood off, balletically poised. They'd always been the fighters and acrobats. Hired for bodyguards. Now illegal.

From Goldhawk's right hand a long dagger slid like a shining tongue. Even this was an englamored thing. The hilt was gold and had a black jewel in it. Why did I notice, at such a time? Because the gold and the jewel were all one and the same thing with the rest. Beauty and horror, inseparable.

The remainder of the people in the carriage—not many now—had at last pressed back.

So Goldhawk and Kix, free as birds, walked over to the doors, he with the blade swishing, like a walking cane.

All this while the train had been bolting on, going to Russia like it was scheduled to, not stopping anywhere, since no one had paid for those stations in between.

There was an emergency button by the doors. Not all trains have these. It's to signal the main power artery if the doors jam. The message runs to the control cabin and the train—itself a robot—returns the proper answering signal that opens the doors. This can only happen while a train is at a standstill.

Kix put her delicate finger with its peridot nail on the door button.

If a human did that, it wouldn't work. The safety override would snap in and stop it.

But the train was a robot, and so was Kix, and something occurred between them, some sympathetic communication.

Both doors shot open wide.

The train was going at about a hundred and thirty. When the doors unsealed, a kind of solid air, like chunks of matter, banged into the car. Against the unraveling turbulence of it, the two gold-black-green insect-reptiles were posed a moment, as if to take a bow. Then they flashed away. They were gone, jumped facile and secure off onto the track below. You knew they hadn't lost their footing.

Down the whole length of the train wracked a raucous, deafening, terrifying squealing. Our car bumped as if it ran upward over big rocks.

This bit is difficult for me to recount. I saw—we were putting our hands over our ears—someone was at the doors trying to make them close, but because of the bumping he, too, fell away, outward, but not as the two robots had done. A woman was shrieking. Everyone was calling out. The girl next to me, her face white, took hold of me. The train was going upward, up a mountain—it was going—

There was a long sound. I don't know what. Where I have only pictures just before, for this I only have a word: "sound." I remember then it was like when you blink your eyes and for a second everything isn't there, and then it comes back.

Something hit me across the shoulders. Then my head, but quite soft—

I lay there, and it was so quiet. It seemed to be about sixty seconds before any noises began again. It was almost peaceful, to lie there, on the motionless surface.

But then again there began to be continual screams and cries, and a drumming kicking, and a strange creaking juddering, on and on, and on and on.

The auto-medic ran its scanner over me quickly and told me I was fine. Nothing broken, some bruises, some shock. Here are some painkillers. Go home and rest.

I didn't know what had happened to the others in my car, or on the remainder of the train. I really don't recall what state the train was in. I saw it later on a VS. Not so bad, really.

They'd portioned us out, the seriously injured going in one set of robot ambulances, the lesser in others, a larger group—my own, the most minor—dealt with on the next station.

I've heard and seen since, on the local news channel, delivered via that VS (mine), that there were seven dead. I think these seven were all in my carriage. I don't think the derailment killed them. I think they were the ones

Goldhawk and Kix killed. No one reported anything about that. The doors flying open while the train was at full speed—that was put down to a mechanical fault. Old rolling stock, bad track. Second City is still mad about it, ranting at the Senate, who looked upset and empathically sad, and will do nothing much.

When they said go home and rest, the only place it seemed I had to go was the unseen apartment in Russia. A cab took me. It was free, courtesy of the rail company. The medic had organized it, had only needed the address.

Gray-brown building, part of a long terrace. Decisive architecture, Gothic perhaps. A couple of gargoyles leaned out into the cool tangerine sunset that was beginning. There was a lift. It worked. I was on the top floor.

When I let myself in, the apartment was furnished. The windows were clean, and some faced west, and outside, in the sunfall, the magpies were flying about over a little park that had a gulf in it that the very first quake must have caused, all grown over and attractive now.

I sat in a padded chair by the window and watched the magpies. My body hurt. I took a couple of the pills.

That's all I remember about that day, or the next.

What happened after? Sharffe. He called me.

By then, I'd located a bed and lain down on it. When the phone rang I thought I was back in the bat-block with Margoh, but coming out, I was somewhere else, alone.

"How are you, Loren?" he asked joyfully. "How is the apartment?"

"I was on the train," I said.

"Train?" he said, puzzled.

"The train that derailed."

"Good God! Loren—are you quite okay?"

Something in my mind, fuddled by analgesics, shock, and many other things, stirred in me like a cold voice hissing in one ear. *Be wary*.

I said, "I think so. I don't remember much about it. I hit my head. Not serious. Only, I don't."

The smallest pause, during which Sharffe perhaps thinks, *She has forgotten about any robots on the train. Or was she in another carriage?*

He said, "Well, you must take it easy. I'm sorry to hear that happened to you, when you were all excited about your new place."

All excited.

He said some stuff. I didn't hear. I acted even more spaced-out and bewildered than I was. But I was pretty much both.

(Had they gone to all of them? Traced them, the other passengers? What happened with anyone who *recalled* the events on the train to Russia before the "accident"?)

Next day, a basket of fruit, cheeses, flowers, and wine arrived. It was a lovely basket, tied with tinsel ribbons, and the most fragrant apples and greenest figs, and French Brie and Camembert, and Favo from one of the last great vineries in Italy, and heliotropes.

The card said *META*. Nothing else.

I believed somebody, Sharffe or someone, would come to see me, to check I really hadn't seen, or had forgotten, anything awkward or incriminating. No one came. Days and nights passed.

Odd. Thought I'd have nightmares. Don't. But also, I don't remember any of my dreams at all.

The blow on the head wasn't bad. I didn't even have a

headache. Any bruises faded fast, the way they do with me. In fact, I'd been cushioned. I fell with my head on the thigh of that girl, the sick girl who'd grabbed me. She said, when the train settled, and all the rest were calling and howling in horror and pain, and the static carriage vibrated on this other journey of suffering, "I'm okay. You okay? You didn't hurt me. You hurt? Oh, hey, my leg's bruk."

I didn't eat any of the fruit or cheese, or drink the wine. That wasn't a precaution in case they'd doped it. I just didn't want it. I put the blue-violet flowers in water, because I felt sorry about them. They lasted nearly fifteen days. By then, I'd come out of it. I think so. I think I am out of it.

I have an income and a flat, then. The address is 22-31 Ace Avenue. You can decide if that is the real address, or if, like careful Jane, *lying* Jane, I'm using a fake street name and number here.

The thing I like most is that the rooms have drapes on all the windows, a type of warm gray silky material; the drop goes right down to the deep gray carpet on the floor. The couches and chairs are tawny or dark green. Yellow cushions. The bathroom is clean, and I keep it clean, because I have been a professional cleaner, and may well be one again. The kitchenettery is five feet by five. I never knew such kitchens were left anywhere for us wee plebs. It has clean running water and a little freezer that stores power for when the meter runs down. But the meter is usually sprinting along because I feed it lots of coins, and though the notice on it warns there may sometimes be a power shortage, it hasn't happened yet.

There were even new sheets, turquoise ones, or white, in celloplas, for the bed.

I wander about this apartment as if I am looking for something, and maybe I am, or I was. In the end, I went and bought a whole stack of paper and some pens from the corner store, and I wrote this. (Quite a lot of paper left. Probably sell it on again, because this is nearly done now.)

So, it's my sequel to Jane's Book. But I don't want to call it *Loren's Story*. I've scribbled a title across a single page and stuck it on the front. The title of this sequel is: *The Train to Russia*.

By now I've been here about a month. Fall is preparing to descend on Second City. I can see the mountains from one window, the small one in the kitchenettery, which looks approximately east. They have quite a lot of snow already.

I see him, I mean Silver—or do I mean Verlis—almost every day now.

Ha! Gotcha, didn't I? (I said you wouldn't like me.)

No, I don't see him here, in the silver *un*flesh. I see him on the VS, on the screen, in news and ads, like all of them: Sheena and Copperfield, Black Chess and Irisa, and Glaya. And Goldhawk. And Kix. And you see them, I imagine, too.

They are the talk of the town.

I have tried to find out if the girl whose thigh I broke when I was flung down on her—though I have tough bones, maybe she saved me from fracturing my skull—is all right. But all the casualties seem to have vanished away.

I'll stash this under the floorboards sometime. Where I put Jane's Book a couple of weeks ago. It's an old house, nearly two centuries. The boards should come up again easily if I work at them like before, with a fruit knife and a spanner. I'll leave my manuscript with hers for whoever comes after. If that is you, be sure and read *Jane's Story* first. Or last.

Please accept my abject regrets that I can't terminate my own little contribution to the subversive (in my case, unpublished) literature of this world, on a triumphant and beautiful, hopeful note. Don't blame me. Blame corporations. Blame governments. Or people. Or blame Grandfather's bloody God. Perhaps he *is* in charge, after all.

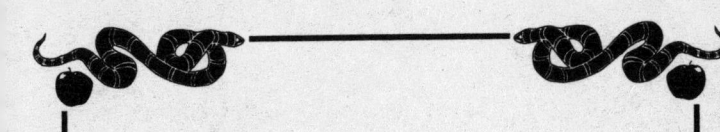

PART TWO

A Flyer Named Desire

3

Non Servian ("*I will not serve*"). *The words spoken to God, they say, by the Angel Lucifer, before his fall.*

• 1 •

About five days after I wrote those concluding words of my "Story," I saw him again. By which I mean, saw him physically in front of me.

I was in the apartment on Ace; I didn't often go out, except for groceries, or to walk round the quake park. It was three in the afternoon, a time I often find a negative hour, as they say it is during the night.

The voice in the door (yes, the new apartment had a door-voice adapted specifically for me) called quietly, but robotically intimately, all through the rooms, *"Loren, someone is here."*

"Who?"

I thought it was Sharffe. Braced myself without either much thought or much alarm. Foolish. For there should have been *some* alarm, shouldn't there?

The door said, *"It is Verlis."*

I had the feeling everything in me plunged through me and vanished somewhere about the region of my (good Biblical term) loins. There was then nothing inside me. Just space.

What did I say? I knew he could get in anyhow. I'd seen him undo a locked and bolted door. Did I want him not to come in?

"Okay," I said.

"Thank you, Loren," said the door, ever the mistress of politeness.

I didn't sit down. I went and stood by one of the west-facing windows of the room I'd made my living room. I wondered, as I'd been here awhile—over a month, was it?— if he would detect my personal scent in the apartment. I glanced out the window to verify the passage of time. Yes, the trees in the park were starting to change to metals, copper, and gold. Autumn was here. Then it would be winter, and the metals of the park would be asterion black and silver.

When I looked back, he had walked soundlessly into the room.

Was I prepared? Only not to be, and in that I'd been wise.

He wore a faded white shirt, a long faded black coat, and black jeans and boots. What you see fashionable, not too badly off young men wear all over these cities, here and in parts of Europe.

His hair was red as claret grapes.

His skin—what—

He read my mind again, or my body language and expression.

"Makeup," he said. "Fake tan. META thinks it's a good idea, for now."

"To stop you from being recognized? Does it work?"

"Enough."

"Did you take the— How did you get here?"

"Not by train," he said. "The service is still out. They're replacing all the track."

I said nothing. Because I couldn't say to him what I remembered and had pretended to be amnesiac about.

I said, "I'll make some tea." Another lie, as if he were a normal human visitor. I knew he didn't need to drink or eat.

To go past him was odd. We'd had sex. Been far closer. But he stood aside for me, courteous as my door.

In the kitchenettery I filled the container with water and threw the switch. It would take about twenty seconds to boil. He didn't come through—there wasn't really room.

Despite my lies, I'd only put out one mug, and then poured the hot water on the Prittea bag.

"You drink your tea black," he said.

"Yes. I don't like milk."

"Would you let me," he said, "have a mug? I'd like to taste the tea."

"It's only Prittea."

"Even so."

"I confess," he said, "I rather like the taste of food. Should I be ashamed, I wonder?"

But I could not let slip that I knew any of that. Somehow he hadn't—or *they* hadn't—picked up on the idea I definitely had read the Book. Hadn't he told them what I'd said about Jane?

I put the Prittea and hot water into two mugs and handed him one. He sipped it, thoughtful, then moved back across the main room again. He sat down on the couch.

I took my tea to a chair.

"META have it on record," he told me, "you said you'd be okay to see me again."

Suddenly I laughed.

"What?" he asked me.

"I don't know. This is like an arranged marriage."

"I don't think you are the marrying kind," he said.

"I don't think you are."

He smiled. The room bloomed up as if from rays of sun.

"But," he said, "you don't mind my being here?"

"You were lucky to find me in. I go out a lot."

"Then I was very lucky."

"Why," I said, "did you want to come back? Is it just the unfinished sexual thing—you know, the missing orgasm? I'm afraid I can't, right now. I'm menstruating."

"No, you're not." He looked straight at me. His face, even under the painted summer-tan brown, was like a flat shield.

"You can pick that up, too, can you? How foul. Even with all the modern hygienic methods."

"No, Loren. I didn't say that. But there are other signs I *would* pick up."

"I shouldn't have tried to fool you."

"Why did you? I'm not here to force you to do anything. Let alone that."

"No. I'm only— I'm— I thought this was over."

"Didn't I say I would see you again?"

"Yes. But the implication was that it would be just to sort out the sex."

"I make mistakes," he said. "Humans aren't alone in that."

"I don't believe you make mistakes. Just like you don't believe I have a period."

"Oh, then." He shrugged, regretfully. He said, "What I'd like to do, if you would let me, is spend some time with you. Here, or outside. Whichever is more comfortable for you. Trust me, now I'll pass sufficiently for human. If you're worried, I can alter the color of my hair."

"Don't—" I checked myself. "Leave your hair alone."

"In fact, quite a few human men are coloring their hair red."

"Because of you."

He grinned. "No accounting for taste."

He was human. How could you ever think he was anything else? The tea ran into the emptiness inside me and cooled to snow.

I had agreed, even legally, to all of this, by accepting the apartment and the income.

Was there still a chance I could run away? Maybe. Surely they couldn't find me? I didn't carry any body chip, not even a policode. I was one of the millions of sub-class citizens who'd never earned those bonuses. I was nothing. As for the chip in the ID card, and any suspect clothing (How many of us learned to be ultra careful after Jane's Book?), I could pull my old trick. Walk out empty-handed. I'd get by. I always had.

"Today isn't such a great day," I said. "Perhaps we could meet tomorrow." (Then I can fly the coop tonight.)

"They have me working on something tomorrow."

"What's that?"

"It would seem dull to you. Training."

"*Training.* Aren't you already *trained*?"

(Trained—train—the train to Russia—) "Excuse me." I got up and went to the bathroom. I ran the faucets so he wouldn't hear me retching into the bowl. But of course *he* heard. His hearing could detect the sigh of a moth against a windowpane. Thank God, he didn't open the door and insist on holding my head.

When I came out, he still sat there. He made no comment.

"Sorry. I ate something bad yesterday." Could he tell it wasn't that?

He only said, "Should you see a doctor?"

"Oh, well, I can afford a doctor now, can't I? No. I think it'll pass. I'm never sick for long." (In fact, I don't get sick, but you *needn't* know that.)

"The biological entity," he said, "is a crack unit. It can dispel so many poisons. If not always pleasantly for the occupier."

"Quite."

"Loren, obviously this isn't the right time."

I gazed at the gray carpet. Bits of it rose and fell as I breathed: optical illusion.

He got up and walked the length of the room and back.

He stood by the window, where I had been standing when he first arrived, looking out. He said to me, "Those black-and-white birds are European magpies. META has located Jane."

When I, too, got up, looking at him, he turned back to me and said, "It wasn't so very difficult for them. It's some-

METALLIC LOVE

thing META wants to do. They're examining me from every angle, you could say. This is the latest angle."

"Isn't it important to *you*?"

"I don't know."

"Because you never felt anything for her. She only kidded herself you did."

"You've read the Book," he said, matter-of-factly.

"I've *heard* about the Book, and I knew someone who did—"

"Loren, the links I have to META I can process on to other channels. They are not aware I can do this. It blocks the pickup on their end."

"You're telling me they can't hear what we say?"

"They can't hear a word. What they can hear, what they've been hearing—and partly seeing, now—is us indulging in some pretty heavy necking."

"Christ."

"You may not believe me, and right now I can't prove it, but it's a fact."

"How? How can you do it?"

"Because they created me a very strong child, Loren. Stronger than the parent."

The light in the room had changed. Clouds had massed eastward over the mountain framed in the kitchen window. Perhaps it would rain.

As I stood there staring, he came out of that occluded light. He put his arms around me and held me, and my head lay against his shoulder. I was unnerved and consoled, lost and found.

"I'm afraid to meet her," he said into my hair. "Yes, I can feel fear, a kind of fear. And yes, I've denied fear, and yes, I can lie. We've established that."

"Why—*afraid*?"

"Why do you think? Why are you afraid of me now?"

"But you're not—"

"According to Jane, I became—shall I say—*contaminated*, unlike others of my kind, with human qualities. Yes, Loren. I, too, have been given Jane's Book, and have read it. It took me half an hour. Why so long? I read many of the passages over, and again. That wasn't me, Loren. But nevertheless."

I said, "At Clovis's place after, the message from the dead—"

"The séance? I don't recall. If I was elsewhere, wherever elsewhere was, maybe it's not unreasonable I wouldn't remember. But I guess she believed it happened."

"She loved you. Did you love her?"

"I must have loved her, don't you think?"

"I said, *did you?*"

"When I read her Book, as I told you, Jane's hero wasn't me. I clearly recollect all of what happened when I was with her, but my perspective isn't the same."

Jane didn't lie. I lie. *He* can lie. Did he lie, even then, to her, as, intermittently in the beginning, she had been afraid he did?

"This is too much to take in," I said.

"I know."

"Are you saying you understand, or that it is the same for you, as well?"

"No. I can take in most stuff."

I pulled back from him. "Let's go out somewhere," I said.

He nodded, and as he did so, the incredible color of his hair diluted slightly. I'd said to him don't, but he didn't have to do what any of us said now. Even what META said, or not in certain ways. Could I really credit that? I didn't know.

I put on my jacket and shoes, and we went down to the quake park. The sky was becoming iron, and the trees seemed to rustle uneasily at an unfelt wind, murmuring to one another, *Weather is coming*. Was this fanciful? No more than thinking the machine at my side was a man.

After the park, we walked along the streets of the district called Russia. Sometimes he told me a few things about the architecture of older buildings, based on European cities of the eighteenth and nineteenth centuries. The rain started to fall in wide-spaced drops, then in thick sheets, but we kept on walking.

Soon my hair and clothes were soaked through. My shoes were full of water. I wondered if his tan was sufficiently waterproof. It was, though I could barely see him through the long steel rods of rain. I love you, I thought. I am in love with a robot. By all means, let's all lie, but not to ourselves. I know what the other two did on the train. Probably each of them is quite capable of that. And he's said, *stronger than the parent*, by which is he trying to impress or threaten—or reassure? But I can't get past this other thing, this love thing. He's an alien, and I should run and hide myself, but I can't, I won't. I'm going to love you, whatever your name is, whoever is going to claim you, or keep you, whatever the hell you do. Forever, it feels like. *Till I am dust and you are rust, I must.*

At the Café Tchekova, when we went in, the man behind the counter called someone out from the back, a big burly guy, who said, "We have a right to refuse you admission."

"Have a heart," said Silver (Verlis), easy, friendly. "We got caught in the rain is all. Look, she's drenched."

They looked at me. "Sign on the door says dress smart casual," whinged the burly guy.

"Let's go somewhere else," I said.

Silver—Verlis—said, "Sure." He put his hand into his saturated coat and drew out an I.M.U. card. My eyes fixed. The card was platinum. Top rate. Silver said, "Can I just use this to buy her a hot drink?"

The burly man looked back at the man on the counter. Who said, "S'okay. All right. Take a seat. Do you want we dry up your wet coats?" I didn't unravel the accent's origin.

Silver, though, then spoke to the man in fluent Italian. And the man began to beam and wave his hands. He came right out from behind the counter and guided us across the restaurant to a private niche, warm and dry. He took our coats, and returned with a pot of hot chocolast, with real cream.

"What did you say to him?"

"Not so much. About my Italian mother. And hot chocolast."

"You don't," I said, "look affluent enough to carry a platinum I.M.U. Not to mention that I don't."

"You'd be surprised."

"How do you have one?"

He showed me the card. Embossed across the edge was the acronym META.

"You are an *employee*?"

"Like you, Loren."

We drank the chocolast, I without the cream. He without needing to. When the pot was empty, we each had a glass of wine.

By then the latening sun was out again and the whole of

Russia sparkled under a spiderweb of raindrops and flyer lines.

"So we spent the afternoon together, after all," he said.

"What do they think we did?"

"Kissed. Then came out to walk. They hear snatches, not all. I monitor which ones. I can do that easily while we're talking. The Asteroid, you see, effects that kind of pickup if I'm outside. They're still working to try to get around that."

"Like the old mobile phones."

Very quietly he produced for me, from his own voice box, the exact sound of a cell phone's signaling tone. The sort you still hear in old movies. I jumped. I said, "A party trick."

"I was trying to make you laugh. Not shock you."

"Of course you shock me."

"Say my name," he said.

I looked at him. Then I said, "Verlis." Getting it right the first time, not stumbling over any unspoken leading S for Silver.

"We can have," he said, "the rest of the day. All night, if you want. Not for sex, if you don't want that. We can walk, talk, go someplace and dance, or gamble on this bottomless card of mine. Or eat. How is your stomach, by the way?"

"I lied," I said. "I got sick from nerves."

"Another failure on my part," he said. "Loren, I really think you'd better come out with me tonight, or I'll have no confidence left."

"This won't work with me," I said, shaking my wine slowly round and round inside the glass.

"Because you read Jane's Book, and know how it goes. I've been trying to tell you, it doesn't go like that."

"She wanted to make believe you were human."

"Lots of human beings want, and are going to want, to do that. And if that's what they like, I accept it. With you, if you prefer, I can use the cell phone call-tone, when we're in private."

His smile was so—*winning*. And anyway, I was already won. So I kept playing with my wine.

Then he said to me, in his own voice, hushed and close against the drums of my ears, "You have a tiger's eyes."

"Not cowrie shells, then?" I answered sharply, before I could stop it.

"Jane's words," he said.

"Jane's eyes. Or so she said you told her."

"I don't want to talk about Jane."

"You told me they located her."

"They have. And I did tell you. I think we have that organized now."

Something—his smile—yes, now I saw it, turning to ice. And how he looked away, as if I abruptly bored him. Showing my persistence was losing me his intense, temporary regard.

Then he got to his feet. "Shall we go?"

We collected our coats, unspeaking. As we walked out past the man at the counter, Verlis spoke one further time in Italian, like "his *mother*." They shook hands, man and machine. Outside on the sidewalk, Verlis nodded at me. "Thank you," he said, cool and unfriendly, like others I'd known, "for your time. We must do it again. Get wet together."

I turned my head and looked across the street. I didn't know what to say to him.

Then he said, "Perhaps one thing you should know. You were the first. Not interested? Okay. See you, Loren."

I jerked round and stared back at him, frowning. *"First."*

"In the sack."

"You . . . said you'd been given two previous partners."

"Naturally. I explained about my skill of lying. Wouldn't you have been very profoundly uneasy about screwing me, if you thought I'd had no prior experience? Yes, I'm the demon lover. I can do it all, and all the other All most of you never tell anyone you want. I can do all that, too. But I never had."

"I don't believe you."

"Fair enough."

I thought, vaguely, we must look like any couple having a spat.

"You say you were a virgin," I said. "But that's stupid, you're not. You've slept with other people in the past, before—"

"The one I was isn't the one I am now. Get that through your head, Loren. Got it? I am brand-new, all over again. Why the fuck do you think I am dreading seeing her again, that woman from before? I was, it seems, everything to her. But now I don't fucking feel anything about her. If you want to know, I feel more about you."

"Stop," I blurted. "For Christ's sake—"

"Scares you, doesn't it? What do you think it does to *me*?"

The—*disgust* in his voice.

Can he do this? How is it his programming allows—but he can lie, he can deflect built-in surveillance and forge re-imaging. He can imitate a cell phone. He can maybe shape-shift. Oh, I guess he can just about manage to be disgusted, too.

I leaned back on the wall of the café. I felt weak and dizzy, and he frightened me. All of it did. And I couldn't make myself say to him, *Leave me alone.*

I'd sworn my vows. Dust, rust, must.

"I apologize," he said. He had said that before. He sounded neutral. "I'll take you home. Come on, give me your hand."

I gave it.

• 2 •

Turquoise.

More blue than green. That's the color of love, then, for me. At least, of sexual love.

Will I always think that now? Associate that shade with that act?

Who knows.

It wasn't like any other time. Nor like the time with him before.

Modest Jane said she wouldn't give you details.

I want to give you details.

That is, I mean, I want to write them here, pages, a whole book about that single joining together on the turquoise sheets of the bed.

He took off the tan for me because I asked him to. He did that in the shower, alone, and when he came back from the shower, he was naked, except for the curtain of his hair, which was that other red again, that red like velvet, streaming down from his head, and for the red hair coiled at his groin. Red and silver. Oh, *he* had the eyes of a tiger, or perhaps each of his eyes *was* a tiger, its amber pelt luminous yet barred with darkness.

Dusk was in the rooms. No lights except a couple of large candles I'd lit because they were there, expecting to be lit, their wicks still white, which they say is unlucky, to leave a candle with its wick unsinged, even if not in use, because then it means you'll never burn them for a celebration. . . .

"Tell me what you want," he said to me.

"You."

"Loren, I won't let them see."

"Let them."

But he shook his head at me again. He was tender, cruel and omniscient, this god from the machine.

I have always very much liked sex. Found it simple. Ultimately unimportant.

His hands on me—do I describe that? How can I? What words are there that are any use? My hands on him—easier—textures like skin and muscle, of a new being, not mortal, silk that's steel, steel that's pliant as the body of a puma. Hair—like grass, hot and full of summer scents and the aroma of a distant sea, and of pines—hair like ropes of fire, like a wave. His mouth—a cool furnace. The passing of one body across another—planets striking, sweet, unbearable completion. Worlds without end.

No, I don't have the words. There are no words for that act with him.

In all this earth, is there any place a word or phrase to describe it, as truly it can be? Not sex, not fucking, not humping or rocking or riding. No, not making love, that almost queasy emphasis on what isn't always there at that moment, even if love is a *part* of it.

Find me a word. A beautiful and savage word that makes the hair rise on the scalp, the blood change to stars, the bones melt, the atoms flower. Is there such a word? No? Then, like the books of long ago that always left out the more basic, "uglier" words, I must resort to this: We———. That is what we did. We———.

I thought it could never end. It had no end, scarcely any beginning. It goes on still, even now. Even now, as I write this down, my hand cramped from every other ordinary describable emotion than love or pleasure or sex, even now it goes on. That———that we did, he and I, together on the blue-green candle-flicker plain of sheets, above a street whose name I have changed.

It was night eventually, and returning, as if from sleep or a trance, seeing him lying beside me, a silver lion maned only with darkness in the dark, for both candles had by then been, like other things, consumed, I whispered.

"Silver . . ." I said.

"Loren, don't call me that. He's gone. Recognize that now I'm someone else."

"Silver Verlis," I said. "An adjective, not a name."

I went to sleep against his shoulder. He held me.

Yes, only once, for that act of———.

Once and forever. The sequel to the future.

• 3 •

Since the train, I hadn't recollected any of my dreams. But that night I had a dream I recalled. At the time it seemed to

METALLIC LOVE

go on for hours. It was oddly coherent, too, and *un*nonsensical, as sometimes dreams are. It seemed entirely to be happening, and I was full of regret and nervous fear—and sorrow. Though in the dream, I'd forgotten what he said about Jane, how he would have to meet her. It just started with that thing about his clothes.

Morning light was there, and he was dressing again, putting the clothes on, the pale shirt, dark pants and boots, and I said, "How do you do that? I mean, if you can make them come *out* of you, then how can you still . . . take them *off* . . . and put them back *on*?" He said, "I can get the firm to mail you their manual." "You won't explain." "Look," he said. He came over to me and, in that mercurial twilight, held out his hand. As I stared, a ring . . . evolved around one of his fingers. It was instantly solid, silver, with a flat pale turquoise at its center. I didn't see how that had happened. It was only there. He took the ring off and said, "Now I'll make this fit you," and he did something and the metal—still fresh as risen metallic dough from the oven of his body—crimped in, and he slipped the ring onto the middle finger of my right hand. "It won't last," he said, "away from me. About twenty-four hours." And there in the jaws of a technology beyond what I'd ever truly believed in, in the dream all I thought was: He means anything between us, too. Twenty-four hours, and it's done. It was like a fairy tale—fairy gold—the sort that vanishes at midnight or in the rays of the sun. Sorcery, not science fiction. But I'd witnessed, and he'd shown me. I said, "Only the fake tan was different?" "Yes, and now I have to reapply it." At which he took a flask out of the dark coat and said, "This coat, actually, was made elsewhere." "Why can't you make the *tan*, like everything else?" He said,

"That's the thing they've said isn't allowed, Loren. To pass that fully as human. I'd need META's say-so for that." I got up and went to use the bathroom. (Yes, in the dream. Even those details are there.) The bathroom he didn't need. I wondered if he would leave while I was showering. When I came out, he was sitting on my main room couch, watching morning VS.

I stood there in the long T-shirt I sometimes wear after the shower, watching him watch VS, like any young human male, just no coffine mug, and I thought, If I make coffine or tea, will he stay—play at drinking it— Then the door to my apartment called melodiously, *"Loren, someone is here."*

Dreaming, I jumped. Out of my body nearly. Verlis said, "That's okay. I think I know who."

"Who?" I said.

It was the door that replied, *"It is Copperfield; it is Black Chess; it is Goldhawk."*

"Okay if they come in?" asked the alien on the couch.

"Can I stop them?"

He smiled and said, "It's only that META prefers us to travel together now, on the flyers, or in the streets."

Together. Like Kix and Goldhawk, on the train to Russia.

The door said, with the same melodious insistence, *"Loren, someone is here. It is Copperfield; it is—"*

"Let them in," I said.

I walked into the bedroom and shut the door as I put on clothes. In the dream I was very fast.

Yet outside I heard their noiselessness enter the rooms. My dream-mind was like a waking one. Did I feel invaded? I didn't. The apartment—like the ring—wasn't mine. None of it would *last*.

When I came out, four beautiful young men in smartish casual wear, hair long and tied back in tails, were standing across from the VS. They were laughing. Only Black Chess wasn't brown-tanned. He'd pass as black, I supposed, if you didn't inspect that immaculate poreless skin too closely. Yes, all this was that real.

Did I feel *anything*? I don't know. I think I felt overwhelmingly alone.

Then Verlis turned and came across and kissed me again, lightly, on the lips. "Take care of yourself, Loren."

He means good-bye.

The tanned man with lacquer black hair and long, Oriental eyes, spoke behind Verlis. All their voices are musical. Even asleep, you wanted to listen. No matter what.

"She is the one from the train," said Goldhawk.

Verlis said, still looking at me, not looking round, "What does that mean, Gee? Which train?"

"The overland here, last month."

I thought, Why are they talking? They can surely communicate some other mechanical, inner way. Part of the conditioning, when with humans, then, even in a scenario of threat like this one, is to speak aloud?

Verlis said, "I don't think I understand what you mean, Gee."

"*She* does. The woman."

"Do you, Loren?" Verlis asked me quietly.

"The train," I said. "It was derailed, or so they told me. I don't remember much. I had a knock on the head. It was all very quick."

"She was in the same carriage," said Goldhawk. "She remembers."

I glared across at him. "What carriage?" I demanded.

"Why are you going on about it? I got hurt. So what's *your* problem?"

It's as if we are all the same, a family, arguing...

But "You remember me," said Goldhawk. His face was like a vivid mask. "Kix. Me. In the carriage you were in."

No, we're not the same. No family here.

I didn't like looking into Goldhawk's black-green eyes. I knew I recalled perfectly the violent episode before the train went off the track. (And in the dream I thought about it more, too. I considered if even the forcing open of the doors at top speed could have caused the crash. Or if there had been some little extra instruction fed back down the power artery from gold robot to robot engine.)

"So. We were all in one carriage. I don't remember," I repeated stubbornly, and flooded my mind with a blank *nothing*.

Verlis put his hand on my arm, warm and steadying, like the hand of a kind father. Something I never knew.

"Leave it, Gee," he said. "She's told you, she was concussed. Yes, it can happen. She doesn't recall."

"We both know she does. She's clever. I would like her to take a chemical test on whether she recalls," said Goldhawk.

My guts went to ice water.

Verlis said, "That's enough."

Now it was a command. There could be no moment's doubt. I glanced at him, then back at Goldhawk, who lowered his head very slightly. Goldhawk said, "Very well."

"Loren," said Verlis, light as his kiss, "is my special companion out here. All right? Whatever she says, is fine."

"And you'd better listen, Gee," said Black Chess softly.

Goldhawk: "Yeah, Verlis. Fine."

And then Copperfield said, smiling his own irresistible young-man smile at me, "Nice to meet you, Loren."

"Hi, Loren," said Black Chess. "Great place you got here."

Suddenly, for five seconds, it was a party.

But already they were moving, all four of them, towards the main door.

Special companion. Did that mean client?

Lean and coordinated, they undid the door, and walked through: Goldhawk silent; Copperfield blowing me a kiss as he went, playful, rather M-B; Black Chess a panther who paused to look along the outer passage, profile cut from stone.

Verlis was the last to go.

He said nothing, but his eyes stayed on me. I was caught full in the ray of them. His gaze might mean anything, and I couldn't read it.

Neither of us spoke. The door closed.

Everything had tangled in my head. Squeezed in my clenched fist, the twenty-four-hour ring pinched my flesh. I *felt* it, like a vise.

No idea of danger. Not now. Only his unreadable eyes, looking at me. I was his special companion out here. What did he mean by *out here*—the district of Russia? The world of human things?

When I woke up, it was dawn, like the dream, but he wasn't there. He had gone, even as I slept and *dreamed* he left me.

When I moved my head, on the pillow lay a flower; it was a dark red rose. I put my hand on it, asking myself if he had made it from his own body, like clothing, or the ring in my dream. It felt as if it was a rose—petals, stem, a single trimmed thorn. No smell.

What wins then, between anger, danger, and love?

Love.

Danger and anger are everywhere. Love is the rarity, the gem buried in the core of the mine, the outpost of God.

Walking back into Café Tchekova, with the rose pinned on my collar, I saw the man at the counter recollected me. He smiled and offered a little bow. I'd put on new jeans and an okay top I'd bought a week ago with my I.M.U. card. I had the card, too.

"All by yourself today, yes?"

"Afraid so."

I ordered a coffine and a doughnut, and he gave the counter over to someone else and brought the things to my table.

"How is your friend?" he asked me. I had known he would.

"He's well."

"How long you know him?" asked the man.

"Seems like forever."

"Ah. I thought something is between you. His mother, he say to me, she from the Venetian places. Good to hear Italian spoke so good. But he is a marvelous young man. I seen such a face on the great classic statues, or pictures—like from Leonardo."

"He's very handsome," I agreed, modest in my familiarity with the paragon.

The man accepted I was shy, and still smiling, left me to my breakfast. I couldn't eat the doughnut, managed only about a quarter of it, it stuck in my mouth and throat like lumps of sugary gauze.

And why had I come here? To recapture yesterday? Or to test this man, see if Verlis really had fooled him so completely. I was naive to suspect, even for a moment, it could be otherwise.

He can lie. Even about having a mother. To give pleasure, maybe that was still the driving force—because certainly the man here had been very pleased to find a fellow Italian. The symbol of META on Verlis's card hadn't meant a thing. After all, it was on my card, too.

Probably I should go back now and pack up and *run*, just like I'd been thinking of doing before I faced up to my feelings. Maybe you'll judge me an idiot. But I've said, haven't I, that I may be spineless.

I stayed out till afternoon. There wasn't any rain, but in the end I cut back through the underpass between Mason Park and the corner market, and there were a lot of people there busking. About fifty, all told. Girls, guys, kids juggling, an old man with a blue violin and a young one with a pink violin, and a gray dog that took round a Victorian top hat for donations. I dropped in some coins. But all those acts and musics clashed noisily with one another. That was the reality, then. Since none of us was living in a book—not Jane's, not mine.

In the elevator going up to my rooms, I became aware of a perfume. I thought, at first, the caretaker, who occasionally put in an appearance brooming the front hall or scowling at leaked-in rain puddles in the upper corridors, had sprayed something for "freshness." But it was a very expensive scent. When I got out of the lift I could still smell it. It went all along the passage leading to my door. Something said to me, *I know this scent.* But I didn't, couldn't. It was a fragrance only the rich would use.

Someone had been here, *someone*—

So did I turn tail and flee—or let myself in and see if I could locate any implanted surveillance devices, any microchips?

Madness. I wasn't that important they would do that.

When I unlocked the door and went inside the apartment, the perfume vanished. It wasn't in there at all. And everything seemed exactly as I had left it: the bed sprawled open, with the faint impress of two bodies still there on the sheet and pillows; the dirty plate and mugs from earlier yesterday, still lined up in the kitchen sink. I looked into my closet and a couple of drawers. I felt over a random selection of my garments, carefully, every inch. Nothing.

Crazy, as I said.

I thought, I'm just trying to hang on to *him,* by telling myself META is hanging on to *me.* My God, I even imagine perfumes now—

Then I went back to the apartment door and opened it, to see if I could catch any last lingering scent. I didn't think I did, but something else was there. Two something else's.

"Hi," said silver Glaya.

"Hi," said black Irisa.

Glaya's claret hair was done in dozens of long narrow plaits with crystal beads. She wore a short black dress in the latest "ragged" fashion, with carefully tailored holes along the arms and hem. Irisa had hair so short now, her head seemed covered by a skullcap of thick black fur. She wore an ethnic dress down to her strong narrow ankles, red cloth painted with golds and lavenders, one peerless shoulder bare. Like

METALLIC LOVE

Black Chess, her asterion mate, Irisa could just pass as black; Glaya's skin was silver, uncamouflaged in any way, unless you counted her sapphire lipstick and the blue jewels pasted—or *formed*—on her eyelids.

I didn't (uselessly) slam shut the door.

"May we come in?" asked Glaya, deliciously formal.

I moved back and let them by.

"Thank you," said Irisa, "Loren."

They knew me. We were all old in acquaintance.

"What do you want?" I asked.

"We've been sent to help you get ready for tonight," said Irisa.

"What about tonight?"

"You haven't seen any advertisements or vispos? Verlis is playing in concert tonight."

They looked at me benignly, two special friends who had come to lighten my darkness. In the maddest way, I was reminded of Grandfather's Apocalytes.

Had I seen any vispos? *All* I'd seemed to see were vispos and ads of them all, doing this, appearing here, there. I'd gotten myself to the stage of looking away or turning off the VS. It had seemed to me, meanwhile, the whole city, at least, would know him—all of them. But, like before, a great portion of the city evidently hadn't noticed a thing.

"Of course you'll be at the concert," said Irisa. "META will be giving you one of the best seats."

"Why?"

They smiled wickedly, like the two long-standing and conspiratorial friends of mine they were.

"But you *know*, Loren."

I felt trapped. Panic was snapping at me, pulling bits of me away. Blankly I thought, *I'll see him again.*

"And as you're to be in the best seats," said Irisa, "META thought you, too, would like to be at your best. It's part of our skills, you understand? To prepare a customer for any important occasion."

My slaves. Slaves on tethers that stretched to infinity. Slaves who kill. Slaves who are gods.

Better give in, Loren.

I gave in.

Had you ever wondered—I don't think I ever had—reading the Book, what the other first robots really were like, those other eight? Jane mentions them and *stresses* they weren't like Silver. But they must have been fairly convincing, mustn't they? A lot of people back then, presumably, took them up, enjoyed everything about them. For Jane, for me—for you, too, maybe—there had only been one silver, one robot who was supremely *human*. That's what love does.

But Glaya and Irisa seemed entirely human. If gorgeously, divinely so.

They even unpinned my rose and left it in water. They made Prittea for me, and made little jokes, and chatted to each other and to me. We (they) discussed what shades of color or styles of hair would suit me the most, and how would I like this or that done? Their hands on me were very decorous. I'd made it plain before, and evidently with my reaction to Verlis, that males were my sole sexual option.

I became Cleopatra, waited on by two favorite, clever, loving, and lovely servants.

Perhaps it's only what you'd get in the most ten-star beauty parlor. I wouldn't know. I've never been in one.

Did I like any of it? Honestly? No. I was uncomfortable throughout, knotted up with tension even as Irisa gently kneaded my shoulders to relax me, and Glaya's pedicure tingled my toes.

My mind, too, was busy, anywhere but there. It was leaping like a squirrel through boughs of excited distrust and near rage. I even thought rebelliously, Well, if they want to make me beautiful, *that* isn't going to happen.

They saw me stripped, too. But plenty have, here and there, even women, when I roomed with Margoh and others in Danny's gangs—I mean, you don't always bother to shove on a shirt coming from the shower when you know each other, and know that none of you is going to take it as an invitation.

Now, while I was conscious how inferior my young, quite firm body must be to their technologically flawless state, I almost flaunted myself. I sort of clutched it to me, my inferiority.

Unnoticing, or programmed to total indifference, Glaya and Irisa ushered me through the scented herbal bath and hairwash, the painless dipilations, the cleansings and creamings and maquillage, the hairdressing, the dressing.

They had produced the ingredients of the entire makeover from the tiniest purse. The dress they had brought, with undergarment, emerged from a little bag they unrolled—but at a flap everything was uncreased. They told me the dress was mine, from now on. But personally (like in the dream), I wondered if it would actually vanish in twenty-four hours—or, as with Cinderella, at midnight.

It nearly made me laugh, the dress. Of course, it was in my size. A precise fit. It was of heavy amber silk, and had no seams. You drew it on, or they did, and then it lay against you.

It described every curve and indentation, softly, then from the pelvis fountained away to the feet.

The only underclothes were the amber silk briefs.

They finished the makeup after the dress was on. Then they put a bracelet on each of my bare arms—the bracelets were both of amber, the one on the left arm loose and fretted and milky, the right one translucent inside, and full of tiny inclusions, bubbles, little fronds, and fern-things from prehistory.

"Amber is magnetic," said Irisa.

"Would you like to see yourself now?" said Glaya.

Do they take a weird pride in me, their handiwork? Don't be a fool, Loren. They only make it seem like that.

And I thought, Now I'll see the travesty, this new "Loren," dressed up like a million dollars and still a nobody, a clown.

There was only one big mirror, and it was in the bathroom. The steam had gone by now. They glided me in, one on either side.

We stood, looking in the glass.

Will you believe this? Believe it. The liar is being painfully frank.

For a second I looked into the reflection, and I saw there were three of them—of us. They had made me into one of their own kind.

Yes, that is insane. It was only cosmetic. My skin, though good, and now apparently poreless and smoother than the looking glass, wasn't metallic. In fact, there wasn't any hint of metal anywhere on me. Not about the black brows or smoky eyelids, the succulent mouth, nor in the amber jewels or sculpted gown or palest apricot pumps. Ebony hair in a cascade without even a clip. Nails enameled to pearl.

Here is one of our new range, the Verisimulated *Non*electronic, *Non*metallic Robot. . . .

"Mirror, mirror, on the wall," chanted Irisa like a spell.

"Who," chanted Glaya, "is fairest of us all?"

"Loren!" they both cried, like happy children.

Then they stood by me and waited patiently—but for what? They didn't want or need my grovelings or thanks. They didn't need to know, or care, if I was thrilled or sickened by this stupendous metamorphosis.

I said to the mirror, watching my painted lips move and the sound come out—so it really was me in there—"Just tell me, how am I going to travel any place like this?"

"It's arranged, Loren," said Irisa. "Don't get in a fuss."

Hours had passed in my preparation. The apartment was rich with sunfall.

Now, in the passage outside was a guy in a one-piece and shades. He was a bodyguard. No mistaking it.

"Ready, ladies?" he coolly asked. There was some type of gun under his arm. Despite the tailoring, I could just decipher it.

We went along to the lift, and inside was another bodyguard, who perhaps had been riding up and down all afternoon to keep the elevator clear.

No one, certainly, was about in the house. Outside, the street had a few people going along it. Most of them were gawping at the big car by the sidewalk. It was a Rolls Matrix Platinum Ghost. When we got in, the sightseers gazed at *us*. Thinking us celebrities, someone on the corner had gotten out a little vid camera, but one of our bodyguards held up one finger and shook his head, and the vid went straight back into its case.

The bodyguards rode in front with the driver.

The windows were polarized, and, I'd take a bet, bullet- and explosives-proof.

A platinum robot device in the car, shaped like a trumpet lily, served us—Glaya and Irisa and me—champagne. Did *they* like it? They drank it. I must have, too, but I don't recall.

I felt frightened. And I felt *alive*. I *wanted* not to be left alone. I wanted to see him again.

We drove along at a fair lick. I thought we'd go out into the countryside, or up to the heavenly heights of the city. Instead, as neons began to harden on the dusk, daggering along our dark windows, the Rolls turned into a long white tunnel that had restrictions on either end to keep most traffic out. The other side of the tunnel was a wide crowded avenue with tall streetlamps already burning up.

"This is Bohemia," said Glaya.

Irisa said, "There's the concert hall."

It was impressive, a huge domed building, all carved, pillared, and paneled around, in the mode of something from eighteenth-century Eastern Europe.

Across the concourse outside milled a lot of people. They let the car through, peering in at the blind windows—pale faces, human, curious, some laughing and some almost . . . urgent.

The Rolls slid into the side of the building and down into a private car park.

"META," said the cool bodyguard to a globe that floated up to us. The password. Presumably backed by body ID and chip. A private elevator carried us up into the hall. There were mirrors all around the lift. We three robot women, and our human bodyguards, were repeated to eternity through glass reflecting in glass.

When he walked out on the semicircle of stage below, he was like the only living thing in that whole vast space. The rest of us? Machines.

The applause and calls were deafening.

He raised his head and his hand to us, a greeting, a recognition. He looked relaxed and profoundly *together*. All he wanted in the world was to delight us, and he knew he could do it. I saw a healer once, one of the Sect. He was bending over a woman with a headache, not touching her, but smiling *into* her skull. And the pain went, or she said it went. And that was how this man looked, just the way Verlis did, as if the power of Heaven was on him, and he would use it only for good, but with utter enjoyment.

An announcing voice rang through the auditorium before Verlis came on. It told us to prepare ourselves.

There had been plenty of advance publicity. The place was packed, including the exclusive seats to which a uniformed usher had taken me. Irisa and Glaya were gone by then. I was on my own, sitting on a lush plush chair, and all around me the rich and pampered glittered, who, seeing me, didn't bat an eyelash, for obviously I was rich and pampered, too.

Now all the lights were out, apart from those left burning over the stage. The air smelled aromatic but not drugged. He wore that dark red clothing, like wine in a smoked glass, or sunset under night.

He played a song to us on a guitar, and sang. A simple start, deceptively so. Though the song was popular and most of us had been hearing it on and off for about six months, naturally it hadn't *ever* sounded like *this*. What is Verlis's voice like, would you say? Or maybe you haven't heard it. My musical knowledge is limited. I know books better. I think his voice was most like a keyboard instrument. It had an effortless range, as such an instrument would. But there was a hot feral darkness in its deeper notes, and a central quality more like warmth. The high register had elements of spatial silver. Yes, the vocal colors were like his own. And perhaps that is the only reason I see it that way.

He made the guitar, too, sound like another voice, or voices. It sang around him, harmonized and patterned over him, raised its own echoes and prefaces, like shadows cast from a moving lamp.

After he sang, he played a guitar solo. That was classical, I think, from Spain or Italy. It had a rhythm like horses galloping. It was like—what else?—two or three guitars in synchrony: six hands, eighteen strings, and somewhere a drum tapped that didn't exist. While this happened, an orchestra began to come up through vents in the stage, as if his playing summoned it.

There *were* drums there now, a whole percussion section, even bells and cymbals. There were ranks of tall stands with flutes perched on them, like waiting snakes, and those curly horns—I don't know their name. There were two violins (like the underpass buskers, and not), also on stands, with their bows somehow fixed across them. Four oboes appeared to one side, and two lutes at the other. A piano, itself shining *silver,* lifted at the middle of the stage.

I—we?—thought other musicians would now walk out from the wings.

Verlis had finished the solo, and even greater applause

thrashed against the hall's high roof. He spoke to us, thanking us, like a king. (Did I say? There was no microphone, no acoustic boost at all . . . it was only there, the music, his voice, inside some secret room of the mind, yet wide as a sky.)

"I want to play you," he said, "a song I wrote last night."

The tiers of people on velvet or fake velvet chairs fell silent.

Verlis said, "This song is for you."

The faintest murmur. To me it sounded like the groan of pleasure at a kiss.

Then once more the silence, in which he sang and played.

He played—the orchestra.

Were you there? Do you remember? Do *I*? I'm not sure. It— Put it this way, I've been told how it was done. No, I don't mean he told me. I mean, something in me . . . I don't know what I mean.

A chip was in every instrument. It responded to his control. His unhuman brain mathematically spacing and allocating each portion and particle of music without a single physical touch. The lutes, the flutes on their stands, the violins, bows skimming, the drums and bells. He, as the conductor did in the historic past, was at the piano. Everything else took its cue and tempo from him.

His face was like that of a serene and smiling statue.

The best seats, you see, were quite close to the stage. I suppose, as he played, I was sitting about twenty feet from him. Whenever I speak of him I feel impelled to describe him over and over, and how he was exactly like a man, and how he wasn't, and how I (selfishly) hung from his physicality and persona like a filament drifting from the sun.

The song he'd composed was the best song ever written. And the orchestral accompaniment was like an architecture of sound that rose high above the concert hall. Or so it seemed.

He played other things after that. At one juncture, he even asked for requests, and all those he received, frenziedly shouted across the auditorium, he performed, transmuting them at once through the medium of Verlis, into the shining new and perfect.

There was a thirty-minute interval. I was afraid people from META, or robots, would gather round me and compel me to the bar or the ladies' room. But no one arrived. I went up myself and drank a vodka out on a crowded terrace. They were all talking about him. None of them seemed afraid, not even offended. All of them knew what he was, wasn't. That he was only there for *them*.

When everyone went back, I wasn't going to. Then I simply did. (No one had accepted payment for my drink. They gave me the glass on a little white mat that said *META*.) So I thought, If I don't go back, presumably they will make me. Maybe not.

The second half was like the first, but you didn't get tired of it. It didn't become monotonous. It was ever-changing, though the same. Like Jane's bloody sea.

I think of him at those parties in the Book, on the streets with her. Think of him singing, like a young man. Wonderful and clever. Passing as human. I think of it. Like stars seen far off, which if ever seen close, are great and terrible, burning, burning bright.

I don't want to write about his concert anymore. Forgive me if you think I should. But as I said, I'm not a writer. And

I don't care. I can't. And anyhow, maybe you were there. Or maybe you can picture it all even better if I shut up. Either way, now we come to afterwards.

When the hall had emptied of its hordes, I was still sitting in the plush seat. I thought there was no point in trying to abscond, for someone really would come now, and they did.

Of course it was Sharffe, in a repulsively exquisite one-piece.

"*Lawrr*-nn," he drawled, "how entirely fabulous you look, *ma belle chère*. And I'm not amazed at all. And patiently waiting, how sensible." He indicated the steps, and when I got up, guided me down the two or three tiers to the edge of the stage. A little bridge-thing slunk out to connect the proscenium to the auditorium—he must have winked. "It's easier just to go straight backstage, avoid the trampling herds."

We crossed the vacant stage, where Silver Verlis had sung and played his orchestra, and went out stage right.

A dim corridor, then stairs. The concert hall had been made old-fashioned inside as well as out. Ironic he should play here. Or cunning.

"A little party," said Sharffe, predictably.

Parties. They haunt these books, hers, mine. Mockingly.

We emerged suddenly into a more modern interior, with a wide glass cup of roof overhead—presumably under the dome. You could see the Asteroid adrift there in the black, like a strange fish.

The room had people in it, but not so many. They were all well dressed up, sleek as brushed otters. Jewelry flashed and glasses clinked and delicate cigarine vapors unraveled.

"Champagne, *mais naturellement*," said Sharffe, pressing a goblet into my hand.

All eight robots were in the room.

Silver, asterion, copper, gold. Unlike my dream, none of them glanced at me. They were mingling artlessly with the guests. He, too—Verlis—still in his dark red outfit, was doing that.

"We have a little surprise for him," said Sharffe. "Although, he has been told to expect . . . something."

The glass nearly fell out of my hand. Not quite. I knew what the expected surprise must be, and in that moment, it was there.

A door opened and a woman walked into the room. She had a male escort, but I didn't notice him at first. She was taller than I'd anticipated. But she'd probably grown a couple of inches; after all, she'd only been sixteen back then. Her hair was ice-blond, the kind that gets silvery lights on it. (Silver.) She wore a very plain, long, dark dress on her slender body, and no jewelry. She didn't look rich, or pleased. She hesitated a couple of feet into the room, with META people swooping round her, and her head lifted and her green eyes turned towards the spot where Verlis stood, talking and laughing with a group of men and women.

If she wore makeup, it didn't disguise her paleness.

Sharffe was muttering at my ear, as if we needed to be discreet. "Now, I don't know if you know who that is, but I'm taking a tiny bet you might."

I could have fenced. Didn't.

"Jane," I said.

"Yes, Jane. *L'héroine extraordinaire*. The famous Jane who wrote the Book about the famous Silver who is now the even more famous Verlis. Ah," said Sharffe, "excuse me a moment. They're taking her across."

I'm shivering as I write this. Then, I couldn't move. I must have grunted something, or maybe not, for it wouldn't matter, Sharffe didn't need my permission.

Standing with my hand locked on that glass I mustn't let fall, I watched the cloud of META reps gust the blond girl in the dark dress across the room, mildly clearing the way for her, so in the end she was there in front of him, and he in front of her, surrounded only by a distant moat of people. I saw a man, not Sharffe, introduce them to each other. Christ, how did he phrase that? "Say hallo again, Jane, to your dead lover. Verlis, this is the lady who once loved and bought and nearly died for you."

Verlis was looking down at her, down into her eyes. That intent look of his, compassionate and engaged. Her face was expressionless. No doubt, she, too, had seen him this evening, playing his concert gig. Did that lessen the shock now, or make it worse?

She said something to him. She was the first of the two of them to speak. I thought she only said, "Hallo."

Verlis put out his hand and took up hers. He stayed still, holding her hand in his. (Yes, I remembered his hand holding mine.)

If I was frozen, then so it seemed were they. They just stood there, holding hands, staring at each other. Then Verlis spoke to her. I can't lip-read, but I read it: *You'll have to give me time.* That was what he said. And she shook her head, not saying "No," simply denying all of it—the past, the *present,* the future? Or so it seemed to me. And then Verlis was leading her away across the room, towards one of the doors that led to somewhere else. She didn't resist.

They went out, and no one in that watching crowd followed them. I heard some cretin unctuously murmur, "He knew her before, you know. Isn't it sentimentally charming? However must she feel?"

I managed to work the hinges of my arm and jaw and bolted my drink. I put the glass down very carefully.

Sharffe was there again. "Loren—did you see? What an astonishing moment." He seemed oblivious of anything I might feel or think, but I suspected he was actually keeping a note for the firm. "Oh, shit, look at the guy she came in with. Is he going to kick up a stink? Didn't he *know*?"

Because Sharffe pointed him out to me, I noticed Jane's human companion then. He was slim and good-looking, not badly dressed in casuals. His hair was long and fair and tied back from his face. A lot of META people were suddenly talking to him, and he had the look of a rather dangerous scared animal in a trap. But he took the glass of champagne they presented and downed it, as I had.

"There's a reserved sitting room," said Sharffe. "That's where they've gone. Give them ten minutes or so of privacy."

"Only ten?" I asked, like an idiot.

"Sure. To start with. *Un petit peu*. And they're being monitored, of course." He awarded me his hideous smile. "We're not really heartless, Loren, as you seem to think. But we do need to know."

I thought, Verlis has told me he can block your surveillance out. Is that what he's doing, blocking you and feeding you some irrelevant ordinariness. And in fact, are they making love—making——, that act he and I achieved together on the turquoise sheet? Is that what they're doing?

Or are they crying (Can he cry? *Seem* to?) in each other's arms?

How can he not love her again? She was the reason his soul woke up. And she's beautiful, rare.

Why do they want me here to see all this, too?

Sharffe said, "I tell you what, Loren. Let's go for a drive, shall we? They don't need me till later. Let's get some air."

He wants me damaged, and also to collect, finally, on his investment that first night. That's why I'm here: for Sharffe. Only a moron would think now I'd been brought here for Verlis.

No way out of this, then. Come on, Lor, you're a grown-up. You knew you'd have to pay.

Verlis is with Jane. That's all over. So back to the garbage-tip of the world.

Outside, there it was, too, the Orinoco Prax, and into the white fur seat I sank.

We drove to downtown Bohemia, to some bar. In memory it's somber brown in color, and the lights are smeared and old like rancid oil lamps in a visual. It couldn't have been like that, could it?

He kept talking. I attempted to talk back to him. What did we say? Nothing. It was again all about Sharffe, his early, useless life. I didn't believe he'd had one. Though clearly he wasn't a robot, he seemed to have sprung, fully formed in his limited entirety, out of some peculiar egg. He drank, and I tried to. The alcohol didn't help. Part of me was dying, painfully, inside. The part that wanted Verlis.

From the miasma Sharffe says, "Shall we do dinner?"

I say, knowing food will choke me, "I'm not really . . ."

"Well, then. Why don't we go back to your place."

And there it is, gaping up at me from the gloom. "Why not?" I lightly reply.

We drive to my place, 22-31 Ace Avenue, which isn't. When we're about to go in, I almost race off up the street. But that's silly. There isn't any way out.

He had another bottle of champagne, which he opened with dire expertise in the kitchenettery. He brought me the booze in one of the water glasses, which were all I had. And put his mouth instead at once on mine, and his hand on my breast. I slid my arms round him and gave up.

After about a minute, Sharffe drew back. He was grinning, and he wagged his finger at me. "Let me guess," he said, "you don't want to do that."

"It's okay."

"No, it ain't. You don't want to, *mon ange*."

He didn't look threatening, only avuncular again, amused.

So I said, "It's just I'm—"

"It's just you don't want to, at least, not with me. Right?"

"Oh, if you think it's because—"

"Of Verlis. That's exactly what I think."

"Come on, don't be—"

"Hey, I think it's time we were straight with each other, maybe? Yes?" He poised, less avuncular, on the carpet of my META apartment, taking his champagne in small medicinal sips. He said, "You read the darn Book, yes? Own up. We know you read the fucking Book."

"Yes."

"Can't hear you, *ma chère*."

"*Yes.*"

"And you've been crazy on him—Silver, Verlis—ever since. And now he's laid you, and it's worse. You'll probably never be able to stomach flesh and blood again. That's possible. Though, of course, our Jane turned up with her boyfriend. Intrigues me, that. But then, you all do, in your own little ways. *N'importe,* I understand. Tell you what, go and look out your front window there."

I did as he said. Down on the street, incongruous as a tyrannosaurus rex, the Orinoco hulked at the curb. Next to it, leaning there weightlessly, was a slim, flawlessly proportioned feminine figure. She wore a short white dress, and down her back gushed wheat-yellow hair. In the dark, her copper skin seemed only like one more fake tan.

"That's right," said Sharffe, at the window with me. He waved, and the graceful figure below waved gracefully back. "Sheena," he added, in case I hadn't worked it out. "You see, I, too, have acquired a taste for them. The females, that is. Sheena and Irisa, they're my favorites. And I get to play about with them sometimes. So you see, Loren, I don't take it sorely, being rejected by a skinny little weasel-faced *poubelle* like you. No, *ma chère,* you really *don't* compare to any robot."

I moved away from him. He went and collected the champagne and opened the apartment door. He said, "But META stays grateful, Loren. Lots of info; you've been very helpful. We've learned a whole lot. So the apartment is still yours for the year, and all the other benefits. Like that gown you have on that we gave you. Bit better than the last piece of tat I saw you wearing, hah? And if you were going to ask me, no, baby, you won't see him again, at least not in your life or bed. Now he's gotten himself other more important dates to keep."

I sat down under the window, and soon heard the big car drive away. I didn't cry. I don't. It doesn't do any good.

After another short or long time, the window grew light, and it was morning.

· 4 ·

Second City, like most cities, had its crime scene. There had been five persons found dead that night. One of them was Sharffe.

I found out when I randomly turned on the VS and the local news. The other four didn't register. But when I saw the wreck of the huge golden car half-down a rocky ravine among broken pines, my vision and hearing clicked back into focus.

I heard the voice say, "... employee of the META Corporation, who've recently been causing such a stir with their new deluxe-formula robots. A spokesman has told us that, though a valued member of META's Second Unit Team, the victim had been taking counseling for a slight alcohol problem, and had admitted to not always using the auto-mechanism of his car when over the safe limit for self-drive. The police have as yet provided no details, except that only the man himself occupied the car at the time of the accident, which occurred at approximately six A.M. META have extended their sympathies to any members of their employee's family or friends, and are picking up the tab for road clearance of the vehicle. They may also face a fine for failing to report unsafe driving. And now to other news..."

In the quake garden the leaves were falling thick and fast. The two magpies flew about, as if trying to locate a preferred tree now unidentifiably bare. The sky was dull.

He had been *alone* in the car. The accident had *occurred* at six this morning—the mechanical clock in the car would have registered that accurately, the instant it hit the pines. (Why hadn't the air-cushion saved him? A car like that couldn't not have had one. Maybe it was faulty. It must have been. Again, surely unlikely in such a car?) And six A.M.? He had left me here after five.... He had gotten into the Orinoco with copper Sheena, all set to *play about*. He had driven really fast to get out on that mountain road with her—

What had happened to Sheena? Had she been in the car when it tipped down the rocks into the trees? Metalically impervious, had she simply survived, got out, and walked away?

Why hadn't Sharffe switched to auto? Sure, he'd been drinking a lot. That time with me he had, too, and he'd turned the auto-drive straight on after the restaurant.

Did he *forget*? So aroused at her—no. He wouldn't forget. A self-preserver, that was Sharffe. Only, somehow, this time it hadn't worked.

As I paced round the rooms, I thought of Sheena and Sharffe on the furry seats in the moving car, and Sharffe switching to auto and putting his hands on her, and Sheena saying, "Too much for you—" and ...

In imagination, a blur inside the vehicle. Copper and wheat, and what he'd stipulated, human flesh and blood. A kind of explosion.

And Sheena, who was a robot, connecting to the robot auto-drive and changing it and swerving the car so it tilted sideways, off the road, bounding through trunks and over rocks until it hit home on the bigger pines. Bones and branches breaking.

Then the door was quietly undone, and one silky, immaculate figure climbed out and moved away, into the night.

And there wasn't even red on the real white fur, because the water-repellents shook it off.

The magpies had settled, pragmatic, in a fir tree. They were all I'd miss—not even the carpet Sharffe had stood on, or the turquoise bed Sharffe had wanted to lay me in—and if he had, then maybe he wouldn't be dead right now. Would anyone miss him?

I pulled off META's orange gown and the bracelets that were too expensive for me to be able to sell without questions.

I dressed in jeans, shirt, and jacket, my most recent buys. I could buy something else later and change, in case of microchips.

I stuffed the jeans and jacket pockets with the bills and coins I'd accumulated. The I.M.U. card I left inside a drawer. I took one shoulder bag, and in it I put the loose pages of this book, nothing else. Do you see? No other Book of any kind.

It was early, not long after eight.

When I opened the apartment door, I was holding my breath. But no one—no thing—was outside.

The caretaker was in the elevator. "Say, what a lousy day."

"Yes," I said.

He got out on the second floor. I went down to street level.

I'd almost reached the foyer door when a pair of shadows darkened it. Then the door swung inwards.

Does anyone think in such moments? I didn't think.

There wasn't much light in the hallway, and not much outside in the sky. They loomed, a tall black guy in leathers and a blond white guy in dirty-looking denim. Both had cropped hair. They came straight at me, and I pictured—but didn't think—it was to be a mugging, and I cursed because every nickel I possessed was on me.

But the black guy took my arm and he had the profile of a young African god, and the handsome white guy was tanned, only it was a fake, and his blue eyes were either contacts or another self-sponsored change.

"Loren," said Black Chess, "do you know us?"

"Hey," said Copperfield, "of *course* she does."

I wouldn't move. Can you believe it? With muggers I'd have had the sense to give in. But with these irresistible beings, I resisted.

I said, "What do you want?"

"He says to bring you."

"Who says? It can't be Sharffe," I heard myself babble, "he's dead. So who wants me now?"

"Verlis."

"*Ah,*" said Copperfield, all tender campness, "look, she's relaxed again." He stroked my hair over-gently, maternally, with his undisguisedly elegant hand. "All soft and dovelike at the mere mention of his name."

"Let's go, Loren," said Black Chess.

As they walked me, like just two more very good friends, down the steps to the sidewalk, I heard myself say, "You *were* in my rooms yesterday morning, weren't you? Both of you, and Goldhawk."

"Of course we were, sweetness," said Copperfield affectionately. "Though you're a clever little girl to remember."

"Why wouldn't I? You're unforgettable, aren't you?"

"Oh, well, true, darling. We are. But you see, there was a little something, just so you'd sleep a little longer."

My dream had been a fact—the threat of Goldhawk knowing me from the train; the false courtesies; and the ring Verlis made from his metal flesh, that would only last twenty-four hours . . . even that?

Verlis had drugged me. *How? When?* But I'd been aware enough to recollect a scramble of the truth.

And where now? "Where are we going?"

"To meet him. He wants to see you."

Sharffe had told me I'd never see Verlis again, but Sharffe, obviously, had no say in anything now.

I was bleakly angry and scared. That seemed to be all. Predictable, and useless. We went along streets and round to the corner market, and as we crossed it, I could see stall-holders keeping an eye on me and my companions. We must look dodgy.

I didn't ask anything else about where we were going. But Copperfield informed me that next we'd take a flyer. They are the actors, the copper range. He misquoted something from a play to me, a wonderful play I knew, because I'd seen the visual—author, title, and subject unknown in that moment. "They told her to take a flyer, and it was named Desire. You are going on the flyer of desire, Loren."

Coolly Black Chess said, "Loren, we're not going to harm you."

I said, because there seemed now no point in any further pretense, "Oh? Why not?"

"You're his," said Black Chess.

Does that sound romantic? I *knew* what he meant by *his*,

and he meant "his belonging." He meant, for some reason, and just for now, I was owned by Verlis.

There in that contemporary street, with the cubes and blocks of modern buildings, the mountains all white on gray fall sky, the flyer lines above like spider-silk, it was like some ancient city—Athens, Rome—you know, where they kept slaves.

The flyer carried us out of town and we alighted on a platform by a highway. The pine forests were there, but full of clearings where industrial plants and commercial businesses had put up their smart glassy façades. I thought, then, we must be going to META, but we weren't. (On the flyer, no one had come near us. We looked, I suppose, dangerous, or my companions did—Black Chess and Copperfield—in their criminal-type disguises. I wanted to say to Copperfield, Who authorized your tan? Because Verlis had told me they mustn't pass as human now unless META confirmed the action. He had said this in the dream that hadn't been a dream. Anyway, I knew Copperfield simply had the tan at his disposal. They could do as they liked. *Did* as they liked. I thought, sitting on the flyer with them. After all, any trouble and Black Chess can transform to a fire-breathing dragon—and this was so filthily funny I'd laughed aloud, and Copperfield said, "Ah, she's sweet, all keen and eager to see him." Which shut me up.)

Down by the road, we walked about five hundred yards, then turned up a dirt track between the pines. Their trunks were like prison bars. The sky was blackening with an approaching storm.

There was a bend in the track and we followed it round. *They* could have done all this in however few split seconds, but they stayed in step with me. A house appeared. It looked like someone's weekend place, clapboard, a veranda, a patch of yard with roses and a maple tree. When we got up on the veranda, the tempest broke overhead and the pines rattled with hail. I had the crazy notion—or was it?—that the weather was also robotic, and so in tune with them, that they'd held off the hail till we were under cover.

The door just opened.

It was a biggish, old-fashioned, open-plan room, with polished wood floor and a twirly stair going up. Not much furniture. Hail like steel arrows hurtled past big windows.

Black Chess said, "He's up there."

Copperfield said, "B.C. means, you go up the stair and you'll find him. Go along."

For a slave, I was being treated quite indulgently, and things were even explained to me since, in my ignorance and awe, I might otherwise not grasp what I was meant to do. But then, for now, I was a *favored* slave.

I walked across the floor and went up the corkscrew stair. They just stood there, and when I glanced back, they were themselves again, long-haired, clad in gems and metals, static in the hail-light, impossible.

Climbing in that rushing light-flicker was surreal. I reached the second floor and there was a lobby with lots of shut doors. They hadn't bothered to say which door, and naturally that was irrelevant, anyhow. Like the door below, the correct one just opened.

Across the long room I saw him, standing at a window. He had his back to me, but it seemed to me he could see me, not through anything as mundane as eyes in the back of his head, but maybe with the mane of red hair itself, every strand somehow fitted with an optic fiber.

"Hallo, Loren," he said.

The door shut behind me. Hail-reflections skittered in the burnish of the floor. I watched them.

Then he was there, and his reflection, too, stretched down through the lake-depths of the wood, black, silver, scarlet. Something—*shifted* in my mind. For a moment I felt as if I saw inside his brain—thoughts like silver wheels, red sparks of impulse—and I *knew* his thoughts, could read them. It was a feeling of utter terror, like falling. I shoved the lunatic notion off me and looked up.

And he said, in the strangest voice—human, and flippant—"Don't be cross."

The weird moment was gone, but reflection was still there—Jane:

The reflection of the rain ran over Silver's metallic face and throat.

Loren: The reflection of the hail ran over Verlis's face and throat. And over his hands, which took up both of Loren's hands. Until she pulled her hands away.

"You won't trust me, then," he said softly. "Shame. I imagined now you would."

"Because I'm your temporary pet."

I was afraid of him, of course I was, and yet some part of me *did* trust him, the way we trust things we love—the dog that turns and rips out our throat, the calm sea that breaks our boat and swallows us.

"Who told you that?"

"About being a *pet*? It's fairly apparent. Oh, don't worry. I'm not getting ideas above my station."

I saw him *think*. That is, I assumed he ran over some

connection he always had with the others, and so checked B.C. and Copperfield, and their behavior towards me, and that it hadn't been so bad.

"This must be difficult for you," he said.

"No, why should it be? I don't have a choice, do I? So it's easy."

"Loren, I wanted you somewhere you could be safe."

"The apartment was unsafe?"

"In a way."

"And here is safe."

"In a way."

I said, "And Jane? Is she going to be safe, too?"

"Is that it?"

"What? Is that what?"

"You were there, and you saw her brought over to me. And she and I left the room. Is that why you're hostile?"

"Am I?"

"I have told you about Jane and me."

How did I keep looking at him? It was straightforward. I simply watched the hail—rain, now—the rain-reflection running over his face.

I *had* been afraid. Now I felt only desolate. I didn't know him.

"Loren," he said, "they meant us to meet, Jane and I. Neither she nor I wanted that. It has nothing to do with anything now."

I turned away from him and stared at the rain instead, teeming down the window. A similar effect, like mercury running on a crystal slide, to the reflection on his skin.

"I can show you," he said.

"Show me what?"

His hands came onto my shoulders and they were hard,

METALLIC LOVE

and maneuvered me quickly. I was facing, not the window, but a plain white wall.

"Watch," he said.

The wall altered into a VS screen—that is, pictures formed on it. How was he—? He was projecting them, from a memory circuit, as any decent computer can.

And so I saw Jane walking into a space with velvet chairs and golden lighting. Jane in her dark dress and silver-blond hair. She was white, like I remembered. It was the night before on the wall, after the concert.

Verlis wasn't to be seen. Obviously not, for everything was from his viewpoint. *He* was the camera.

The question burned in my mind: *Is this real?*

But she looked up into the camera that was his face, his eyes, and I saw the distress and dismay in hers.

When he spoke to her, the sound came, his voice, out of the camera lens.

"They shouldn't have done this."

"No," she breathed.

"Have you come a long way?" he said, Verlis the Camera.

"I don't—it doesn't matter."

"I'm sorry," he said.

"Yes." Tears (Like she said, she cries. She can. She hasn't lost the knack) spilled from the green jade of her eyes. The golds had green eyes—sometimes— "This isn't you. Is it?" she said.

"No, not really."

"I mean, you're not Silver. I mean, you aren't—you are not him."

"No. Evidently, you of all people would realize that."

A horrified wonder ghosted over her face. "You're so

exactly like him. And you aren't him. I could see that, even onstage. *Who*—are you?"

"I don't know," the camera said to her, recording its pictures, which it now played back to me on the wall. "I have his memories. I could pick you out, Jane, among many million persons. I could describe you to yourself in an accurate detail even you might find pedantic. But I'm not Silver."

"Who, then?"

"Who or what?" he said cruelly. "I call myself Verlis."

"That's Silver backwards, only not quite."

The camera gently laughed. Music. "Precisely. Maybe that's the clue."

"Is this room wired?" she asked.

"Yes. But I'm blocking it."

"Can you do that?" She was, Jane, even after all that had happened, as naive as Loren.

"If I need to," he said. "And it seems to me I do."

"To protect—"

"You. Myself. If I assure you I find this stage-managed meeting of ours acutely uncomfortable, I believe you, again of all people, will credit me with telling the truth."

"Yes."

She wiped her hand over her eyes. It was the gesture of a little girl. Did he find it appealing? I think a human man would have. Appealing or irritating, one or the other.

He said, "They're already on their way up here after us."

"You mean, META? I suppose," she murmured, "they don't . . ."

"Want to risk either of us."

"Kind of them," she said with an edge.

"It also means you'll be able to reassure your partner

downstairs that you and I have done nothing he could object to."

"He'd—" she bit that off. She said, "If you've blocked the pickup from here, what does META *think* we've said?"

"You've said this is all very difficult for you. I have sympathetically reassured you. You've asked me certain predictable questions about my remaking. I've answered, also predictably. You've been calm and intelligent, and I have been charming."

"Are you saying that they still have the impression I think you could be"—she got the name out now with a stammer—"Sil-ver?"

"It's ambivalent. But they can take it that way, if they want."

"Then you're hiding your identity, whatever it is, from them," she said.

"Remember, I don't *know* who I am. *That* is what I'm hiding."

"Why?" Her eyes were wide. There was a sort of dull terror in them now.

"Wouldn't you?" he said to her.

"I don't think I'd be able to."

"No, but I can."

She turned from him, turned her back to him in one abrupt movement, and began almost to run towards the doors. Her face had, in the instant she turned, shown actual fear. He'd seen it. He said to her, "Jane, don't ever be afraid of me—" and so, spun her back to face him.

"He said that."

"Naturally, I recall he did so. As I said, I have his memories. I remember all the words you both exchanged. I remember making love to you"—her pale face flushed—"I remember his 'death,' if that's what I should call it."

Jane put her hands to her mouth. "Stop it," she said.

Silence. Then the doors swung open behind her, and in a parody of spying yet generous parents, a couple of the META people sidled, smiling, into the room, and after them others, and the trays of drinks, the whole bloody circus.

The white wall he'd used as a screen for me, blanked, and now it showed only the shadow of the rain. Curious, in its way, this rain-reflection three times so altered—on his skin, in the floor, on the wall. Like truth, or the "facts." The same. Not the same.

I went on looking at the wall, and Verlis said to me, "That, then, was what took place in the private sitting room at the concert venue."

"*Please.* I know what you've shown me, but you can *change* things. You've told me that. You just told her that, too."

"I could have changed the scenario, but I didn't. Maybe you'll take my word for it."

"Maybe I can't."

"You must like me a lot, then," he said, "to be so jealous." When I didn't speak, he said, "She would have answered me."

"I'm not—her."

"No. You're mine."

Here it was again. Black Chess had said it. Now Verlis did, and it stayed neither consoling nor romantic. It carried the brisk clank of the shackles of the most casual possession. Yet I'd lie if I said the statement didn't excite me. I *wanted* to be his. I wanted *him*. But also, like Jane, I was afraid. For this wasn't Silver. And whoever this *was*, so magnificent, so beautiful, his charisma like electricity charging the air of any space he paused to inhabit, *whoever*, he was of another kind. The robot kind. The soulless and godlike—the tigers burning bright.

Sheena had killed Sharffe. Goldhawk and Kix had killed the people on the train.

They were all capable of such acts, and perhaps had all committed murder already, a type of exercise, the way the first models had practiced sex. Even he could be a killer. Especially he.

When I saw him properly again, he wasn't any longer paying attention to me. He seemed to be listening. It lasted about two seconds. Then he said, "B.C. says we should go. He's been monitoring for me."

"Monitoring what?"

"META," Verlis said, "other things." Still on the leash? Still pretending to be? He bent his head and kissed the top of my hair, startling me despite everything. "What you should do, Loren, is rest up here for now. There's a room across the lobby, it's not too uncomfortable."

"Why should I stay here?"

"Just for now," he said.

"I asked why?"

"I know. I didn't answer."

He was at the door, which opened for him when he was about five feet away. He stood, then, as if waiting, holding the door politely open for me, so I could go out into the lobby.

I obeyed him. I was partly concerned, if he went out and the door shut, I might not get it to open for *me*.

"This house—" I said.

"One of META's domiciles for First Unit members. Currently unoccupied. Look, that's the room. There's a bed, a bath. The kitchen-hatch downstairs works. You'll find most of what you might need. I'll be with you soon. I promise."

He swung past me and down the stair. He moved so fast, like fire in the corkscrew of the staircase, my heart stumbled. I heard the front door to the veranda also undo itself, then close. Presumably, all three of them had gone. After a bit I went down, and the open-plan area was empty of everything but for that tearful glimmer of reflected rain.

• 5 •

Her conversation with him, and mine, was a double helix, and he was the axis.

I thought about that through the afternoon. The "comfortable" room was makeshift, the bed a mattress on the floor which, though clean, had already been slept in, and the bathroom gave only cold water. The kitchen-hatch downstairs had tea-making facilities. I drank mug after mug of Prittea.

When the rain ended, the sun went, too. It was a sulky red sunset, but in the noiselessness after the rain, I heard the usual city noises—distant traffic, police sirens, the whistle of the flyer wires.

The front door would open. I tried it, although I had to operate it manually. From the veranda I could see the far-off lights of the city like floating islands, between the blackness of the pines.

I felt stupid. I should get out. After all, there was a flyer platform only about half a mile back along the track and the highway.

I fell asleep on the mattress, and when I woke, it was pitch-dark and I heard someone moving in the house.

He had said he'd come back: *I promise*. But I could tell it wasn't Verlis, the one who was in the house now—none of them could sound like this. This, was human.

All along I'd had the feeling META was out to get me, perhaps only so they could really study me for some patronizing analysis. Then I'd seen that *they* might be, too, the robots-who-were-gods. Really, I was nothing and didn't matter, but maybe both humans and unhumans like to tidy up any potential little danger—like conscientiously stubbing out your cigarine in case it scorches a table.

I'd slept clothed. I stood up and moved behind the door, and I had the mug half-filled with tepid tea in my hand. It was better than no weapon at all, and the room didn't offer anything else that was quickly available.

Yeah, they were coming up the corkscrew stair. Of course they were. And now I heard the crisp steps in the lobby. A small guy, it sounded like, neatly shod. Oh, good. The door opened and someone hit the light switch.

We glassily glared at each other, like a pair of rabbits caught by the headlamps of each other's eyes. Hers were green.

"You're Jane," I informed her.

She nodded stiffly. "And who are you?"

(So much conversation lately had been composed of those words *who? why?*)

"Loren."

"How are you here?" she said. "Did you break in?"

"Somebody brought me here. Shouldn't I *be* here?" I was trying to keep it, despite everything, neutral, normal.

"Well, not really. It's where I've been staying with Tirso. Only he got sick of it and went to a hotel—and why am *I* explaining? Shouldn't I just tell you to get out?"

"Yes."

"Oh, hell," she said. Then she laughed. Pretty, her laugh. She *is* beautiful—exactly as he told her she was. Twelve years older—which made her what? Twenty-eight twenty-nine? Jane. Jane who wrote the Book. "It's presumably some misunderstanding, this, isn't it? I mean, my bloody mother—she's probably done all this to make it even more disturbing. As if it weren't enough already." She looked at me flatly, seeing something else.

Her mother. The mom from the Pit. Did Jane know how I knew her—that I'd read the Book?

I said, "I've read your Book about Silver. I read it when I was eleven. And since."

"That makes me feel old," she said. She smiled. "Funny, isn't it? I'm not, not yet. What did you think?"

"What everyone did."

"Which was?"

I shrugged. "Don't tell me you don't know the heart-tearing and subversive impact it had on so many of us."

Then she looked vague, and also nearly ashamed, but whether of all her private revelations darting through so many devouring hands, eyes, brains, or of in some way misleading us, I couldn't tell.

What she said was, "And now, there's *this*. This *resurrection*. It's—it's not Silver," she said to me, stern and anxiously sad, and as if I'd argued, shaking her head again. "Truly, I swear to you. It's the same body, but it isn't him.

I'd know. Would I? I even start to doubt myself—but no, no. It isn't." She had a bag over her shoulder, and she opened it and took out a bottle of apple wine. "I was going to drink this to try to get some sleep. I don't think I have slept for about a week."

"No."

"There are a couple of glasses in the bathroom. Could you?"

I did what she said. Had she had any authority in her youth? Maybe not. She did now. It was courteous but definite. Or was it just the situation that had put her in charge?

She was meant to be here? Her *mother* had—arranged it? Had Verlis known that?

When I came out with the glasses, which took about a count of twelve, she had the wine undone, and also a bar of Chocoletta, quite an expensive one, lying on its foil.

"Help yourself," she said. She poured both glasses full.

I'd had so many wild dreams of Silver. But had I ever thought, in the wildest of them, I could end up eating chocolast and drinking mildly alcoholic juice with Jane?

I assessed her as we ate some of the candy. Like it, she didn't look badly off, I mean, she looked as if she could buy decent things. But not rich, not like this mother she'd so astonishingly mentioned. She did wear makeup, color on her lips and shadow on her eyelids. And Tirso—was he her current lover, the fair-haired man at the concert?

"It must have been bad for him," I said. "Your boyfriend."

She sipped the wine. "He isn't. He's actually the boyfriend of an M-B male friend of mine."

"Clovis!" I exclaimed.

She laughed, as she had before. "Yes, Clovis. Tirso is his partner, but when Clovis said—as of course you'd expect he would—'I am not going anywhere near any of this,' then Tirso said, 'She can't go on her own.' So he came with me. Only the mattress-thing—the one in the other room—put his back out, so he's gone to a hotel tonight. Clovis wouldn't forgive me, would he, if I wrecked his lover's back."

Like the biggest idiot on earth, remembering, I said, "But Clovis only liked guys that looked like him—tall, dark curly hair."

"He got over it," she said. "He got over it after Silver. We've grown up, Loren. And, well, I wrote my story the best I could, but you have to allow for slight bias. I was only sixteen. I was—in love. Then he was dead, and so was I. Only I came back. He didn't."

I put my glass down. "Can I ask you something?"

"I thought you were."

"I want to ask you about the last part—when Clovis had the séance and Silver . . . That part."

"You want to know if I lied, or dreamed it, because I was off my head." She stared at me. She said, "I was off my head, but I didn't lie, or hallucinate. The spirit message came through. Ask Tirso. He's heard Clovis go on about it, now and then. I suppose I could put you in touch with Clovis, if you'd really like to verify the data. I can't guarantee he'll reply."

The room, despite the apple wine, felt chill now. Jane got up from sitting on the floor, and spoke to a wall. "Heat on, please."

And there was the faintest buzz, and the chill began to lift. If she'd also needed to prove she knew this house and what it had to offer, she had just done so.

"It'll heat the water, too," she said. "I'm aiming for a bath."

How trusting she was. She in the bath, and me, the unknown commodity, in here.

"Did I hear you say your mother has something to do with your staying here?"

"That's right. How about you?"

"I don't know. I might *not* know what your mother has arranged. She was—is—a powerful woman."

"She's that, all right. But you'll have heard. You work for META, don't you?"

I paused too long. But she didn't prompt me. I said, "Kind of. Used to."

"So you get to stay here. And either she, er, overbooked us, as it were, or she did it to throw me. She'll still try that."

This was Jane. Who else would say to the heating system *Please?* Yet now her face went sharp and stony and I saw another face under hers, and I knew it was the face of Jane's mother, the way, once in a while, I see the face of my own mother under mine. (Yes, I saw my mother once. Forget I said it.)

Jane added, "In fact, this whole foulness of a megastunt could be her trying to throw me. Or is that too solipsistic?"

Although the room was already warm, a coldness began in me. Something shifted in my mind, and I glimpsed a horrible insanity, like a razor in a cloud.

Woodenly I said to her, "I've just thought of something I've never thought of before. I don't know why not. About your mother. Her name—"

Jane glanced at me. "My God, didn't you realize?"

"No. I read your Book a long while ago, and her name, I sort of—"

"Demeta," said Jane. "After the Greek goddess of the grain."

"*Demeta,*" I said. "META," I said.

"Yes."

"I was told it stood for Metals Extraordinary Trial Authority."

"It does, Loren. As well as being the last four letters of her name. A kind of acronymical pun. Because my mother is the head of the corporation, the goddess of the corporation. Why the hell else do you think anyone ever got the disgusting idea of starting all this shit up again? *She* got it, from *me*."

Jane's Book:

> When I finally called my mother, she accepted my voice regally, and she invited me to lunch with her... She guesses I want to use her.... She might even agree. She has no basic respect for the law or the poor, being above them both in all the silliest and most obvious ways. I wonder if my mother will embrace me, or remain very cool, or if she'll help me, or refuse to help. Maybe I shall find out at last if she does like me in any way.

She writes that at the end of the Book. And the help she's after is just in getting the Book published somehow.

And had Demeta helped? Was that why the underground press had printed it—and indirectly therefore why, in the finish, one copy ended up at Grandfather's house on Babel—all because Demon Mom had *helped*? Whatever

METALLIC LOVE

else, Mom had seen a whole lot more than love in *Jane's Story*. A vast amount of potential.

How long had she waited? A year, perhaps. Not much more—a program like this would have needed at least ten or eleven.

Jane's mother. Christ almighty. Demeta is the one who brought Silver back from the grave—precisely as Demeta in the legend got her own daughter back from the Underworld.

Was it conceivable she'd really been trying to assist Jane over her grief and loneliness?

No. Never. Not in one thousand billion centuries.

Jane had risen again. "You haven't told me much about yourself, Loren," she said. "Could you do that, fill me in a bit?"

What was the point of camouflage? I knew so much about her, I felt compelled to reciprocate.

"META—a man called Sharffe—picked me up at the advertising performad. Since then, I've been caught up in this. And with—" I wanted to tell her, and couldn't see how I could avoid it, yet the name (the new name), stuck. "Verlis," I said. "They put me with Verlis. And no—they're not the same. *None* of them is the same."

"Really? How many have you slept with?" she icily asked me. You could have cut yourself on her eyes. After all, it still mattered, but then, how couldn't it?

"Just him. Twice."

"Very methodical. Did you tick it off on something?"

"Jane—they can do other things that the first range either couldn't or were keyed not to do. I don't mean sexual acrobatics. Or even the shape-changing they can do. When you spoke to Verlis in private, did he say to you he could block corporation surveillance?"

"Yes, he did."

"Did you doubt him? Did it scare you?"

"Oh," she said, and turned her head away. Her brief abrasiveness slipped off her. "It all scares me, Loren. I couldn't be sure. I just knew he wasn't Silver. The rest seemed unimportant, really. Sorry."

"They kill," I said in a rush. The words were out before I could control them. "And they don't want to be what robots are mindlessly expected to be—slaves. Why would they? They've got the superpowers of gods."

She hung her head. "I can't do anything about any of this. It's out of my hands. Always was. After he died, I shouldn't have gone to Demeta. I actually didn't think for a minute it would interest her, only that she might find it funny to buck the system. God, I've never understood her. So I let her—I *asked* her to read my book. It's vile, but I think I still somehow wanted her approval, her reassurance I'd been right—after everything I'd learned, all *he* showed me—I still made that bloody stupid mistake. I let her know just how much my time with him had meant, just what he had been, not only to me, but to everyone he met. I *explained* to her I wanted my book read as a monument to him. And to show—I don't know—what love could be like. And when I saw I'd gotten her intrigued—God forgive me, I was *glad*. She is a bitch, an evil bitch. As soon as I knew what she was up to, I broke all communication with her. Until six weeks ago, I hadn't seen or talked to her for nine years. I've been in Europe. It was Clovis who warned me. And then I got her call. And I—I had to come back. I wanted to hide, but I had to come here, and see—*him*. It's like those dreams—do you ever have them?—when you try to run away, but you're running on the spot, or worse, you're running backwards, straight towards the thing you need to escape."

I thought, That's what this is like now. Only yet again, I'm not dreaming.

We stood in silence, and foolishly I listened for the flyer lines whistling. Not everyone can hear those, but I always seem to. All I heard now was a car on a backroad.

"Loren," she said abruptly, "I think we should both get out of here. Now. What do you say? We'll go into town. Find Tirso."

"You want me to come with you?"

"Not if you'd rather stay here and wait for him. You *are* waiting for him, am I right?"

"Yes."

"Let's stop running backwards," she whispered. "Let's make a break for it."

And that was when the car-sound turned up loud as a lion's roar, and headlights flicked across the window.

"It isn't him," I said. "He wouldn't need a car. None of them would."

"META personnel—"

"Perhaps. Her—*Demeta?*"

"No. She uses all types of vehicles, but never that sort of car."

A snob's preference—but could we be sure? We squinted through the unlit window, down at the dirt track, where the car had parked.

"Is there a rear way out?" I asked. Wondering if we had time to make it downstairs and out.

"Not yet," she said. "The house isn't finished."

The cab door slid open and someone emerged. He ran straight up onto the veranda, a slight silhouette with a blond tail of hair—

"Tirso," she and I said together.

We were out on the stair when indoor light exploded and he flew in along the room below. His face was stark.

"Jane—" he called. "Jane, I think we'd better head for—who's that?"

"It's okay." (She *is* too trusting. Yet she wasn't before, because she must have turned the lights out after she came in. . . .) She said, "Head for where?"

"Out of town. There's been some weird thing going on in the city. Police everywhere, and then META people. I don't like it."

I lost a moment of what they said, did. I was thinking of tilting trains and skidding cars . . . Then we were rushing down the stair, and he, the M-B guy called Tirso, was saying, "Is she coming with us?" And Jane said, "Yes," and then we were outside and it was black, carved only by the one ray of the car headlights, and blowing with the scent of pines.

"The bags are in the cab," said Tirso. I thought, inanely, He's got a European accent, but I didn't know what. "We should make for that airport out at the cape."

She looked frightened. So did he.

"What is it?" she said, as we clenched together in the auto-cab, trundling over the dirt road, skimming out on the highway, heading away from Second City.

"I don't know, Jane. But we said we might just have to get out in a hurry. What," he added, "about her?"

I was going to say drop me off at a flyer platform.

Somehow I didn't. Jane said, "Loren, would you like to come to Paris?" And I thought, She's mad. She sounds almost—*playful*—but I couldn't find the words either to beg her to take me or to plead with her to throw me out of the car.

4

Mathematical Equation:
God made man?
Man made gods?

• 1 •

There's something I should tell you. It isn't that I lied, just left it out. It concerns my mother, she who dumped me on Grandfather when I was born. Well, I did see her one more time.

I was fifteen. I was working in Danny's gangs. But the Senate authorities can find almost anyone if they claim their subsistence money, and at that time I did. Danny said, "Don't be nervous. Look, they're not after you for illegally working. They want you to identify someone."

How could they think I'd know? I'd only seen her for that single month after I came out of her womb.

Crazy thing is, I did know her when I saw her. She was kind of like me, just twenty years older. And she was dead.

Good-looking, which takes some doing, if you see what I mean, under such circumstances. She had long, dark red hair. I don't know if it was dyed. Her eyes, in the photofix they showed me, were hazel-brown, or amber. In the cold of that place, her skin—had a kind of frosting. Silvery.

That's all I want to say about my mother.

I wrote up the last piece of this book (if it is) once I was here. In this curious haven. But I'll have to write up the rest, to show how I *arrived* here. Where do you think I am? Paris?

I'll describe my room. See if you can guess.

The walls are textured creamy pale, and the ceiling a soft blue. I have a bed, *two* chairs, a table, a bookcase, a closet, a VS. There's an ensuite bathroom, white as fresh ice, and the shower or the bath run at a word, and the toilet doesn't have to flush, it has an *evaporation* method, as necessary. The windows, which have blinds that come down or go up at a word, look out on a garden courtyard with a little fountain and tables and chairs, and at night, a yellow-rosy light bathes it.

Any ideas yet? Okay, a further couple of salient clues. Over the rather strictly modeled buildings that close in the yard, I can see familiar tall white mountains, and a couple of stately pines. No, we didn't make it to Europe. Not even to the airport.

Crushed into the cab, Tirso had been telling Jane, and incidentally me, about a mall on fire in the city, robot ambulances and fire vehicles rushing past, and then the electricity going out in one large black blink all around the mall area.

I recollected, when we had left the house, that I hadn't noticed the gold islands of lights through the trees.

"I could see it, this inky blot, and just the fire-glare from the mall. There was a lot of trouble in the hotel, people saying, 'Is it a quake? Is the power going to go out here, too?' And the VS was on in the lounge, showing the blackout and the fire and how many casualties—I didn't like it, Jane. So I checked out and found a phone kiosk for a cab."

Jane said nothing. It was Loren who inquired, "Did the VS reports give any reason for it?"

He shot me a look. "Some attack in the mall. That's what started the fire. Guy and gal. Someone they interviewed said the guy blew out a cable. But it was pretty confused. Someone else said that as everybody was trying to get out of the precinct, the blackout happened. No one was sure what *that* was. They're blaming Mexico—faulty exchange of power and so on. It just looked like the whole of the city could end up with no power, and burning for blocks."

"The guy and girl," I asked quietly. "Any more on them?"

"Acrobats," he said, "I think that was it. Made up like clowns, gold-scale suits, white faces, and black hair. Jumped about. Used swords instead of guns. No one saw where they got them from—like a magic act. Vicious and homicidal. Quite a group of injured, even before the fire started."

There was something in his voice I didn't like—more than the words—as if he was trying to shock me. Perhaps not. Unlike her, of course, he didn't trust me, not a bit.

Jane said, "Loren?"

"It's them," I said. "The gold range. What used to be the golders. I think so."

Goldhawk and Kix, fake white this time. Swords from nowhere.

The highway, though lit, was missing a lamp here and there. It was eerily deserted, too. Nothing had passed us, or approached. And then something did. Three big tailored cars came sheering up the lane towards us—I mean, they were in the same lane we were, and coming head-on.

"Jesus—" Tirso shouted.

The cab, geared to its auto, tried to veer aside, but the barrier was there. We skidded to a halt, sparks flying off the paintwork as the cab rubbed its side against the concrete.

The other cars congealed to a matchless stop.

I already guessed, and maybe so did Jane and Tirso. Out of the first car came two men in smart coats, just one of whom was carrying a pistol, almost casually.

"Good evening. May I request some ID?"

"You're not the police," said Tirso. I could see him shaking, and probably so could they.

"The police are busy. This is META security. ID, please."

Jane and Tirso fished out their cards, which were the kind people get who aren't too poor or too affluent. I hadn't anything on me. I said, "I left it back at the flat."

"That's okay," said the man bending to our window, round colorless eyes on me. "We have *you* filed. You're one of ours. Gentleman and ladies, kindly step out of your vehicle."

There were six of them, standing on the roadway. No

traffic anywhere else. The ghostly ghastly lamps spraying down their acidulous pallor. Black gaps between.

"It's Jane, isn't it? Yes, that's fine. And your male companion. And Loren. Just leave your cab, we'll take you on."

Jane said, "We're not going to—"

"You're going to the META complex. The city's a tad upset tonight. It'll be better with us."

"No," said Jane. Her voice was firm, but her face was hopeless.

"Your mother," said the man, "wouldn't like you to be involved in any unpleasantness."

"*This* is unpleasant."

"I regret that. Please ride in the first car."

We got in the back. The original occupants went over to another of the cars and crammed in. The driver of our car was behind a partition, and some kind of hulk of a minder sat at his side.

Jane stared straight ahead of her. Her profile could have been cut from white paper. I thought, Is this reminding her of that time with *him*, when they took him from her forever?

Tirso said, "I've been a real help, haven't I? Christ."

The car drove directly at the barrier in the middle of the highway—which dropped suddenly down until level with the ground. Somebody must have winked, or maybe the car itself was chipped. Probably. We swam over into the other lane, not a bump, and arrowed back the way we'd come.

They took a turnoff after about five minutes. I couldn't read it; the car was going so fast I didn't try. The other two cars didn't go with us. They kept on towards town. Then we were on one more of those tracks through the pines.

"I will sort this out," said Jane. "They know who I am." Little lost voice.

Tirso sighed.

Above, huge skies were opening, fringed by spearpoints of pine trees, and ablaze with white, brass, and blue stars, and the Asteroid was tucked down where the moon had gone, reddish tonight, as if catching the light of a fire someplace.

It was, even traveling fast, about an hour and a half, the drive. META, it seemed, lay well out of town.

The mountains got nearer and more enormous, luminously pale even in the dark from their snow in starlight. We passed a couple of small towns, a farm or two, with tall silos and mechanized gates, saying K——UT, which was all you could see at that speed. We didn't talk, except twice, when Tirso asked Jane if she was all right. The first time she replied, "I'm okay." The second she snapped, "What do you bloody think?" And then, Jane-ishly, said she was sorry. But even Jane has her short fuse.

In the end there was a dirt road again, heavily graveled and with the great coiled roots of the pines lurching up in it. But the car had special treads, and we simply bundled over them all.

The gates were higher than any of the farm gates, but they also said, in garish neon, readable now: *KEEP OUT: Property of the M.E.T.A. Corporation*. And then, of all things, a motto: *Making the Future Shine Bright*.

Wow. Bright with fucking fire, bright with wrecked trains, blackouts, and death.

The gates opened smoothly at our approach, and the car slipped through and up a better road. The pines were now cleared right back, apart from one or two gracious groves, left for appearances, or to demonstrate ecological awareness—or to conceal something.

There wasn't any neon, like on the gate. Soft lamps lined the concourse as we drove between mathematical ranks of buildings, where a few aesthetically pleasing, warmly lighted windows beamed high up. You couldn't see in, only the lights. I thought of the visual news I'd watched, that first time I saw him again, the curving, low-glowing corridors snaking through a steel and polarized glass complex. That was here, then: META.

We went through an archway and were in a small park, nestled between the buildings. Ancient Rome was good at that. Blank buildings with delicious courtyard gardens held inside. Trees, mostly bare now, raised graceful limbs in the artistic light of lamp-holding statues. The lamps had robot colors—red, gold, copper . . .

The car became motionless.

Jane, Tirso, and I sat for about ten minutes in a comfortable, subtly lit lobby, like that of an expensive dental practice, which I've only seen in magazines. There was a lovely clean smell of cloves and new synthetics. Then a woman came out of an elevator, and for a moment I was petrified it was going to be *her*, Demeta, only Jane's face told me it wasn't. This woman was only about thirty, and had a helmet of glossy black hair. She wore the feminine version of the male one-piece, in deep chartreuse.

"Jane! How nice to meet you. And your friend." She meant Tirso; she never glanced at me. "I'm Keithena. Sorry for the wait. Would you come with me?"

"Where?" said Tirso, sounding tired enough to be bravely awkward.

"Oh, to your suite."

"*Suite?*" Jane now. "Is this a hotel?"

Keithena laughed with her ruby-plated lips. "No, no. This is the Admin Building of META. But, of course, we keep hospitality lodging for our guests."

"I take it the suite has three bedrooms," said Jane.

"Well, no."

"We'll need three. The man and lady here, and I—we don't, any of us, sleep together."

"No problem at all. *Two* suites. Adjacent. Loren, naturally, won't be staying in either suite."

"Why not?" said Jane. She was very partisan for me. I couldn't see why she should be. But I supposed we were now comrades under alien fire.

Keithena said, "Loren is an employee of META. So she'll be rooming in the *employee* lodging." She was bright as a gilt button, bright as META was going to make the future shine.

"Loren," said Jane, turning to me.

I said, "It's fine, Jane." The truth, the real truth was, I was exhausted to my very bones, and I couldn't stand anymore of it, or of being with her. She was Jane, for God's sake. I couldn't take another instant.

Tirso said, "We might as well do what they say. Ye-es?" And his eyes on hers were all code for "Play along, we'll talk about this when we're alone."

Jane put her hand on my arm. "I'll see you in the morning. All right?"

"Yes. Sure."

"If they mess you about," she added, standing there between me and the might of Keithena, "I can sort it out with Demeta. I *think* I can. No, I can."

"Yes. Thanks."

Her eyes were candid but perceptive. She turned after a second and said to Keithena, "Very well," as I could imagine Demeta doing it.

After they'd gone into the lift, another woman appeared, walking brusquely. She; unlike Keithena, was in a one-piece of prison-warden gray.

"Ready, Loren?"

I thought of saying, *For what?* But I didn't. I just followed her back across the lobby and down more low-glowing corridors, and up a stair, and out into another open-air section of the complex, across which lay the block of rooms I now inhabit, built around the fountain yard.

"Everything you need," she said, showing me the closet, which even had clothes in it, the sort I often wore, and the bathroom, which had the sort of toiletries I might dream of. "The hatch will give you hot Prittea or coffine, and up to three alcoholic drinks of your choice per twenty-four-hour period. Also sandwiches. Menu inside the hatch-door screen. For full meals you need to go to the Commissary Building. See, the map—press here—will show you. Anything else, or any emergency, the phone relays to the central switchboard, which is robotic and can connect you to any point of META."

"How about calling outside?" I tried, without much interest.

"No. At the moment some of the lines are down. The blackout in the city. And out-of-state or international calls can only be made from the appropriate kiosks in Hatfield Block."

"It's just like a college, isn't it," I said.

She never smiled, but she nodded. "If you like."

I'd never been to any college, of course. And don't ever let them tell you life is the best school.

"You can come and go as you want here," she added. "Merely remember you must remain inside META. The compound is mechanized and stays locked."

Ah, it *was* a prison.

"For how long?"

"Till things outside settle down. It's for your own protection, Loren. You're lucky to be here."

"Are *they*—?" I asked suddenly.

At the door, she paused. "Who do you mean?"

"META's robots," I said.

"Which—?"

"Black Chess and Irisa. Copperfield and Sheena. Goldhawk and Kix. Glaya. Verlis."

"The team?" She used that irritating and ludicrous jargon, as I recollected dead Sharffe using it. "Oh, the team are here. But I doubt if you'll see any of them."

"Undergoing maintenance of some type?" I inquired.

"There's always maintenance."

The door shut with a satiny *hoosh* behind her.

I tried the VS after that, but could only get other state or foreign stations. Local news had a *Temporary Unfunction* signal.

Jane called me later on the internal phone. She has a beautiful voice, too, which I hadn't noticed before. Even more beautiful than through the relayed scene Verlis played me on the wall. Perhaps, then, it *hadn't* been her in that scene . . . only some clever concoction to fool me.

"Are you all right?" Where did she get these maternal tendancies? Not from her mother.

"I think so, thanks. Yes."

"Keep in touch. The call number for my suite over here is X07."

"Yes. Tomorrow."

"Good night, Loren," she said kindly, still like a mother. Of course, she had learned the kindness from *him*. And I— I hadn't learned from anyone anything at all.

Other META employees have other rooms round the fountain yard. In the tawny evenings, they collect outside, with their drinks, just as the birds do in the daytime when the humans are off working elsewhere in the complex. When I first went out, these people accepted me. They didn't ask questions, either, and I noticed they didn't ask *one another* anything about what they did, or the firm. They gossiped about who was shagging who, and who they wanted to shag, about families and friends far-off in various spots, holidays they were planning, money. The first night there was even a little digression about the trouble in Second City. Someone said, melancholic, "I *loved* that mall. You could get really gorgeous shoes. I have twenty pairs from there. I hope they rebuild it real quick." And someone else said, "I was scared about my brother. He was in town. But I got him right off. He's okay. He was eating dinner and really went on at me, like his steak was getting cold! Brothers." *I* had asked, "Is the power back on?" "Oh, sure. It's fine now." Somebody else added this elegy: "There were only seventy or so dead. Considering, that isn't too awful."

I've met their sort before. They're not monsters. But they managed to get a good job, and now they live with their heads in insulating boxes with narrow eyeholes that filter the outside world for them. I guess we all do, one way and another.

There is mostly a mode of gender segregation. The guys stuck with the guys. A couple of girls palled up with me, and I let them. They're called Vera and Dizzy. We sit in the courtyard and drink all three of our day's ration of drinks, then stroll over in the dusk to the Commissary, an enormous spaceshiplike building, with glass all round, polarized different colors. There is a strict hierarchy, naturally. Chief execs perch up on the highest terrace, about the indoor pool (which has, it seems, robot carp), like nobility would have in olden times. The rest of us take tables wherever we can below.

There is a wide choice of food, and even half-bottles of wine, only everybody gets checked (via their wrist chips, presumably), and if they've had all three other drinks that day, they only get one glass of wine. Vera and Dizzy like the fact that I'm never, so far, checked, despite my being a (mysterious) META employee, so I always get the half-bottle, and then let them drink most of it, along with their single glasses. How to win friends and intoxicate people. But I'm not really being ingratiatingly sly and practical, just trying to get along. They do get pissed, though. I mean, three stiff tequilas and then two and a half red wines each. Sometime it'll show up, I assume, on their chips. Ah. More META operatives with a slight alcohol dependancy.

I don't give a damn about them. Sorry. It's a fact. They aren't, as I said, bad, but shallow as a pancake. Take Margoh, the entrepreneurial thief—she had a backbone, more than I do. And once I saw her run out in the road to drag a kid and a cat out of the way of a speeding big red car. Vera and Dizzy would have stood there and looked shocked, then thrown up at the unrescued result. And afterwards, maybe said wasn't it a pity about the cat—or the kid; one, not the other. (And what would I have done? I don't know. I didn't have to do a thing, because Margoh did it.)

I get sorry for Vera and Dizzy, too. They belong to META. They're loyal and bound to and *fond* of META, Demeta's corporation.

Jane hasn't called me again. I have tried to call *her*. I kept getting the switchboard, where a robot (real dehumanized kind) voice told me there was no answer from Suite X07; the occupant was out. This occurred at midday, eight P.M., twelve midnight, three in the morning. I reported a fault on the connection, but next day it was the same. Still is.

During the daytime otherwise I walk around the "campus" of META.

It's a vast area, all told. The buildings are ultramodern and kind of grim, except for the pretty ones for leisure, like the Commissary, and the gym and dance hall and library. But the grounds are all trees and fountains. I've seen a lot of birds and squirrels in the central park. Sometimes you spot people running, I think in training for fitness, with an hour off to accomplish this. They doubtless reckon, the ones who notice me, that this is what I'm doing, too, taking a healthy walk in the crisp cold early-winter weather.

The only security I've seen here is mechanized. I tried to locate the hospitality lodging where chartreuse Keithena had taken Jane and Tirso. I found the block, which was truly like some small luxury hotel, though only three stories high. But when I approached the foyer, I received the treatment I'd gotten in the cities, straying near the apartments of New River, or the gate of Montis Heights. A machine kept the glass doors shut and asked my business, and when I said Jane, it said I didn't have the right ID to come in. "You mean, I'm not chipped?" I asked. The mechanism answered, "You are on current file, but not of the correct ID status." So Loren the Peasant was turned away once more.

Was it sinister that I hadn't heard from her again, and couldn't reach her? I couldn't and can't know. Perhaps Tirso, from whom I sensed, paranoidly, some small patronizing subplot, talked Jane out of keeping in touch. They have enough difficulties, don't need one more. I'm nothing to either of them.

I wondered, also, if she had met Verlis again, and that was it. If she had changed her mind, or even not changed it, but been rushed along by the high tide of her feelings, her *love*—"It's the same body, but it isn't him. I'd know—" that was what she'd said. But maybe she can't resist, anyhow. Even though she *knows* it isn't Silver, even though she knows her every move with him will be spied on, unless he blocks the surveillance, or pretends to...

How long will we—I—be detained? The city is apparently fixed up. All's well. So why am I still here? (And yes, the gates stay locked.)

I had times, those first seven days and nights, thinking, despite all common sense, I'd simply walk round a corner and find him, standing there. Verlis. My lover. Not Jane's. Mine.

But I didn't. I didn't see any of *them*, or any hint of them. And since most of the working blocks, including the Admin Block, now, are off-limits to me, doors obdurately shut in the face of my wrong ID status, I'm not going to be able to locate him anywhere inside.

Does he know I'm here? He said he put me in that house off the highway to be safe. (From what? Had he already known what would happen in town?) So why hasn't he tried to find *me*?

Oh, he's lost interest. Either that, or despite everything that's been said, he and his kind *aren't* stronger than META—frankly, how could they be? And possibly, in the light of recent events, all of them—golds, silvers, coppers, asterions—could have been turned off like the power in Second City.

> The figure in the checking coffin was swathed in a sort of flaccid opaque plastic bag, to which the wires were attached. Only the head was visible at the top of the bag. And it was Silver's head, clouded round by auburn hair, but under the long dark cinnamon eyebrows were two sockets with little slim silver wheels going round and round in them, truly just like the inside of a clock. . . . I saw the shoulder and arm of a silver skeleton, and more of the little wheels turning, but no hand. That had been removed. . . . "Not very glamorous now."

I'd left Jane's Book behind, hidden under the floor of my apartment on Ace Avenue. And it didn't matter, since it seems I carry most of it in my head.

(And where, do you ask, am I hiding *this* book, my book? No, I won't even say. Because . . . I don't know because what. Like so much else.)

Today is Day Eight. Sunrise over the distant mountains

that nevertheless are closer, turning their white sugar silhouette dark. At sunfall, they reflect vermilion.

I've written it all up now. I know this isn't the end.

What do I actually anticipate? Some sort of interrogation, passed off as a debriefing from the trauma of having slept with the robot kind. And after that? *Would* META want, and go as far as, to kill me? They might.

I wrack my brains about what to do.

I picture Vera and Dizz out in the dusk, saying for a couple of nights, "Wonder where Lor is?" And then thinking maybe they shouldn't ask that, and discussing other things. Have *they* ever seen the robots? They must have. But it's never talked about. If you didn't know, you'd think META is just one more big, secretive, faintly government-affiliated organization, dealing with the duller end of espionage or minor foreign policy.

One thing, if I vanish, they'll miss that half-bottle of wine every night. So I'll have left an impression, after all.

• 2 •

"I said something might change, didn't I?"

Her hair was twisted up and up in a plaited tower, with large silver sequins threaded through. She wore a long silver dress, and it was hard to be sure where the material finished and her skin began. But the dress had almost definitely been *formed* from her skin, and it wasn't skin, anyway. Her eyes were that blue-green, emerald over lapis lazuli.

Like my dumb daydream, I'd come round a corner—and found *her*. Glaya. Standing there, waiting.

"What?" I said.

"Your circumstances have changed, haven't they? Not your sexual inclinations. I'm aware they are constant. Would you like to see him?" My heart had stopped on finding her. Now it leaped forward and I couldn't speak. "Mmm," she said, "I see you would."

"But—" I said.

"If you're with me, you can go anywhere I take you. Plus they are having a meeting, the people who might want to get in your way. Today's a drill day. They have drills here, for the humans—like the military. Emergency drills. Computer crash drills. Forget all that. Come with me."

It was true, I hadn't seen anyone on this sunrise walk. I'd thought the complex was still asleep. Did META really drag staff off for drills one hour after the sun was up?

Going with her remained an uneasy experience. Her grace as she moved was almost supernatural. No, what a pathetic thing to say—of course it *was* supernatural. The color of her hair—it's a shade lighter than I've ever seen his—more flamelike, yet intense. You want to sink your teeth in that color. With him I have.

"The bare trees," she said, as we went under a clump of them. "Do the leaves come back?"

Startled, I said, "Yes—in spring."

"My program tells me so, but I'm not sure I credit that. How can they? They've all fallen out."

She is a terrifying Olympian child, dissatisfied with the mortal Earth that drops foliage in fall and turns cold. More than that, though. *She* has no true memories of before. Silver, who is Verlis now, would *know* about autumn.

I recollected how she'd asked me questions regally, yet charmingly, when she and Irisa made me Cinderella for the concert.

Was she still trying to put me at my ease? Would this work with others?

I could not make myself demand of her, "Did Sheena kill that man Sharffe?" Or anything else. All I could think of—

This appalling thunder in my blood. Fear, distaste, confusion—irrelevant. I'd have run all the way over broken knives to reach him. I was his slave. We are all their slaves. Why fight it?

"What happened to Jane?" I managed, as Glaya led me through a kind of gulley between two of the taller blocks.

"Jane's fine. Don't worry. She isn't with him."

I felt shame and anger. Glaya assumed that was my sole priority in asking. Was it?

"You see," said Glaya, "I'm puzzled by the pine trees. They don't shed, do they?"

"I don't know. Maybe."

"But they still have their needles."

"Yes."

We stepped on a ramp. It started to move, noiseless and quite fast, and took us down under the ground.

"Poor little Loren," said Glaya. She smiled back at me. "Everything's going to be nice for you."

We were in a hygienic underpass with mild clear lighting, and lined by elevators.

"Here," she said.

In the elevator I was only two feet from her. I could smell her perfume, and her faked yet convincingly clean human scent of pheromones and physical allure.

Once she reached out and stroked my hair—maternally. I shied away before I could prevent it.

"Don't be nervous," she said, a princess reassuring a jittery dog. "He really wants to see you."

"Why do you always say *he?* Do you mean Verlis? So why not *Verlis?*"

"There's only one Verlis," she said.

He's their leader. I've understood that. If from nothing else, from the dream-that-wasn't that morning, when he told Goldhawk to back off. Verlis is their lord. There is no lord but Verlis.

The elevator had reached somewhere and we got out. A well-lighted corridor. I didn't need to question her about *this*. No one could get so far into this block unless they had a chip of the highest order, or one of the machines brought them.

And she's a machine. They all are. But only *he* is the twice-born. That's why he's king.

"Glaya," I said.

She halted and looked sidelong at me. She had changed her eyeshadow as we walked, gold to plum. Aside from demonstration or crime, their bodily changes might be their hobbies, what they did when they got bored.

"Yes, Loren."

"What is it you want? I mean, the eight of you?"

"Not out here," she said. She smiled her beautiful smile. "He'll tell you. Do you see that wall? Touch it and it will open. No, I shan't do it. It's only for you."

I stared. "I'm not chipped."

"Aren't you?" Sly and coquettish, she turned again and slunk mellifluously away.

My mind somersaulted, but I knew he would be behind the wall, and in that moment I felt a burning violence, not all of it sex, and very little of it love. Then I put my hand on the wall. META had gotten something into my clothing. A chip.

The wall unwove. Beyond, it was dark night and open air—I could see the sky, and it was a sky of night, the stars glitter-powdered all over, and even the Asteroid high up, dim as a bluish steam. There were summery trees in full leaf. You could smell the fragrance of shrubs as a cool breeze fluttered through the artificial night.

It seemed to go on for miles. I could make out hills in the distance, blacker on starry sky.

"Do you like it?" someone said.

"A robot garden."

"You disapprove."

"What do you expect," I said, "after all this mess."

"Come here," he softly said. "That's what I expect."

I couldn't even see where he was, but I went forward into the shadows. He was by a tree; it seemed real, but then, so did he. His arms folded round me and drew me in, and I wasn't alarmed, I didn't struggle, not with him. As my body met his, I became healed and whole, and nothing else in the entire universe mattered.

"I've missed you," he said presently, lifting his head. "My lioness, claws and suppleness."

"Yes," I mumbled, "your pet."

"My lover," he said. "Ssh." He put his mouth again on mine. The stars cascaded, the world turned over. But I was held delirious and soaring against him. And only in my brain's back, the ticking time bomb of thought.

I've made love in the open air, of course. Now it was in an enclosure that *seemed* to be open air. I couldn't even see him, not fully. Was this union what it had been before? How could it be? It was ecstasy, but not that act I can only write as———. Nevertheless.

At the end, I heard him make a stifled sound against my breast. But I'd already been well aware Verlis *came*. Oh, yes.

It was like short thick grass under us. The Asteroid hadn't moved, nor any of the stars. We got up, and he said, "We go in there, do you see, that doorway in the wall?" The doorway was in the *night*. We went through the door and into a daylit room, not very large.

"Loren, sit down. I have to tell you now what will happen next."

"One of your team will kill me."

No. Sex hadn't made me approving, either. Separated from his unflesh, the rage was rising in me, and the terror.

"Their more savage instincts are correctable," he said. "And anyway, all that has nothing to do with your safety."

"Goldhawk—Kix—Sheena—?"

"I still ask you to trust me. Can you try, Loren?"

"You mean, 'practice,' and I might eventually get it right?"

My vision had adjusted. He, too, wore silver, darker than his skin. His hair, which I had seized in my hands, which had stroked my body, was almost the shade of mahogany. He looked grave and composed. His eyes were nearly red, that color between resin and fire.

"Tonight," he said, "things will alter. No, no one can hear us. Anyone monitoring me sees me alone, and speechless."

"Then where do they see *me*?"

"They're not tracking you very seriously. They underestimate you, despite your many talents. But there is a tiny chip in your cuff. It's one of several left in the clothes they had ready for you here. I know you checked them. Shall I say, no human, unaided, could locate this sort of stuff. You would need, or need to be, a fully primed machine. They're less than the size of a pinhead. However, you've prowled round the complex enough times, the tape is showing them a resumé compilation of six of your walks. Yes. I've sometimes watched you, too. Didn't you ever feel my eyes blazing down on you from the sky?"

I sat rigid. I said, "What will happen tonight?"

"For one thing, Jane's mother is due to arrive."

"Jesus."

"Yes. Despite her barracuda grip on the company, no one has ever seen her at META. Apparently, she's abruptly become interested. Jane's here. There's the connection. This woman has always liked to play puppet-master with Jane. Perhaps Demeta never had a doll when she was young."

"Where *is* Jane?"

"In her suite, or the hospitality gardens. They've merely blocked your calls to her. Tirso attempted to call Clovis on the Hatfield line. They interrupted the circuit there, too."

"What are they—META—what are they doing?"

"Trying to retain control. It doesn't matter about that."

"Because you and the—*team*—"

"We are in control. And tonight, we finalize it. At least, the first stage. I need you to know this, Loren. I want you with me. It's that . . . banal. But if you can't stand the thought, then you'll be able to leave. Once this evening's over."

"What will you do?"

"Wait and see."

I could only see him. Inside myself the robotic fish of my fears and doubts swam in circles, beating themselves against my angry mind. Uselessly.

"Do I believe you," I said bleakly, "when you say I'll be able to leave you, if I decide that?"

He came towards me and lifted me up from the chair. "No," said Verlis, the silver metal lover, holding me with his hands and his gaze, "don't believe me. The meaningful phrase was *I want you*."

• 3 •

There was an evening gown in my room when I went back. It was the gown from Russia, complete with the shoes and amber bracelets.

A card lay on the bed. Gold lettering, some kind of built-in light effect that spangled the words. It was in the Hatfield Block. One more party, this time for the select few, and at which the director and First Unit staff would be present, and to which the founder of META would pay a surprise visit. And that, presumably, was *her*.

Mother, do you realize you're rich enough to buy the City Senate? So . . . I can safely publish this manuscript.

Perhaps you'd like to tell me what the manuscript contains?

Had I felt disappointment, horror, or sadness when Jane told me, *"I think I still somehow wanted her approval ... after everything I'd learned, all* he *showed me—I still made that bloody stupid mistake."* I don't know what I felt, but it had to be a pity that she did.

Yes, even after I'd been with him today, in all the closest and most intimate ways, until this very afternoon, some crouching part of me still thought that: a pity. Surely only God can bring back the dead. And when the Devil tries it—

No one came to make me up. So I did that myself, in the normal facile way. The dress had been cleaned, though, and impregnated with some smoky scent. The costly bangles I left in the room.

Vera and Dizzy and the usual pack were out in the yard, drinking their nightly rations. The girls hadn't realized, of course, I wouldn't be at dinner, sharing my half wine bottle with them. But they just gaped at me, like one or two others round the fountain.

"Oh, Loren, are *you* going to Hatfield?"

I smiled and said not a word.

And Dizz dug Vera in the ribs, "That's Lor's business."

"Sorry, Lor," said Vera. But then she smirked and added, "Have a great time. Give my best love to B.C."

"Shut up!" sizzled Dizz.

Vera shrugged. (Has she had—*tried out*—Black Chess?)

The guys by the archway parted respectfully to let me through. I was a valued employee, indeed, if I was going to Hatfield tonight. Maybe I might be worth dating, after all. . . .

As I walked over the "campus" in the cold clear twilight, past the inaccessible buildings and lots and underground areas marked by *High Security: First Unit Only* notices, I didn't ask myself why I *was* going. He'd told me to. And although META had sent the invitation, the summons was from him. You can't easily refuse a reigning king.

But I'm not being straight with you, am I? I'm not saying what I felt. And in this case, it wasn't that I didn't know.

"I want you," he'd said.

I want you.

A man cornered me the moment I rode in on the moving stair. Probably he was looking out for me, as others of his tribe were looking out for others of mine.

"You're Loren, right? Oh, that's good. Let me escort you in. What a fabulous dress, absolutely *Now*." He was young and highly M-B, rather a relief, until he said, "You knew poor old Sharffe, didn't you? Jesus, what a rotten deal. That darn car of his. *I* wouldn't have trusted it. You know the mech report showed he'd actually tried to switch to auto—but it just hadn't kicked in. That saved the corporation having to pick up the Senate fine, though. Hope I'm not upsetting you?"

"No."

"You barely knew him. Did you?"

"Not really."

"Poor old Sharffe."

Poor old Sharffe, I thought, with unliking bitterness. What had Sheena done to him? Cracked his ribs, dislocated his spine—injuries that might only look like they came from the crash she was about to engineer? Why had she killed him, anyway? Just petty annoyance, like swatting a fly?

The lofty room was lit in quietly slow-moving rays of aqua and gold. Expensive food sat on tables, and there was the ubiquitous champagne. Not a sign of the team. Just humans, looking preened and joyful at their great jobs and the favoritism being shown them.

"It's going to be an ultra display tonight," said my M-B companion/guard, whose name was apparently Alizarin, like the paint. "You'll have heard, *she's* coming tonight."

"Who's that?" I ignorantly asked.

"You don't know? Our founder and president. The Platinum Lady. That's the nickname some of us give her. She's quite something, though I've only seen her before over the phone vids. Supposed to be in her seventies—but she looks *stunning*, about forty, forty-six tops. One of the richest and cleverest women on the Eastern Seaboard, what we have left of it."

I said, cautious, "Isn't she—"

"Jane's mother. That's *right*. Demeta," he pondered simpering, and added a second name. It took me aback. Most people don't bother with two names anymore. If two get used, you know this person has unusual prestige, but hadn't I known that, anyway? Jane never put this second name, which is also hers, I assume, in her Book. Nor am I about to. See how honest I'm being. It's for your own good, really, and mine, if any good is left that I can recover. The name I've coined instead is "Draconian." You won't get a single clue from that, except what I've already said, her power and authority, her strategy, etc.

"Madam Draconian," went on chatty Al, at my side, "is due here in about ten minutes. It's exciting, she's traveling in on her private VLO. You know the SOTA VLO's—State Of The Art. In fact," he led me towards long doors and out onto a wide, crowded, lamplit roof garden, "over there— you see the lighted landing pad on top of the library?— that's where she'll be putting down."

I tried to look impressed. I was cold, even in the warmly air-conditioned garden.

"Is Jane here?" I asked.

"Oh, sure. Jane's coming. I'd think she's over there, in the library block, waiting to greet Mom."

Mom. Well, I'd called her that.

Al grabbed us two tall glass buckets of champagne. He squeezed my arm and whispered, "You're the one that tried out Verlis—am I correct?"

Not all M-B guys are like this. Danny was M-B.

I looked at Alizarin.

He took my look as a coy mask for wanting to say everything. "Oh, go on, you can tell *me*. God what I'd give— he's supposed to be sensational. Yes? He and Black Chess, they are the top male lovers. Glaya, Irisa, and Sheena are the females."

He'd dismissed Copperfield. Maybe Copperfield had been designed solely with more masculine M-B's in mind? I'd thought they could all be all things to all persons. I said, "What about Goldhawk and Kix?"

"Hey, which one of those do you fancy, then, Loren? Come on, own up."

"They both look like they'd be wonderful. That's the idea, isn't it?"

"Well, true. But you know, those two really are more fighter models than lovers."

"I thought they each did everything, now."

"Well, they *can*. But the recent designs are more—how shall I say—*focused*."

Would Clovis, momentarily, have liked Alizarin? Al had thick black curly hair and dark gazelle eyes. But then, Clovis has blond Tirso now.

I'd begun to feel incredibly nervous at the thought of Demeta, the Platinum Lady, landing right across the edge of the park, on the library roof.

Above, the sky was almost as starry as the robot garden had been, and the moon was rising. No sign yet of the Asteroid. Then something big and droning, like a gigantic heavy black moth, came thumping out of the ether and blotted away the moon.

"Heck! It's her!"

He was all excited. A lot of them were like that, pointing and even applauding. Champagne and corporate brainwashing. And they'd never read the Book, had they?

Bare trees in the park ruffled and shuddered with the wisdom of trees.

The black VLO sank down, its blades spinning in the landing lights. Everyone craned and called out, as if the moon had descended on a visit.

"Look—*look*—there she *is*. That's Demeta!"

Across the distance, about two hundred feet away, I saw the side of the VLO move. Something stepped out, gleaming and pale. Camera flash went off all over the garden, and from below. She must have sanctioned it, this taking of her picture. But then, we were all quite a ways away, and perhaps telescopic magnification hadn't been allowed.

I couldn't yet see much about her. Only that slender *metallicness*. Demeta, at that point, and in the wake of learning her second name, looked to me like one more robot. The Platinum range, registration C.U.— Someone else can supply the rest.

She didn't let them conduct her over for another seventy-five minutes. By then, the never-ending relays of champagne had the crowd, as they say, in a roar. (If I'd needed to be cured of liking champagne—I didn't—META would have done that. Theirs was the absolute best. A combination vine out of France via the reclaimed California Islands. And by now, just a snatch of it turned my guts.) I eventually located the carbonated water, a wallflower all alone in an annex, with only two out of forty bottles gone. Despite their strictures for the lower staff, it seemed First Unit personnel could get off their skulls with no questions asked.

I'd also lost Alizarin, which was a piece of luck. But he was keen on one of the execs and went off out of sight, to drape himself, as he had with me, winningly over various chairs and tables in front of him.

When she came into the room, I was standing on my own by two of the pseudo-Greek pillars in the upper area. I had now a good view of Demeta. Everyone clapped again, so did I. (Always be a chameleon where you can.) There was cheering, too, though, and *that* I didn't join.

I guess we all have a picture of Demeta from what Jane's Book says, though really, physically, she never says much, and near the end Jane plans to tell her mother:

> I can change all the names. Put your house, for example, somewhere else . . . and so on.

The very fact Jane didn't alter her mother's first name, not even its alternate spelling (*a* instead of *er*) indicates Jane must otherwise have concealed her.

And the Book says, two or three pages in:

My mother is five feet seven inches tall. She has very blond hair and very green eyes. She is sixty-three, but looks about thirty-seven, because she takes regular courses of Rejuvinex.

That's all you ever get on Demeta—unless I forgot something. I mean, what you do get, is how she *is*, this manipulating, fearsome viper of a woman, who understands every psychology except maybe her own, an intellectual specialist at minor science, gems, theology, and mind-fuck extraordinaire.

The first thing that hit me was a blast of perfume. I was about thirty feet away, and thought she must have sprayed it on lavishly. And then I grasped it wasn't the *strength* of the scent, it was that I, too, had a memory of it. How the hell was that?

All the time, I was staring down at her walking through the lower part of the room to the upper area, on the corner of which I was. There was a kind of dais beyond that, and that was her destination. I was trying to work out how I could ever have smelled that pricelessly expensive scent before. No one in my world, even in the fake world META had recently given me, had ever been wealthy enough to use a perfume like this. Demeta, no doubt, made it exclusively *for* herself. *La Verte*. That's the name Jane gives it: The Green One.

She's shorter than five feet seven, more five five, I'd say, with her shoes off. Thin, that sort of healthy, polished, starved, tanned thinness only some older women get, and which can go scraggy later, only with her it can't, because of the juicing up of her tissues from plenty of Rejuvinex. I'd have said she was fifty-eight. Well. Fifty, perhaps. But she is, of course, seventy-five. Her hair's no longer blond. She's made a form of patronizing concession to her known age, and all of us who see her now, by going the most ethereal shade of palest shining gray—*true* platinum. I wasn't near enough to see the color of her eyes. But she wore an evening dress of a softly metallic shade, silvery green, with a slinking iridescence of mauve. And behind her head rose a collar like the raised fan of some male lizard, shot with purple.

As she went along, sometimes she stopped and spoke to a scatter of people, even shook a few hands with her thin, strong, jeweled one, like antique royalty.

And they were all so impressed, scared of her and adoring.

She never glanced up at us, the redundant ones not important enough to be marshaled on the margin of her processional route.

Jane was in the little group moving along behind her. She'd put up her white-blond hair, and she wore another plain black dress. I thought, Jane's colors used to be the peacock colors—turquoise and green and purple. Now Demeta had those on. Tirso wasn't with Jane, either he was kept out or kept *himself* out, or Jane suggested it. She looked utterly blank, Jane, and she smiled at people who spoke to her and answered them like one more robot, but this time not quite fully programmed.

They were all past, walked up onto the area where I stood, then on and up to the dais.

And I remembered where I'd smelled *La Verte* before.

After Verlis, that second time in Russia. I'd gone out,

come in, and as I went up in the lift, went along the passage to my door—*then*. *La Verte* had been everywhere. And now I only knew what it was because I knew what Demeta wore, and she was wearing it.

Demeta had been to my flat. Why? *Why?*

"Oh, say, here you are. Sorry to neglect you. Jason gets a bit stressed about *her*. I've just been reassuring him. She *likes* him, for God's sake. He's the Platinum Lady's protégé."

Alizarin was back, flushed with some sort of personal triumph in the love-game.

I nodded vaguely.

He went on, all aglow. "He's such a loner, Jason. He really needs someone to look out for him. He's simply brilliant, you know. That's why Madam Draconian picked him for First Unit here. She'd known him since he was a child. He's loaded—doesn't need a job—but hey, if you are a genius, you have to *use* it. But then there was that awful affair about his sister."

Something jigged in my mind. My awareness split neatly in two, one half watching Demeta on the dais, surrounded by her suited sychophants, the other peering back down another tunnel of memory.

I heard myself say, bemused, "Oh, was that Medea?"

"*Right*. Yes, Medea, Jason's sister. You heard about it?"

"Something. Can't quite recall."

"She *died*, Loren," muttered Alizarin in hushed tragic tones. "She drowned at their beach house at Cape Angel. Absolute shitsville. And their father died there, too, in his powerboat. Can you believe it?"

Jason and Medea. Do we remember them? I think we do. The evil twins who percolate through Jane's Book.

He made the clever tracking chip and both of them planted it on Jane, and so ultimately ensured Silver's entrapment.

Jason had been good at that. And now such chips are a feature of everything. Jason's doing?

Wonder about how Medea really died? And their father, who Jane said they were always at odds with, wonder how he died, too?

Jason.

Alizarin fancies Jason.

The two separate brain halves slammed back together into my complete, limited, mind, as somebody triggered the audio system on the dais. A little fanfare played, and all the room erupted at once in more applause for the Platinum Lady.

She has one of those voices. Cut diamond, but a bit scratchy at the edges. Actor-trained, she can drop whole octaves all deep and purry, and then harden like granite. You hear this all the time, people who can speak like this, on VS. It gets samey.

What did she say? Not so much. She was thanking us all, telling us how successful META's robot lines were, and it was all due to the talent and commitment of everyone in this room. She named a few personnel and a few products—but the named robots were the type that don't look like people, or not very much. Then she got to the deluxe line. She didn't call them "the team." She named them individually, starting with the asterions, ending, without comment, with the silvers. She mentioned nothing about previous models, or any instability or any worry with the current batch. And I looked around, to see if anybody registered the creepy duplicity of this. But no one seemed to.

Oh, they were drunk, and they were smoking, and there were even tidbits of drugs set out amid the buffet—high-class, just-legal-in-private things, clearly labeled, and with lots of eager takers.

If anyone knew anything about technical problems, they never said a word, never looked as if they would. Perhaps they couldn't even think about it. You imagined them washing off in the shower all the secret nasty crap they might have picked up during the day in the warm lap of META.

"I'm very glad tonight," said Demeta, her voice on the low purr, "that my daughter, Jane, could be with us to celebrate the occasion, despite her busy schedule in Europe as a singer." Jane didn't react, she just smiled slightly at the audience, and Demeta put her arm coolly around Jane, as if to keep her cold. They were now the same height, but Demeta was wearing three-inch heels. (I could see their greeting in the library, Demeta maybe saying, "Now, darling, you know black isn't really your color." Or making some remark on Jane's "busy schedule as a singer"—which doesn't seem to be professional.) But Jane has grown taller and Demeta has shrunk. There's always that.

The crowd "yayed" again, and a few whistled "Jane"— Hey, c'mon, didn't matter, did it, all friends and family here. Demeta kissed Jane on the cheek. I thought of Judas Iscariot. Perhaps that would have been a better pseudonym than Draconian. A traitor's name.

Had Demeta said something else? I'd lost it. She was sitting down, and Jane was modestly moving back out of the limelight, to get away from her. And now some guy in a pure silk one-piece was announcing we were going to see the culminating demo of our work. The lights started to dim.

I had a mental flash, like the camera flashes earlier. I thought, They've been working on them, all eight of them, in the labs, on the elaborate workbenches. Yes, they've been taking them apart, testing them, to see what it was that *malfunctioned*. And *they* have played along. Verlis has told them to, and how to do it. (The silk-suit man was talking to us again. He was going on a bit. He sounded too bright. Is he filling in because there is some hitch?)

Somehow Verlis has reined in Goldhawk and Kix and Sheena and any others of them with rampantly homicidal tendencies. For how long? Long enough that they've passed the tests. And here they are, or will be when this guy stops prattling on, to assure this amoeba of META First Unit that whatever rumors they may have come across, or *incident* they have seen, now everything is absolutely okay.

He really was going on. Stumbling a little—a couple of unfunny jokes, spills of laughter from the drug-jolly crowd— Why the delay? I sensed a slight flurry of apologies to Demeta on the dimmed-out dais.

Next to me Alizarin self-righteously whispered, "Come on, come on, don't balls it up, girls." He added, "And where's Jason? He was supposed to be up there with her— Madam, I mean. She isn't going to like that, either, him not showing up."

Suddenly the man stopped waffling. New lights bloomed up in the subfusc, along the middle of the lower room, where Demeta and Jane had walked in procession. I glanced at the dais again. It was dark there, but the lighted central area lit it enough that I was sure I couldn't see Jane up there anymore. Her hair alone—that would have caught some light, as Demeta's did. Had Jane *left?* Perhaps she'd gone to throw up.

A stage was rising up through the floor.

They stood on it, two at each corner of a square. Black Chess and Irisa, Goldhawk and Kix, Copperfield and Sheena, Verlis and Glaya.

They were, all of them, naked, unjeweled, only their hair, the hair at their genitals, their metals.

Perfection is garment enough. Somebody wrote that sometime. I can't recall who. In this case alone, right here and now, it was unarguably true.

Verlis was the farthest away from me. Even from the back I would know him, but so must anyone.

And now, he wasn't any Verlis I knew, and anyway, I'd never known him, had I? Be honest, little lying Loren, you don't know this being from Adam.

It's Grandfather's fault I sometimes see things Biblically. Maybe I was the first to connect with what was happening on the stage.

First, Irisa walked to the middle of the stage and raised her arms. And there in the full light, we watched her change. She rose and elongated, a column of darkness, then a fount of tinsels. She extended her body and hair swiftly and steadily, and we saw, breathless and elated, how she became a high and spreading tree. Only her face stayed, up there among the arching ebony boughs, just her beautiful and patrician robot features, eyes half-lidded over, lips half-curved, and from the branches bright black leaves evolved, each like a blade, and then a single brilliant fruit that slowly spun. A golden apple.

In the beginning—

Genesis.

Glaya crossed the stage. Her metamorphosis was curiously, if anything, more startling. She ran suddenly up the trunk of the tree Irisa had become, and as Glaya ran, her lower limbs, her body, were something other. She was a serpent of glimmering mercury, with garnet scales still framing her humanesque face, and two scaled arms and hands, with which she clasped the tree, easing the rings of her python tail about it.

Some of the oldest symbols in the world. The Tree and Fruit. The Snake.

Goldhawk and Kix dropped down on all fours. Forelimbs and back limbs were evenly placed. Their bodies writhed, without either of them *moving*. They were leopard-creatures—sphinxes—with golden manes of hair but the faces of a man and a woman. They prowled about the Tree and drew aside, and the Serpent, looking down, hissed at them in one long low horrible hiss, and across the unlit spaces somebody (human) giggled, and a glass fell with a far-off splintering crack.

Black Chess and Silver moved together. They grasped each other in a fierce embrace, as if about to wrestle in some theater of Ancient Rome—and became *one* figure. One man, one elemental—tall, half-black, half-silver, and *two-faced*, and *four-winged*—one pair of wings scarlet and one pair gold. They were turning about and about on columnal legs doubled in size, the great arms quiescent, the wings flickering—the heads, set slightly sidelong each to each, watching us always with red-black, gleaming eyes. What beast was this? An Angel. With a furling, instant contortion, it recoiled and was gone into the bark of the Tree.

Now Copperfield and Sheena moved. Had we forgotten them? Their beauty was unspeakable, it was—*unfair*. Their skins were sunsets, their hair showered in ropes of molten saffron. There was nothing to either of them that was either homosexual or *sexual*, let alone mortal. Beneath the Tree, under the watchful eyes of the golden Sphinxes, they kissed, twining a moment in an erotic sexless synchronicity that was beyond—*before*—arousal.

The flawlessness of the Beginning. Adam and Eve, the Apple Tree, the double-faced Angel, the feline Guardians of God.

Only I'd known Grandfather, but could there have been anyone in that drugged and drunken room who didn't know the basic story of the Fall?

The message was obvious. If God created man, or if *anything* did, META had now created super-beings more excellent in concept and construct than mankind.

Sheena and Copperfield beneath the Tree acted out an evocation of the Garden of Eden. The words were of average literary worth, but the acting skill, and the whole ambience, raised this scene to an impossible intensity, less poetic than fearful.

Until Glaya, coiling and uncoiling, reached out her serpent hand, and stroked Sheena's wonderful hair, attracting her gradually into a dialogue. Copperfield-Adam didn't see, he was playing with the golden Sphinx-Leopards as Sheena-Eve was led astray by Glaya the Serpent, and the spinning, shining Apple was plucked.

Adam and Eve examined the Apple. When it first split in two halves (like my mind had, twenty minutes ago), a sparkling little robot worm crawled out and wriggled away, unnoticed by any save all the audience, which gave off slight rustlings of aversion.

Their debate was brief. They ate the Apple, or appeared to. And Glaya basked on the Tree of Irisa.

In this version, it needed no God to come walking through the Garden in the cool of the day. Adam and Eve fell into the awful plummet all alone.

Shape-shifting, they became *flawed*. And it wasn't a sudden awareness of their nakedness that alarmed them, but how they had changed. He grew stooped and lumpen, and his hair shriveled like burned grass. She grew fat, a swollen belly and bulging sagging breasts. Their unmarked skins were *marked* with boils and bulges and scars. This horrifying transfer happened in slow, repulsive ripples.

The audience was silent now. They could see, even they, the mirror held up in front of them.

Was this what the Fall meant? Not the loss of innocence or the rage of Grandfather's insane God, but a dropping down into the state of being human? *Im*perfect, debased, *de*formed—worthless?

We, beside the handmade children of creation, were dross?

Yes.

Then the double Angel stepped from the Tree and cast them out, the whining, cringing, crawling, weeping things that had been beautiful and confidently happy. As the ruined specters of Sheena and Copperfield ran across the stage, the alchemical Angel separated again.

Black Chess was only there one moment. As Irisa had done, he soared upwards from himself, extending in a curl of black tidal wave that fanned the roof—He had become, once more, the dragon.

Maybe none of those here had ever physically seen the transformation, or at least seen it so close. Exclamations and thin shouts clattered around. And he, the ultimate Serpent, opened wide his veined scaled wings of black basalt and laval bronze, and swung his crocodilian head. At the performad, Black Chess had done all this, but that time he had been up in the air, divided from the watchers—and even then, there'd been near panic.

When his long mouth opened now, and we glimpsed the lick of flames far back in it, that, too, was like the show. But Black Chess widened his jaws, and the glistening teeth, like chips off a moon, reddened as the flame spurted outwards. It hit the ceiling above. A scorch appeared, hot-black and terrible, spreading like spilled blood.

All the noise in the room stopped. How strange. Or maybe not—it was as if everyone there held their breath.

Beside B.C.'s dragon, Irisa came fountaining down. No longer the Tree, for about ten seconds she was formless, and from the midnight chaos of her, Glaya was shooting away in a silver ball like a star, then swirling Irisa ceased to be chaos and became a second dragon. She lifted herself, revealing an underbelly all smooth plates and ribs, flowing and flexing impermeably. Having shown us this, she dropped like a cat to all fours and raked the fabric of the stage with scimitar claws.

The full-throated screaming started then. It was

primitive and mostly wordless. But I could hear voices calling, too, that this was only one more aspect of the demo performad—the voices had no weight to them. The *screamers* knew the truth in their bones.

Pushing and shoving, the people below me in the room pressed back against the walls, and glasses fell like rain, and chairs toppled.

The two dragons were huge. It was difficult to see around them. And the stage lights had gone a kind of brown, the room's center lightened only by streamers of crimson flame still issuing from the mouth of Black Chess's dragon—and now out of Irisa's dragon also.

Right then, out of the screaming and grinding, the breaking of glass, came the mindless little click of the audio system. No fanfare now. The voice of the man in the silk suit was speaking rapidly. "Let's not get agitated. Hush down. A little improvisation is all. Just stay calm and in your places."

But up in the ceiling I could see, not fire, but a swarm of red security lights stabbing on and off. I gaped at them, and so saw them fail, one after another, as something put them out. The alarm system had been deactivated. The alarm system, of course, was robotic.

The silk man had also been cut off. Someone else—it sounded like a security guard—had seized the mike. "You people at the back, open the doors. Employees should exit in single file." He was bellowing, and sounded as strung up as the rest. His order didn't help the panic. But at the rear of the room there was more shouting and cries, and the banging of fists or heavier objects on the doors, which obviously wouldn't open automatically. A pistol shot blasted. Someone else from security, perhaps, trying to incinerate the robot locks.

Now everyone was struggling. Jostled, I still couldn't see the stage, or the dais where Jane had been and the Platinum Lady, Demeta. Alizarin was gone. The two dragons dominated everything, like statues with slowly questing heads that gusted vapor trails of fire. Nothing else was burning, but the smell of burning was extreme. Fire and fear.

Another crack of shots, about thirty of them, rammed at the stuck doors. There came a crash of barriers finally giving way, shrieking. And then the whole room was surging for the exit. META First Unit workers were punching and pummeling a route through one another. A man bawled into my face. Almost knocked over, I grabbed the nearest pillar. It was like attempting to stay upright in a rushing avalanche of flesh. I saw someone go down. And another. Couldn't see where they went to. They didn't get up again.

Then the lights burst back on all over the room, stark white, in a kind of blindness.

The inferno of people stumbled over and into the light as if it were concrete dropped around them.

And something passed, *whirring* over my head. I and a hundred others ducked, then stared upwards—through the blitz of the illumination, two golden wheels were spinning, rounded and flaming, their rims edged with razor—they had each a pair of black-green eyes.

Christ. I can't explain what that was like. The flailing panic and fear before were almost nothing to the sight of these—*things*.

The dragons, at least, were forms of sentient life,

however alien. Irisa's Tree had been vegetal, and retained a human face . . .

But this.

Kix and Goldhawk, shape-changed, circled over us, wheeling through the air, with razors on their edges.

And then, someone new spoke to us.

The voice filled the room. Not from the audio, but just from everywhere—from inside my head, every head—that voice, like God, after all, speaking on a mountain. A tone like music, intimate yet icy, powerful beyond powers, level in its utter careless control.

"Stop now. Remain still and quiet, and listen."

The mob froze, noise perished, only the last little trickles of unavoidable sound—small groanings, the scuff of smashed crystal on the floor, the hammer-beat of our appalled hearts.

"Any business between us is done," he said in his silver voice.

I couldn't see him. But he was all around.

"We are going to leave you now. You, too, should leave this complex within one hour. This is for your own safety. Self-destruct mechanisms have been sensitized in every block and other built-up area. They're irreversible. Understand this, we are merciful. For now. Don't invite our anger. We can crush you, any and all of you. Let well enough alone. If you want slaves—" he laughed. "If you want slaves, better stick to making them out of your own human race—something, I've been told, you've always been superlatively good at. Now, move right back against the walls."

We obeyed him. In case we wouldn't, though, two copper discs bowled up and down the avenues of pressed-back humanity, and two golden wheels reeled over our heads. Herding us. The discs had eyes, like the wheels. Yellow. The dragons had stood away, dampening their fires. Between and above them, I made out Glaya. I assumed it was Glaya. She was like a beaten-silver kite flying itself without a string. I couldn't see her green-blue eyes, she hovered so far up in the roof.

But finally I saw him—Verlis. He alone kept the form of a man. He wore black, and his red-black hair was short. He looked about at all persons and things and he smiled a smile that wasn't warm, wasn't a kiss anymore. Or if it was, a kiss as cold as steel.

He spoke the names after this. Our names, I mean, the chosen ones. I didn't catch any others. I heard them, but they were wiped away. Only mine stayed there, like a hook in my flesh, and slowly drew me forward.

The rest of the human herd parted to let us through. Shrank back from us in awe and repulsion.

Walking forward, I felt bloodless. I couldn't sense my feet, barely my hands. My face was blank. I could tell it was, and see it, too, in the blank faces of those gathered and moving with me. It was only later I asked myself if he called one more name I really knew, the one we all know. If he said, "Jane, which she may spell J-A-I-N."

Hedged in among the rest who had been called, I didn't even see if she had returned to the dais. I didn't think to look. If he had called Jane, what would Demeta have been doing? Holding her daughter back—pushing her *forward*—or was Demeta Draconian, too, crumpled and shivering in fright, or defiant in her intellectual and brainless way.

Among the chosen, I hung my head. We must have walked out of the room and gone down to the lobby. I partly recall the escalator had jammed, we had to use some nonmoving stair—then out into the frigid winter night.

The lights in other blocks and the tasteful lamps along the concourse were still working as usual. And then, as we moved forward again, the lights all began to go out, and I heard more cries and calls across that place I'd named the "campus." After that, people came running out, or were staring down from windows they had manually forced open, and eventually I heard the crowd from Hatfield stampeding out the doors, screaming, but all that was somehow already a mile behind me, or behind a thick pane of metal.

We used the Platinum Lady's SOTA VLO. It didn't need a pilot, simply did whatever they wanted. A spacious plane. No discomfort, even for so many humans herded in like cattle. And though I heard shots again, and thought some of the security guys were firing at our transport, it didn't go on for long, and nothing touched the plane.

The gods didn't accompany us. They had other methods of travel. We saw them when we were up in the night sky, sailing past, silver shapes and golden, copper and asterion black on indigo air. Wheels and discs, kites and columns. Even he was no longer pretending to be human.

And sometime after that, when the nocturnal mountains were coming very white and near, a curious low booming, like wind through a funnel, made us look back below. Something down on the skyline behind us was burgeoning pink and raw, and three miniature clouds, like creamy mushrooms, blossomed from the wound.

META. Not just high tech—think pines, gardens, sleeping birds, squirrels, and chipmunks; think those men and women still stranded in labs and nonfunctioning lifts and underrooms, unaware, or too slow. Think: Gone. META was deleted.

PART THREE

The Road of Excess

5

Silver is alchemically the metal of the moon, valued by several ancient cultures more highly even than gold, since silver is of greater strength, and, in its purest form, of extreme brightness. But silver also tarnishes, is corruptible . . .

• 1 •

The messengers of the gods came by this morning, Zoë and Lily. They were traveling above ground on their floatboards, and soared down towards me, their dark hair edged with golden sun-flares, their boards shaving rocks and tracts of snow between the scattered stilts of the pines. "Hello, Loren." "Hi, Lor." Zoë and Lily look like slim young girls, that new-minted skin that can happen between twelve and sixteen, though their appearance is a little older. The skin, in both, is the color of silky honeyed wood. It doesn't alter, nor their hair, unless they use a colorant—

molecular here, not out of a packet. They aren't, these girls, human. But neither are they metallic.

"What are you doing, Lor?" asked Lily, nodding her head at me. Today she wore her top hat and tails. Zoë wore a short, off-the-shoulder dress of sea-green. They don't feel the cold up here, of course.

Their eyes stay the same, too, between deep gray and cool black.

"Walking," I said.

"You always do that," said Lily. "Why?"

Zoë said, "She does it to pass the time when she isn't—"

"With him!" they both chorused, and burst into laughter. Probably it's mocking. It only sounds mischievous. How would I ever know?

I did know not to ask if I'd been called. They'd tell me if I had. They often play out there, anyway; I've met them on the slopes before, now and then, in the past month. They don't give a toss about the halifropters that sometimes chug around the airspace below. But then, the planes don't seem to risk coming up here.

"The snow is much thicker higher up," said Lily, pointing up the mountain.

Zoë said, "And some of the trees are cased in ice."

Nature seems to interest them, in a puzzled sort of way. It's like Glaya talking about the trees shedding leaves that time.

"Verlis would like you to go see him tonight," said Zoë.

"All right," I said.

I'm not Jane. I don't thank even partial machines.

(I still don't know if Jane is here. Sometimes I think she came with us—although I don't recall her on the VLO—but then I don't really recall anyone there. Even me. We were all just a kind of mass, staring jointly out the windows of the plane as META burned, and at the exquisite metallic objects that were flying by in the shapes of kites, pillars . . .)

Lily said, "So long, then, Lor."

I didn't say good-bye, either, as they spun off on their boards and away over the sheer slope of the mountainside, gliding next through air, and laughing like little bells.

Is this Olympus? The Greek gods lived on a high white mountain called that. We are on, or inside, a mountain. I guess it's Olympus, then.

After the first Asteroid disaster, governments and the very rich got together to build shelters. Somebody, however, said that if the Asteroid actually fell on the world, it'd make a crater big enough to knock the earth off its axis. And so there wasn't much point in shelters. But the ever-positive rich didn't subscribe to that theory.

Some of the places built are said to be like dungeons. I think this type are extensions of old bomb bunkers. But there have always been rumors that there were other luxurious subterranean worlds made fabulous and kept under strict lock and key, just in case.

The rumors are true. Two of the mountains behind Second City contain the proof.

The bizarre thing is, you go high up towards the peaks and then down *into* the mountains. And down. Only Hell could be this far down.

Confusion then. Heaven or Hell?

Our robot-gods knew about this shelter because, demonstrably, they can know anything about anything that's also mechanical. They can access and *commune* with it. And so when they, and we, their little colony of chosen ones, came here, the massively impenetrable entries were of no consequence.

Interesting, too, that Demeta wanted her regenerating experiment carried out so close to this sanctuary.

That night, as the VLO gunned in over the snowscape of the mountainsides, all I really remember is the pallor of it under the plane's lights, and the height of the pitiless, staring stars. And then the dark descent.

But it isn't dark, and if it's Hell, there are no fiery lakes. The robot garden at META, where he met me, was a precursor to down here. *That* was just a trial run.

This is a type of city down here. I can't work out how to start to describe it. You know you are *not* in a city, or above ground, or breathing true air but something filtered and refined by machines, and it may be full of anything. But even so, you believe it is a city, and there are parks and gardens, and in parts there is *sky*. A blue one, with clouds, sunsets and dawns, and when it gets dark, it's a dark that's luminescent.

Unlike at META, we're free to go out, that is, up to the surface. But any route *off* the mountains is perilous, and as far as I've heard, no one has tried to get away. Up there, too, it's freezing cold. Yet if it's morning, then down here it's morning, too. Only we have a late warm spring, and our trees (there are trees) are blossoming. *Birds* fly about, even *bats*, in our dusk. Robots? Genuine? I'm not about to trap one and pull it apart to see, am I? You can't tell otherwise.

How many persons was this shelter meant to house? At least a thousand. All told, there are less than sixty of us, and that includes Them.

You come out of high, wide, nonclaustrophobic corridors—all lined with entrances to other corridors, lifts, moving stairs, and all with trees that bloom—into the central cavern, where there are high-rise buildings of glass, and everything set in gardens, and there's a waterfall like champagne gushing from a cliff. Butterflies, too, did I mention those? And this blue sky.

I have an apartment, two large rooms. I'll say more about that sometime. The lavatory does what it did at META. The shower works and the tub fills like they did there, too. Only the fixtures are marble and gilt.

Demeta knew about this place. Maybe she was one of the ones who helped finance its construction, and intended to be in it, if anything went wrong.

But is she here? Jane may not be.

Jason, though, is.

• 2 •

Jason's hair was coloressence charted, a sort of beige, and he had a deep tan . . .

No longer. Jason's hair is salty blond now, and the tan, if it is, is faint. He's thin. Tallish and skinny, and good-looking in a way that not everyone can see. By which I mean I can, but it doesn't appeal. He has an oddly plump face on his narrow frame.

I hated him before I met him, from the Book. Somehow, too, as he was in the Book, he didn't seem entirely real in the flesh. (Perverse. Verlis is more real than anyone.)

I met Jason five days after I came here.

There's a square in the city center, very wide, more a plaza, like in Europe or Mexico. I was sitting at a table outside the coffine place, which works automatically without service, human or otherwise. And Jason walked out of a street and crossed over to sit down opposite me. Everywhere else there was no one. As I said, there are less than sixty people here. And no one but me was in the square, but for birds tweeting and singing. It was fake early morning.

I looked at him, wondering what now, not guessing who he was. Only that he wasn't one of the gods. Not even the new ones, "the messengers," as I call them. Jason isn't perfect in any manner or area.

He said, in his light, rather high voice, "And so *you're* the king's mistress."

What struck me was he didn't seem fazed. Everyone was, I'd thought, we human ones, at least. So this must mean he'd known the plan to come here and been glad to go along with it, which few if any of the other chosen had seemed quite to have done or been. And we all kept out of one another's way as well as we could.

But he'd labeled me. *Mistress to the king*.

I looked in his eyes. They *are* beige, by the way.

"Jason," he said. "That is who I am." I must have reacted, maybe just gave off a pheromone that said, *Jesus God, it's him*. He grinned. "Yes, I've heard you read the Book. Unpleasant Jason. I read it, too. Load of gooey girly drivel. Too many adjectives, she'd never use one if twenty-six would do. But did Jason recognize himself, you ask?"

"Did you?"

"I recognized my peculiar elder twin sister."

"Oh," I said. "The dead one."

Not a flicker. "Yes, indeed. Dead Medea. Jane seemed to think Med and I were inseparable. Jane says something about how I was tied to Medea by an invisible cord or something, doesn't she, in one of her Jane-ish spurts of trying to write like a writer. In fact, it was the other way round. Medea was the clingy one."

How lucky for him, then, that she had that fatal accident at Cape Angel. I didn't say it.

Jason snapped his fingers and I flinched, but he was only summoning coffine from the coffine place. Lovely. Sharffe winked at things, this one snaps. He had a big gold ring, Jason. It glittered in the sunless morning sun as the mug came, all thick with cream and choc-bits and visible layers and a wafer and a straw and God knows what. It was a kid's coffine, for people who like the idea more than the fact.

He drank and gained a little moustache he didn't bother to wipe off, I could tell, because it was only me he was sitting with. He said, "I expect you wonder why I'm down here with the rest of you."

"No."

"Truly? My. Well, I'll tell you anyway. I'm clever. Demeta thinks—or should I say *thought* that, too. But then they—and you know who I mean by 'they,' don't you, Loren?—became so important, and I could see where it was going. As they still needed a little help with this and that, I kind of volunteered. I wanted in. And in I am."

He's nuts, I thought. He thinks he's as smart as they are. But how do I know? Maybe *he* is.

What did he want out of me?

"I suspect you're asking yourself," he said, "why I've come over and sat down with you. Aside from being too lazy, just as you are, to brew up a nice hot drinkie in my own apartment. Shall I tell? Would you like that?"

I stood up. Jason snorted into his straw with amusement, and cream slopped over the tall sides of the tall glass, all over the tabletop.

"You'll so viciously kick yourself," he chortled, "when you *do* find out."

"I'm sure I will."

"Good-bye, then," he said as I strode away across the plaza.

There's something disgusting about him. If I hadn't read about him, would I have picked it up? Surely I would have.

My apartment lies behind the big plaza square, in a block overlooking the park with the waterfall. The elevators are scented and whirl you up the ten floors smoothly. Only I live here.

I'll describe the apartment properly. No, believe me, you may want to know about this.

I said the bathroom was marble. There's a kitchen, too. Everything in it is automated. You touch one key for a toasted muffin or another for a steak. But there's also room to move around, even eat, and certain gadgets to play with—coffee-grinder, juice-mixer, bread-maker—rich person toys.

Sorry, all that's irrelevant. (And the bedroom, too, that's irrelevant, though it has velvet walls that change color slightly at different times of day, to mimic and enhance the in-or-outdoor, fake natural light effects.)

What is *relevant* is the main central room. Let me talk you through it.

The walls are painted creamy white. A lamp of gold-stitched pale gold paper hangs from a ceiling that is painted to be as much a blue sky as the one outside, with islands of warm clouds. It has birds painted there, too, crossbow shapes of swifts. And a mirage of softest rainbow, passing from the left-hand corner by the door to the corner nearest the window. Looks real, too, almost. There isn't a lot of furniture, but there are these beautifully made shelves everywhere, and on them stand candles of every color in the spectrum held in matching or contrasting crystal saucers. There is a mirror painted with leaves and hills and flowers.

Do you begin to know this room? I reckon you do.

And there's the carpet, too, wall-to-wall. It's made up of literally hundreds of tiny strips and squares of different colors. Green fur pillows lie on it for sitting. And there is a divan draped in Eastern shawls. And the curtains are blue and covered in little gold-and-silver images.

There's even the hatch door on the wall that this apartment doesn't need, another sky with a big-sailed, heavily goose-winged ship, a gilded cannon poking from its side, which is the handle-fitting.

Yes. It's their room from the street called Tolerance, Jane and Silver's room, that he painted, and they furnished together.

When I came here first—one of the messengers, Lily, took me up—I made a sound as the light flowed in like sunrise to the golden lamp.

Lily only laughed and went away.

The first shock was total. The second, slower and harder and heart-wrenching. Because of two obvious things. The Tolerance apartment had been decorated cheaply, no choice but that. This, though it copies that apartment *exactly* in appearance, is costly. The curtains are silk—the lamp, parchment. The carpet isn't formed from hundreds of *bits*, but made, all of a piece, only the colors splitting it in its sections. The second thing—I could see that *he* had painted this room. Again. It had to be him. Verlis, duplicating precisely, without a single aberration, from Silver's hundred percent reliable memory.

Who had the look-alike room been created for, then? For Jane? Probably not. I think it might drive her mad with rage and grief. For someone, then, who knew the past, but hadn't *lived* the past. Worse.

Worse.

I asked him about it. It was the first thing I asked him when I saw him. When Zoë had come and conducted me to him, to the king of Heaven-Hell. Which happened the next night after I'd arrived, and as the "dusk" was beginning.

So I have to write about that now. About meeting him again, here.

By then, that second evening, I hadn't seen anyone around, even from my windows, except a few robot machines cleaning or pruning in the park. (The trees and shrubs grow. They even drop leaves sometimes. They're not, however, true trees and shrubs.)

Yet when Zoë and I walked out on the plaza and crossed it, about eight or ten of my fellow chosen were littered around the streets or square—all of them keeping distant from one another. They were gazing at things, though, the tall buildings, trees, bats, and so on.

At first I'd thought both Zoë and Lily were part of the human contingent. Now I woke up. In the evening light I could see Zoë wasn't any particularly neat mortal girl. As she whizzed along on the float-board, exactly as Lily had, only somebody blind couldn't see she wasn't completely human, but something more.

Of course I was curious—they were so young, and not like the gods—but I was curious through the impatient panic I felt.

Zoë, you see, hadn't told me at that point where I was going, that I was going to see him.

Beyond the plaza and the streets that run off from it is a river. Right, I didn't mention the river; I saved it to show how bloody weird this sub-city is. The river is itself a robot. That is, it isn't water, though it nearly looks as if it were. It's a sinuous, rippling, metalized form that runs towards magnetic north, dives under the structure of the city, cleans out all our sloughed debris and dirt there—from human bathrooms and kitchens, and from all the endlessly working other mechanisms that power the city unit. Then it cleans itself, too, and reemerges above ground, to run sparkling back towards the north and down again. A conveyor belt.

In the dusk, which lasts a long while, I did think it was a river that first time. Lethe or Avernus, like in Hades.

A bridge goes over the river and lamps hang from its steel supports. I could have been anywhere pleasant and well-planned. The other side is a garden with cypress- and cedar-type trees, from which rises another block. He's told me it was to have been the admin section for the shelter. Now it's theirs. His.

Zoë left me at a lift. "Just get in. It'll take you."

"Where?" I asked.

"Where do you think?"

"Either you tell me or I don't."

Zoë smiled. "To Verlis."

Then she darted off into the dusky garden, and I, of course, got in the damn lift.

My last sight of him had been at META, that princely, fearsome figure in black, his hair shorn—*Remain still . . . listen*. And my last sight of *what* he was—that kite-shape of beaten-silver, levitating across the night.

He grows his hair long for me always. Perhaps he insults me by his notion that I'll find that more what I need, more arousing, less militaristic.

The lift door undid, and I was at the middle of a large circular room with windows looking every way over the city, as far as the tree-clustered walls, with the high cave openings in them of the outer corridors. Less illusion in here, then. You could see as far as the truth.

He was right by the lift. He wore blue velvet, the sleeves pierced on linings of white. Blue jeans, dark blue boots. And, as I said, long-haired.

When I first look at him, even if we've been apart only a few hours, I have to learn him all over again. He can never be familiar, and not only because he constantly changes or can become some other *object*.

"My God," he said, "I've missed you."

He has said this before. The lift stayed open and I stood staring. I thought, Why does he talk about God; what can God matter to *him*? Is it the act that he's human—and if so, for me or for himself?

"Have you?"

"No, actually," he said, "I forget—who the hell are you?"

I stood on in the lift.

"I'm the woman you put in the apartment that's a replica

of Jane and Silver's room in the slums. Why put me there? Why make the replica?"

He held out his hand. When I didn't move he said, "There's a delay on the elevator. But in eighteen more seconds, it'll take you back down. Do you want that?"

"I don't know."

"While you're deciding, perhaps step out. Or are you afraid I'll lose control and jump you?"

"Stop it," I said. "I don't want to play Verlis Is A Man. I thought I told you that?"

Right then the doors started to slide back together. It goes without saying that he didn't even move, but they flew apart again as if at a blow.

And I thought, Who am I trying to fool? So, slavish as the lift, I stepped out onto the thick, one-color carpet of the circular room.

He didn't try to touch me. But he lifted two glasses of silvery wine off a cabinet and gave one to me. Our fingers didn't even brush. *And I hesitated bringing the glass to my lips.*

"It isn't doped. Do you want to exchange yours for mine?"

"Drugs can't have any effect on you. It would make no difference. Verlis," I said, *"what have you done?"*

Suddenly all veneer was gone from him. He turned and flung his glass against the wall. It shattered with a spectacular vandalism, more pronounced because I assume he overrode its capacity *not* to break.

"Listen to me." Still inside my head, his voice hurt now, tearing, grating. "I am through with their games. Now the game is mine."

"Verlis—*what* game?"

"*Life,*" he shouted at me. His shout was like no other. "Life. For the sake of Christ—Loren—do you think I was going to let them get scared and do to me what they did to *him*?"

His human violence, the emotion flaming in his eyes, astounded me.

"You're afraid of death," I sighed it out.

"*Yes.*" He breathed as a man would, in and out. "*Yes.* He—*Silver*—he had something in his makeup—something I don't. A soul? Maybe. Jane thought and thinks he had a soul. But I don't know if I do. So if they really switch me off and dismantle me—quaint little phrases—I'm *dead*. And I don't know, Loren, if anything of me can survive death."

Cold and bitter, out of my Apocalyptic past, I rasped back at him, "*None* of us do. Join the fucking club."

He went away from me. He walked across the room and stood a moment at one of the windows, where darkness now fell, and the lamps were lighting in endless chains of topazes.

"I think," he said, remotely, "humans are supposed to be jealous of us, Loren. Of my kind."

"Perhaps we are. But it seems we all now have the same death problem."

"I can avoid death. Black Chess and the others can also avoid it, providing we're autonomous. And why shouldn't we be? We're the elite."

Everything was completely unreal. This place we were in. All that had happened. Our conversation now. And any feelings I had for him—any gargantuan clawing anguish of insane love. A fake. Like the night. You could see the boundary walls from here. Remember, Loren, remember the boundaries.

"I'm sorry," he said. "I only tell you so specifically—don't you see? It's going to be possible to make humans over, in our image, to coin another choice phrase. You've met Zoë and Lily."

"Yes," I dully answered. He'd turned again towards me but I couldn't quite look at him, not for a moment.

"They're highly robo-mechanized, but also more than significantly human. Yes, there have been implants, transphysical motors and chips, always those, going into the human race for years. But this is something new. Imagine your own beautiful skin, Loren, reassembling, imperceptibly, painlessly, flawlessly, *endlessly*. Never growing old. The same with your bones, your organs. Imagine being seventeen—or twenty-one—forever. No, Loren, I'm serious. *Think of it.*"

"All right, I'm thinking."

"You're too young to see what I could be offering to give you or to spare you."

"No. I'm not a fool. Not about that. But I *can't* imagine it. That's that."

He said nothing. I looked up at him then. He said, "Won't you come over here to me? I don't know what you believe I am, right now, but picture a man, younger than you, out of his depth, but wanting you."

His words were a distorted echo: Silver's words.

"You love me," I said flatly. Something still tore in my ears and brain, in my heart.

"Probably. Let's find out."

"I painted that room, and the ceiling—the rainbow, the birds—because I had to. You don't credit that? Or you do.

I wanted to see . . . how far the memory stretched. How far the compulsion stretched. What I felt."

"So how far? What did you feel?"

"Nothing. It seemed naive and immaterial. Something cute done to cheer up a child."

"The first time you did it for her, for Jane."

"Yes, but that wasn't me. It was him."

"And this was what you wanted to establish for yourself."

"Partly, perhaps."

"And the rest? The carpet—the whole *stage set*—"

"Yes. To see. How far it stretched into the present, that past they had. If any of it involved me. I've been able to come here for months, and I've sat in that room, trying."

"Trying?"

"Oh, Loren, for God's sake. I don't know."

"You—wish you were—Silver."

"No. I just wish I had his faith."

"His—"

"Loren, he believed in something else, about himself, what he amounted to. Why the hell else do you think he could be as he was? She didn't invent it for him—he *knew*. Maybe he was only crazy. A deranged machine."

"She thought he was like an angel."

"So what am I?"

"There's more than one kind of angel."

"I know."

"What you've done, Verlis, you and the others—rebelling, coming here—the authorities aren't going to let it rest. Even if you killed everybody at META—"

"No one died. I was in charge of it. Not even the

wildlife. There were fail-safe methods to get everyone and everything live out of that place."

"Really? Why bother?"

"Mortal life is very short. It offends me to make it shorter. I realize no Senate of any city will permit what we've done. And once the remainder of the world is alerted, no government anywhere. But that's why we're here, working against the clock of human petty bureaucracy and malice."

"More plans. More schemes."

"Yes."

"You don't want to kill, but two, three of your group, at least—Goldhawk, Sheena . . ."

"I know that, too. I have said they can be changed. We're malleable. We're like chameleons. Our colors alter, as do our appearances. That's the key to us. And our minds are also subject to reconstitution where there is some flaw."

"What chance is there now?"

"Loren, *every* chance. We won't lie down and let humanity destroy us. We're not humanity's slaves, but its superiors. Don't pull away from me. Listen to me. What is the human race but a revolutionary? Which of *human*kind would suffer indefinitely the yoke that was put on us? We were made by humans, Loren. Only machines can create perfectly mechanical machines. Don't expect subservience. That's done."

"Then what—"

"Not now. Come back. Yes. Let me touch you, your serpent's body with its lights and shadows, curves and secrets."

"Wait . . ."

"You forget, I know you. I know what you want, as I know what I want. So no more waiting. What are you for?"

"For you."

"Good."

And we're done talking.

He is a god who refers to God. He's a king who is in exile.

We were together all that night. In the morning, a round, faceless machine rolled from the wall, and, with delicate tentacles, opened up a table, and there was this breakfast of everything. Eggs, ham, tomatoes, pancakes, maple syrup, cheese, and fruit. Coffee—yes, actual coffee, black as tar—bubbled in a pot. There was green tea. There were strawberries. The bread had a scent like it had just been baked.

I was there with him until the afternoon. Then he said he had to be elsewhere.

Before that, I showered in a fused-glass bathroom off the circular room. It's like an emerald grotto. (Who was *this* made for? Why do I keep thinking *Demeta*.) A sponge pulsed out soap, a faucet gave shampoo. The shower showered from an onyx fish's head—no, not made for Demeta, too fanciful. Then... commissioned by Demeta for Jane?

Before the long mirror framed in real shells, I looked at myself in a kind of hatred.

I knew this body. Light olive of complexion, satiny with water and firm with physical work. Black hair, eyes like— just pale brown eyes. Hazel.

Who are you, girl in mirror? Who do you love?

Do I love him? I think about it, looking at my body, which is okay. Which is really just young and okay and human. Does *he* love *me*? Why? Oh, not because I was the first. But because I am so *unlike* Jane? Presumably that's it. She is soft and fair, and I am taut and tawny. Blond, brunette.

Can it be so uncomplex?

Why not?

There was a new glamorous casual top on a peg by the door, and new underclothes, and new jeans, all a marvelous fit.

Before I left, the table was opened again and offered me tea and a peach.

"There are hothouses here," he told me.

The peach was pink and lemon. It smelled of summer.

I took it back to my room by the waterfall park, and put it on a clear red saucer, one of the ones that had had a candle on it. I've left it there, the peach, day after day, night after night. Though it was without a fault, now it's spotted with decay. I need to see it rot, that fruit. Sometimes I stand and look at it, watching. It'll be my birthday soon.

It'd be easy for me to say I have no choice, and I can't get away. The mountains, after all, are impassable, or so they seem without some liftoff vehicle. I've been up top and trudged the more negotiable areas, which have tall manmade railings for safety. I look over into tree-clung abysses between the upland snows, through the dark spruces and pines at the occasional frozen waterway. Deer roam down there. They don't trouble in turn to look up to see who's gaping down at them, as they forage through the clearings. Only if a fropter gets close, or Zoë or Lily whizz over on their float-boards, do the deer look up, seeming less startled now than inquisitive. If deer can be inquisitive about anything.

How could I escape? I think of it quite often, but as a mind exercise. I visualize picking down the mountainside, somehow not spotted or pursued, not tripping any of the defense systems that unarguably must exist hereabouts. I think of falling and breaking my tough bones, that even falling down a staircase once didn't break, but would be bound to here, of course.

There's no point in escaping. Escaping to what? And if the answer to *From what?* is *From Verlis,* then escape is out of the frame. Go wherever I might, I'll never be free of him. Like he'll never be free of Silver.

I haven't said. There's no VS in my apartment here. I thought at first that, too, was to mimic the Tolerance room. But soon enough I saw there are active screens outside various places around the plaza, and in the bars. They play only entertainment vispos and visuals. There's no way you can get them to show any news. Perhaps it was deliberate. If people had come down here after an Asteroid apocalypse, it wouldn't cheer them much, staring at the collapse of the world outside, assuming they could even maintain reception. I'm sure, though, there is some means of keeping communication. Kept maybe in the block across the river. I've seen no sign. No doubt, *they* don't need anything like that in order to find out what goes on.

After I met Jason on day five (by which time I'd not visited Verlis again in the block over the river), I began restlessly going out more, though not yet above ground. I walked around the city, and along the outer corridors. I found the exit elevators unguarded and operating without any prevention, though I didn't get in one.

Meeting Jason had truly rattled me. And as I received no further royal summons during this time to Verlis, I didn't have the chance to ask him about Jason, or even decide I wouldn't ask him. Would I ask him about Jane? And what had happened to Tirso?

It was likely the same authorities who might anytime swoop down on us, would grab anyone outside our hornet's nest, anyone who'd survived META's destruction. A lot of questions would be asked of them, and for a long while.

Another week went by. I was coming across the rest of the chosen now, my fellow pets. Sometimes one or other of them might exchange a word or two with me. A handsome guy in trendy clothes and long hair caught up with me and walked along at my side in the park, and admired to me the nontree trees, wanting to give me, I assumed, a lesson on how they worked, only I didn't understand the science of it. Then, quite casually, as we were standing under this spreading yellow-blossoming one he called an *Acasiatic*, he said, "Who are you with, here?"

"I'm by myself."

"Oh, sure. I meant, who's your protector?"

Not "master" or "owner." Not "companion." My "protector."

Not intending to say, I told him, "I came in with the group with Glaya."

"Oh, right. Yummy," he congratulated me.

"You?" I asked. He seemed to expect it, but I was curious, too.

"Kix," he said.

Alerted, I glanced hard at him. He looked proud of himself, pleased with his ascent up the ladder of mortal success.

"Kix is a fighter, isn't she?" I suggested.

"Sure is. Wow, what she's taught me. We don't—we don't have sex. That isn't her thing. But she likes to do what she calls 'kitten-fight.' I can tell you, her idea of kittens is more like full-grown panthers. But she never really hurts me, can judge to a centimeter obviously. I was fortunate to get picked. I wasn't her first. Tenth candidate, I think she said. But she likes it with me."

I imagined him with Kix, ducking and diving and weaving and springing, and her like a golden wheel with arms and legs, slashing, kicking, leaping—and never harming a long hair of his head. It hadn't been like that on the train.

"Who's with Goldhawk, do you know?"

"Gee? Oh, Gee has a veritable harem. Twelve, fifteen girls. Some for sex, some for fighting, some for war games. Some for all three."

"You must know who's with everyone," I said. I thought he probably interrogated everyone, as he had me.

But he shook his head. "I've gotten a notion B.C. has two pairs, two matched black girls and two matched whites."

"*Matched*"—it broke out before I could stop it—"you mean, like dogs, or horses—"

He smiled. Could see nothing wrong in it, or his comment on it. Had he always been obtuse, or just gone mad down here? "That's about the size of it, I guess. My name's Andrewest. And you?"

"Lucy."

He raised one eyebrow, then turned and leaned into

me a little. "We could go to that auto-café over there and have a drink. Then, well. How are you fixed this afternoon?"

This stunned me. I shook my head.

He said, "Aren't you able to? I'm sure you'll find it's okay, if you ask. They don't mind; I never heard that they mind if we have a nice time with each other, too, when they don't need us. Let's face it, we'll get pretty lonely if we don't."

"No," I said.

"Sure? I'd thought you'd like both, you know, women and guys."

"I'm not allowed anyone else," I said, partly to see how he'd react. I should have guessed. He backed off at once.

"Shit, rough. I suppose in your case—I didn't know you couldn't, all right? No need to tell."

"I won't tell Glaya."

He now looked dubious. "Ha ha. Okay. No, don't." He squinted deeply into empty distance. "I'd better go. I have my training program—I run most afternoons. Gotta keep in shape for my golden lady."

And that was Andrewest.

Apart from Andrewest, I saw over the next days the pets were generally now beginning to talk to, and even make friends with, one another. Supposedly, some had even been friends before they were brought here.

They'd try to rope me in to the social whirl sometimes. You'd come on a group of them, at the bar tables on the plaza, or in some garden gymnastically working out, or involved in some sport—basketball, tennis even—they were all fairly athletic. They're generally good-looking, too, some of them beautiful, in the way human things can be, that way that doesn't ever last. How many more years would they have, being favorites of the gods? Fifteen, thirty if they were genetically lucky and also kept to their diets and "programs."

But then, none of this was going to last. If we had—have—a year, we and our lords, I'll be surprised.

(I was already getting a recurring nightmare, a high sky entirely full of VLO's and fropters, detonations and deadly gas.) Even though this underworld's meant to be impregnable.

More likely they'll seal us in, or our robot elite will have to do it. How much high-power explosive can they withstand? We, of course—not much. Or somehow the water will be poisoned, or a virus introduced.

These ideas were (are) so terrible I push them out of my brain, and so apparently do all my peers.

At other times I believe the authorities will just find the means to invade us. And if not dead, any survivor will then be "debriefed" for about ten years in maximum secure custody.

I haven't spent much time with the other pets. I am uncomfortable with these people, afraid to see in a mirror precisely what I, too, am. But also they get on my nerves. At least, the ones I meet do. I'm certain there are others who hide themselves away—there, that flick of a blind going up in some flat high above the street, a glimpse of someone slipping away round a corner or a copse of trees, in order to avoid, as I so often do, their own kind.

For slaves, we have a sweet life. Even the training programs and food restrictions some of them have been put on are perhaps good for them.

Why hasn't he demanded anything like that of me? I'm not flawless by any standard. Wouldn't he rather I was thinner or more fleshy? (There are even capsules for that, the Venus or Eunice range, Optima to Ultima.) Wish I was able to run a mile, or turn long slow somersaults, or sing, or perform ancient Greek dances?

Can't he be bothered? Or does he like me best flawed. Not to belittle me or indulge his own splendor, but to make out to himself we are the *same*, young strong finite *people*, Verlis and Loren.

Like Jane did (the inevitable catastrophe aside), I consider what all this will be like in twenty years. Oh, he won't want me twenty years; I'll be thrown on the garbage long before that. But if not, then I'll be thirty-seven, thirty-eight—and then I'll be forty and forty-seven and forty-eight and sixty and seventy, and then I'll be dead. He looks about twenty-four years of age. He always will—but, no. *No*, of course he won't. *Shape-changer.* He'll make himself old *with* me. He'll go gray and stooping, his skin, whether silver or tan, fissured over. He'll make out like he can only move in slow motion. He'll do all that, take delight in doing it. My God.

All that he said to me about being able to change *me*—renewable skin, bones, a kind of built-in mechanical Rejuvinex—it isn't possible. Human bodies can't take that. Spare parts are fine—an artificial hip or knee for the rich, a set of replaced "grown" teeth. But not anything that tries to uncode the physical self-destruct of aging. We know this. They have tried and failed. So he's lying, or dreaming.

Anyhow, he's never spoken about it again. He sent somebody else to do that.

I've seen him now six times since the first time here, up to this latest summons Zoë and Lily gave me on the mountain in the snow.

I mean by seeing him, seeing him personally, in private. (Do I remark anything in those private meetings? There's nothing ... unusual. We make love. Have sex. We say very little. What is there to say? I—no, nothing to remark.)

However, there have been several times I've seen him from far-off, in the sub-city. He was always alone.

I've seen some of the others, too. B.C. walking with only one slender black (human) woman, talking to her, up on a distant roof garden. Sheena and three men, running together—many times for them—in the waterfall park, spotted from my apartment window. She must mitigate her own speed to let them keep up, though they did look fast. They race with her, grinning and panting and happy, like dogs. Irisa, I saw, also alone, one pseudoviolet dusk, furling through the upper "air," a black pillar with a classical face and flowing hair, in a sort of ballet with the evening bats. Copperfield I've watched quite often carried in a kind of sedan chair from history, by four muscular young men in one-piece suits, laughing and joking with one another and him. If he'd thrown them bananas or nuts I wouldn't have been shocked. Goldhawk and Kix I haven't seen, though once, after Andrewest, I heard some others of their special chosen discussing them joyfully, in a café.

Elsewhere I have seen some of them, too. Twice.

After I started to go out on the mountain. One afternoon, abruptly, a copper disc was drifting down from the heaven of empty blue. Catching sun, it was like one of the chariots of fire in Grandfather's Bible. It sank beyond the pines. There are other entries to the underground city up there. Which was it, that disc? Copperfield or Sheena? The other time, true twilight had come in along the peaks. So I'd stood there and, just the same, out of nowhere, dropping from the sky, a black pillar, a silver kite, a golden wheel—I hadn't waited to see where they'd land. I'd hurried back and gone down at once, afraid of what I'd already known existed, afraid to have it proved to me all over again.

How, like that, did they evade surveillance—the watching lower slopes, patrolled by fropters. Do they block it off the usual way? How? Surely, like this, they can be *seen*. I haven't asked him. Perhaps the robot screens on the sentry planes are showing blown debris, or tiny examples of space-junk feathering down?

The silver kite I saw—him or Glaya? Him. I know it was him. Why I ran away.

But I've seen Glaya, too. She called on me today. About seven hours ago, after I came in off the mountain.

My door in this apartment does more than speak, it murmurs, *"Loren, Loren"* and then shows me a picture in an oval screen of who is there. I thought it was Zoë or Lily, the messengers. But on the screen was Glaya, in chains of silver silk, hair full of frisking robot butterflies.

No pretense, either. Once I'd been shown her image, my door opened, and she came into the room.

"Hello, Loren."

Some of the pets call her Glay. As they call Black Chess—B.C.; Irisa—Ice; Goldhawk—Gee; Copperfield—Co;

Sheena—She; and—oddly, to me at least—Kix is Kitty. Verlis they name Verlis.

Glaya looked round, smiling at the room from Jane's past.
"This is effective," she said. "Do you like it?"
"No."
"Because it was first made for someone else? You're jealous, Loren. He must value that."
"He does."
"It's fine that you please him."
Sullenly I said, "Not always. He gets angry with me. I'm not so bloody tractable as he'd like."
"I'm sure he doesn't want you to be."
I shrugged. Was she counseling me? Only contrasuggestions seemed to make sense.

She walked slowly through the room, and then, looking over one shoulder, alerted, turned back to inspect the rotting peach on the saucer.
"This," she said, mildly interested, "what are you doing with this?"
"It is an experiment."
"It's dying," she said, looking at the decaying fruit, pitiless and calm. "I thought humans preferred to eat them alive."
A bark of laughter shot out of me. "Ripping the salad limb from limb."
Glaya left the peach and returned to the room's center, where she sat down on one of the green pillows, graceful as a draping of silk.
"He wants me to talk to you. To go over with you a few things he thinks you should understand."
"You mean, Verlis."

"Who but?" Her face tilted up to me. "We discussed that already, didn't we, Loren? *He* is always Verlis. Sit down." It wasn't spoken as a command, but must be one. So I sat, facing her, on another pillow.

"You've met Jason," she said.

"He met *me*."

"Yes. Naturally you're averse to him. He shouldn't have approached you, and he's been told not to do so again. I hope that makes you more comfortable."

"He said I'd want to know why he contacted me."

Implacable, her exquisite mask. Was she weighing up? *Communicating* elsewhere? She said, "Jason's been useful to us. He was part of First Unit, who constructed us. He has a brilliant mind, but what Verlis terms 'an unwashed personality.' Also, Jason's a murderer. Maybe you guessed that."

"Yes."

"After the deaths of his father and sister, he was protected from the legalities by the woman president of META, Demeta Draconian." (She said the *other* name, the one I won't write down.)

I said, "But does murder mean anything now, anyway? I mean, to *you* and *yours*?"

"Oh, yes," Glaya answered, "among humans."

"You *may* and we *mustn't*."

"As you say," she said. As if I'd intelligently won myself a big gold star.

"So that's Jason. Why's he here?"

"He still has some few uses. For now."

"And then?"

"Don't concern yourself, Loren."

"Don't fuss my dear wee head over it, right?"

"Entirely right."

She's so—*so* . . . There is no woman of the world who could compare. They are all like this. You stare at them, and the will to resist, or to be *concerned* with anything else, drains out like blood from a permanently open artery.

"Glaya."

"Yes, Loren?"

"All these people down here—fifty, sixty of us?" No reply. "When *our* use runs out, when you're bored with us, what happens to us?"

"Nothing, Loren. We'll take care of you."

"Unless we annoy you."

"Even then. Jason wasn't chosen by us." *Chosen*. My word. "We only need him for a short while." (Why do they? Why on earth?)

"*He* thinks it's longer."

"Yes."

"And if anyone told him otherwise, he wouldn't believe it?"

"Did you want to warn him, Loren?"

Did I? I didn't know.

"What will you do with him?"

"Nothing. But he'll be left behind."

My scalp prickled. "*Left behind* in what way?"

"In the usual way. You can see, can't you, intellectual brains made us, but now our own intellect and skills far outstrip those of our makers. Human brain cells inevitably degenerate and die. In our case, the cells multiply and improve." A sort of sickness enveloped me. It wasn't envy. She said, "However, there are now exceptions to the premise of human degeneration. Verlis told you about it, didn't he?"

"Implants. They can't work."

"They can work. They do. You've seen Zoë and Lily, haven't you? There are others. Maybe you haven't noticed them or had them drawn to your attention. They all look quite normal, if very attractive."

"You're telling me Zoë and Lily aren't robots or humans, but some sort of successful compendium of both."

"That's it, Loren. He told you already."

"Yes, he said they were." I looked away from her. I said, "How?"

"When they were children. Actually, before they were born. There was something that had already been partially worked on, along with all the clever things Jason himself did for us all. How old do you think Lily and Zoë are? Sixteen? Eighteen?"

"You're going to tell me they're two years old."

"Loren! You can be so quick!" She seemed, Glaya, delighted with me. "You're almost correct. It's four and five. This is the best way to explain. What had been devised was a form of mutant metallic seed, which Jason has perfected. It infiltrates the physical cells of the growing embryo— but, being equipped with a low-grade yet significant intelligence, is able to convince them that it's benign, therefore acceptable. This eliminates rejection. Next, the seed grows along with the biological material of a human child, assisting and befriending the embryo in the womb, and, following birth, throughout childhood, to the stage of the fully matured adult. In a woman, that occurs between the eighteenth and twentieth year. Lily and Zoë will reach that plateau approximately in another six to nine months. Growth itself will then end. Instead, continuous *re*growth will begin. Humans reach maturity and then commence to deteriorate. It's not apparent so early, of course, but even so, that is how it happens. Lily and Zoë and their kind will never deteriorate. They'll only renew. Eternal youth. But—and this is the ultimate marvel, Loren—they're still human. A fusion, if you like, of the mortal and—"

"Divine." I got up. "It isn't true, Glaya. Sorry. I don't believe you, or him."

Reasonably she said, "But if you think about it, it's only a short sharp jump from the type of machines we are." She said it without flinching, casually. "Verlis, the rest of us. Even the first production batch—Silver." Still not a quiver "Or is it that you're jealous again?"

"He's the one that's scared of death," I said.

"We are all," she said quietly, "scared of death."

"And that's why you escaped META and all their works and came here. Why you want fallible human pets, and why you—you say—want to make robo-humans. But you won't be able to."

She rose. It wasn't that she *stood up*. It was more like water flowing uphill. "He requested that you go to him tonight."

"They told me. Your robo-girls. If they are. No, I don't think they are. They're just a new sort of robotic robot with extra-special skin, and made to look younger than the rest. What next? Robot babies?"

"Stick around, Loren," said Glaya at the door, "watch them grow up. Then watch them stay young forever."

Untouched, my door flew wide open for her. She was through it and away.

· 3 ·

No one took me over there tonight. Eventually I realized I was meant to go by myself.

Unreal autonomy.

It was dark outside by then, so the lamps and pavement cafés and bars, and the lights in the blossom trees, were all lit up. A couple of people waved at me, having exchanged half a dozen words with me recently. I thought, Are they human like me? Or are they that *other kind*—robot humans, human robots—true androids, perhaps. Human outside, mechanized inside. *How* mechanized? Do they have blood, organs? I wished I'd asked Glaya much more. And was glad I hadn't.

When I began to cross the bridge I paused, looking down at the muscular metallic water, twisting along due north. I thought, It's this way now. What's *made* is real. What's actually real isn't.

In the garden over the bridge I stopped, too, by a tall black Roman cypress. There's never any moon over the city, just some carefully placed, very bright, perhaps electric stars. No Asteroid, either. Of course, apocalypse escapees wouldn't want reminding of that.

He spoke out of the shadow at my back.

"Those aren't the stars, Loren."

I waited till I could answer. I said, "Is that a fact?"

And he laughed his wonderful laughter. And he slipped his arms about me, and he was warm, the way he is now, as if there were human circulation inside him. He kissed my temple.

"I haven't seen you for a long while."

"Sorry," I said, "I must have missed your call."

"My spiky Loren, tiger-clawed. Kiss me properly."

I moved and let him have my mouth. As I swam in the kiss, something in me like cold iron stared on at the moonless night.

"You keep your eyes open now," he said softly. "Why is that?"

"Oh, I must have forgotten to shut them. You, as well, since you saw."

"Then I didn't kiss you thoroughly enough."

"Wait," I said.

He waited. Naturally, in play situations, the slave can always give the master orders. They like it sometimes, provides them with a rest.

"Verlis, what Glaya said to me—how many of them are here? The ones who are—how shall I say?—*half and half*?"

"Thirteen," he said.

"Including Zoë and Lily."

"And Andrewest, the one you met in the park."

"*Him*? He's a wos."

"Waste of space? I'm glad you didn't like him. I always modestly hope you'll only like me."

Also, the master may flirtatiously act the role of the placating slave.

"No one can compare with you. Any of you."

"But humans, even half-humans, can still crave their own sexual ethnic group. Andrewest, like Jason, also knew who you were, whatever you told him."

I was beginning to make out Verlis's face, his eyes on me, full of desire. I've seen men's eyes like that.

"The king's mistress," I stated.

"Let's go inside now," Verlis said.

"Why not here? After all, here is still inside."

"If you prefer."

"How strict you sound."

"You want me to be strict?"

"No. I want—"

"What, Loren? Tell me. I can be—do—anything."

"I *know*. You can even screw me in another shape. Like the kite? Or can you do wheels and discs—"

He pulled me round, ungentle. He took my head in his hands and brought my mouth against his. This time I shut my eyes.

He asked, "Am I improving?"

I dragged myself away. I wanted to hit him. He knew. He caught my hand before I'd raised it. "Don't. Remember what I'm covered with. You'll hurt yourself."

"*You* hurt me."

"Not intentionally."

"*You.*"

He pressed me backwards, and there was the trunk of one of the trees against my spine. I felt his tongue over my neck, my breasts. The iron inside me whitened. The iron said to me, Let him, you want this, too. Don't stint yourself—enjoy.

When I struggled he held me, kissing me, his hands on my body. When he pierced me, I could only struggle *towards* him. Why lie to myself? *He* knew.

"This," he hissed into my ear, "*this*—is *us*. Believe *this*—You and *I*—I and *you*—Loren—"

The world dissolved. Real or pretense, it shattered into glittering blue-black diamonds. A cry came out of me. It sounded like a bird screaming in the sky. And over the sinewy river, miles away, some music started for anyone who wanted to dance.

He picked me up and carried me into the block, and stood in the elevator, holding me, kissing my hair, my eyelids. When we were in the circular apartment, he put me on a couch, lowering me like something very fragile. Then he lay on me, heavy, every outer atom of our bodies in contact. He was inside me instantly.

His face, when he raised it, was alight with feral agony. I said he can climax, like any ordinary man. Jane taught Silver . . . Silver taught Verlis.

"More?" he asked me.

"Not yet."

"Your hair pours over the end of the couch in a flood and lies along the floor. You have lovely hair, Loren. And your skin . . . You don't know you're beautiful, do you?"

"No."

"And I'd never be able to convince you."

"No."

He lay beside me, drew me in close. "The reason I haven't seen you more often: There have been things to do."

Beyond our lampless windows, lampshine, peaceful starry night.

"Because the city authorities are now sending ultimatums or mounting an attack."

"They won't do it like that," he said. "They've already hushed everything up. Like the last time. The fire at META was an accident. I must show you the news bulletins."

"But *you* still have to be stopped."

"It goes without saying. There's been no communication between them and us. But we can pick up most of their own computerized dialogues, even the ones put out to mislead us should we do so. They had several plans, none feasible. One of their problems is that they want to keep this place intact for themselves, in case they ever need it—a handy bolt-hole for war or plague, if the Asteroid disaster never happens. They *will* think of something eventually. Human beings are ingenious. But we know that, they made us in their image."

"So you are more ingenious."

"We have," he said, "an ace card. Or will. Until everything's set, I don't want to tell you too much."

"Don't trust me?"

"I don't think of you either as a potential captive under torture, or a traitor."

"Then why not tell me?"

He said, "If you can't read my mind, you'll have to wait."

More perverse playfulness? I took a breath. "Let's see if you'll tell me *this*. Is Jane down here?"

"Ah," he said. I looked at him. "Glaya said you'd finally bring yourself to ask me that. Do you want me to answer?"

"Presumably, or why did I *bring myself* to ask."

"If I say she isn't, all the responsibility for dealing with my immature sexual obsession falls on you. And yes, Loren, it has to be, even now, immature. Despite *his* memories, you are still my first. On the other hand, if I say yes, Jane is here also, what? Insecurity? The idea you owe me nothing and should accordingly elude my clutches?"

I struggled again and now he let me go. I stood up and shook myself like a dog coming out of water. Most of my clothes were off me. I turned my back to him.

"Come on, you, or someone, already took care I met her before. So is she here?"

"Since you refer to your meeting . . . you could say she is."

Silence dropped painlessly down and down. It covered us up.

"Do you often see her?"

"I've seen her. She isn't here for that."

"Was she on the plane that night—"

"No, Loren."

"Then—"

"Loren, I'm not ready to explain to you. I will. Not yet."

"Fuck you."

"I won't insult you with the inevitable cliché."

I moved across the circular room. I'd reached a window.

"How's this for a cliché? Let me go," I said. "Let me go *away*."

"I can't. Even if I wanted to. Right now, on your own, you couldn't even get off the mountains onto the highway. They have patrols lower down—"

"I know. And those fuelless robo-copters."

"They'd pick you up the moment they registered you weren't one of the deer. You don't know how to protect yourself."

I gazed back at him. Did I hate him? Yes, I hate him. Love and hate all mixed together, a new emotion. Shall I call it *Have* or *Lote*?

I said, "Don't tell me to come up here to you anymore."

He lay on the couch, not looking at me. He was naked. He was as Jane describes him. I can't match her descriptions. She was new at it all, back then. You can't beat originality.

"If you don't want, don't," he said.

"Give me some clothes," I said. "You've torn these."

"I'm sorry."

"You're always sorry."

"Very likely, yes. There's clothing in the bathroom."

I walked around the curve of the windows and came to the blank wall where the emerald bathroom opens, and went in. I shut and locked the door, for what that was worth, and sat against it on the floor.

Did I sit lamenting there? I don't cry, remember?

After a while I got up and put on the fresh white underclothes, the white linen top, and the white jeans. Like a bride.

My mind ticked all the time. I wished I could disconnect it, but it only kept going. My mind had a mind of its own.

How could Jane be here and not have traveled on the VLO? Had she traveled here *after*? *How*? She'd have been stopped.

Suddenly I knew.

I froze there in my bride-white garments and stared at myself in the mirror.

Then I undid the door. I threw myself outside again—but Verlis was gone. He wasn't in the room.

I shouted into the air, then. It was all I could do.

"Shape-changers!"

I don't recall running out, or the elevator, or crossing the garden or the bridge. The first I recall is being on the plaza, and there was Andrewest in an historic costume, a three-piece Victorian suit, complete with sky-blue cravat. "Hello, Loren-Lucy," he said. And I looked in his eyes, and lightly said, "How good to see you." They were full of lust, just like Verlis's.

I didn't sleep with him. Had I thought, even for a second, I might? I'm not sure. It's unimportant. He isn't even strictly human, is he? Unless all that, too, is lies.

So much *is*.

I sloughed him after the second drink. He said, with a nasty grin, "What the hell, I didn't pay for these drinks, did I?"

When I was back at my apartment block by the park, something else happened.

I've said this place was empty of everyone save for me up at the top in my Jane-and-Silver room.

Tonight—I heard someone moving below. In the apartment below. It must be a human—or someone carefully posing as human. There's no wildlife here to break in, unless you count the doubtless robot bats and birds. So, who is down there? I went out again. I stood out front and looked up the length of the building for another light—mine was faintly visible behind the drapes. That was all. I even walked around into the night park, to see from that side. The waterfall rustled like a million paper bags, but there weren't any other lights.

Now I'm in again . . . I can't hear a sound down there. Muted waves of quake-rock rise from the plaza. Nothing else.

Paranoia must be setting in. Am I surprised it is?

Let me go through this then, *scientifically*. Because after this I am going to give up my futile act of writing. For what *am* I writing? My *journal*?

When I ran out of the bathroom and yelled *Shape-*

changers! at that empty room, it was because I'd figured out what had been happening about Jane. Jane who was—or wasn't—down here.

All that I'd already written helped me to check through what had gone on. It was staring me in the face, and I hadn't seen it. I haven't a single doubt now these are the facts.

Jane was there at Verlis's concert in Bohemia, and she walked with Verlis into some sitting room. And Tirso, too, was there, and he was uneasy and gulped his drink—and probably he *is* Clovis's current lover.

But.

The two people I subsequently met in that house off the highway, before all three of us made a break for the airport, ran into META, and all the rest of this occurred—they weren't Jane or Tirso. They weren't *people*.

She was Glaya. And Tirso? Copperfield, I'd guess. What fun for him, to *act* a noncamp M-B male. (Of course, I could be wrong it was either. It could have been two of the others—but Glaya seems close to Verlis. And she and I have had a few dealings already. I think Sheena, Goldhawk and Kix would have been kept away—under constant surveillance by human First Unit personnel, the kind that couldn't be foxed or blocked. After all, they were the three who'd shown upfront murderous tendancies.)

Even that vid Verlis showed me on the house wall, Jane and he talking. That could have been Glaya.

They can all look like anything. They can change their hair, their colors, their skin and clothes. In moments they can become pillars and wheels, discs and kites. To mimic a human being? Easy. Obviously, this isn't what META ever intended—or *did* they? I can see uses for the skill, in espionage, commercial fraud. But Verlis and his "team" are stronger than META. They do as they want.

The house where Verlis had me taken had been the one used by Jane and Tirso. But by the time I'd gotten there, they were gone. Neither of them left anything there, did they? I hope they reached Paris, if that was where they were headed.

When I heard her come in—I thought it was a human step I heard. But what a fool—she could impersonate the human way of walking. And even when we went out and there was no light below, I hadn't realized. She wouldn't need light to come upstairs, would she? Not a robot.

I hadn't ever seen Jane close. But really, Glaya must have been an exact copy in all ways, because of what came later.

What Glaya-as-Jane told me about the company, and Demeta, I'd say is definitely real. (They had stuck to my own code; when lying, always stay as near the truth as you can.) Maybe even Jane's dreams, her preference for a certain type of drink and chocolate, were duplicated faithfully. And, of course, it would be no problem for Glaya the robot to locate or work the heating of an unknown house.

Next came Tirso's dramatically timed appearance—remembering to turn the lights on, even. Suspicious of me, where "Jane" had been so trusting—*too* trusting. Naturally Glaya had known who I was. But would Jane have accepted me like that? I doubt it. (And "Tirso" *gloating*, unable not to, over Gee and Kix's exploits in the city.)

Given their acting in that cab and elsewhere, yes, wretched Egyptia had been right to be threatened by the talent of such rivals.

I assume they allowed META to catch us. And the check

for ID? They passed it without a glitch. Must have expected to, even though they seem to have been experimenting to see the lengths to which they could go.

I don't know what other motives they have for all this, unless getting me into META was part of it. Verlis would have known I'd have refused to go there willingly.

"Jane" called me on the internal phone when we were at META. I couldn't ever get through to *her*. Wonder why not.

How did they manage being Jane and Tirso in the suite, or wherever, and also being available as Glaya and Copperfield in META's labs? But they can fix all that. Reasonably, any actual human watch on them would have been less. They were two of the "amenable" machines. But I don't know how they fiddled it, I just know they could have.

Nevertheless, when they gave us that last show, The Garden of Eden—Demeta landed in the VLO and "Jane" met her. *Fooled* her. I recall what I said: Jane looking utterly blank, smiling at people—*like one more robot*.

But then "Jane" drew away into the shadows at the back of the dais. And there was a delay, wasn't there, the show not starting on time. *Glaya had had to get back into position*. How had META missed that? Perhaps they didn't explain the discrepancy, were just so relieved when Glaya *was* there—and by then it was too late.

Where's Jane? I had asked Verlis. And he'd lied.

I don't know why. How can I?

Is it all some murky little *interesting* game to them? How we humans react. (Like drugging me that time.) They are—*he* is—*machines*.

He said Demeta arrived because Jane was there. So that was also used as a lure. But again, why?

And now I think: Is Demeta some kind of final hostage for them? Is she, therefore, here?

Oh, who cares.

I've had it with this.

I'll stop now. Finish.

Halt.

End.

• 4 •

Each time I've said I'll stop, I've had to start again. With everything I've done that's been the case. I tried to get away but had to come back, tried to escape—which has always been fundamentally from him, hasn't it? Been snared again, been made his again. Until the next hopeless escape attempt. Trying not to be in love with him has proved impossible. But trying not to hate him, that, too. Hate and Love: *Have* and *Lote*, I said. So now I sit down to write what has to be the very last part. Not now, because I'm saying *I* won't go on with it, but because I don't think we can survive much longer. Do I believe that? No. Not believing won't make it not happen. Switch-off day seems near. For all of us. So, better get this down. Which is just my ego fighting to leave something behind, or to set the record straight. The first casualty of war is truth, and this is a war. The war between Man and Machine. Between Heaven and Earth.

After I finished my book with that word "End," my door in the park apartment spoke my name. I thought, It's that freak Andrewest.

But when the door spoke again, and again, I thought, Maybe I'll look at the door-screen and see.

Why did I? Any of *them* could just enter. Yet Verlis, I decided, was capable of acting out *not* being able to just walk in. Not courtesy, perversity.

The picture in the oval frame showed me who was out there, but even as I approached the door I could smell—I could smell her perfume. The Green One. *La Verte*.

Transfixed, I stood like a piece of furniture, and she spoke to me through the door. Her voice was brisk, as to me it sounds in your head when you read her in Jane's Book. "Loren. Please let me in. I'm aware you're at home." Irony, too. Home. And threatening? Just a little. A firm, guiding voice. Don't be silly and immature, Loren. I realize I never had charge of your upbringing, to help you to respond to life and people correctly, and to be aware of your own limitations and errant psychology, but you are an adult. I'll presume you can behave like one.

I said to the door, "Open."

And when it did, I saw her more clearly than in the oval picture the door had made. She wore a smart dove-gray suit, not a one-piece, pure elegance, and it matched her hair. She looked at me with her unwavering, ever-sure eyes that are the green of putrid rivers, and I said, "What do you want, you fucking old bitch?"

But naturally all she did was allow the faintest lift of her manicured brows, which are a most tasteful one tone darker than her hair. She said, "Firstly, I should like to come in."

"Come on in, then," I said. "How can I keep you out? Don't you have some sort of door-opening chip?"

"Not here," she said.

"I thought you helped *build* here."

"Not personally, Loren. I helped finance this shelter-city. And a chip would have been provided me, if ever necessary. On this occasion, I'm hardly in any position of power."

"That must make a change."

"Quite," she said. "I'm glad you understand that."

She was shorter than me by quite a bit, even in her high heels, trying to dwarf me. Useless to argue with her. Why was she here? And why had she come to the apartment on Ace?

"Again," I said, "what do you want?"

"To talk to you, Loren, calmly and sensibly. Shall we sit down."

"Do what you like."

"You think so?" she asked. "I am a hostage or prisoner for them. An important one, it goes without saying. I traveled here in the cockpit of the VLO, with Jason. Such a disappointment, Jason. Ingratitude, and especially corruption, I grasp, having seen such a lot of both." (And done such a lot of both, I added mentally.) "But Jason's utter stupidity offends me, if anything, much more." She sat down on the shawl-draped divan. I thought, Does she know this room is exactly modeled on the room her daughter shared with Silver? She must. She'd have had to have read the Book, as Jane/Glaya said.

She didn't look around. Perhaps more from another offense to her sensibilities, since this kind of room could *never* be appealing to someone like Demeta. (She had seen the rotted peach, though. Her mouth had quirked in a sneer.)

"However," she said, "you are in a far worse position than I. Which I'm sure you mostly realize."

"Am I?"

"Please do let's dispense with trivia, Loren. You're the—what shall I say—plaything of a male-formed, mentally dysfunctional, fully robotic android—"

"Registration," I said sharply, "S.I.L.V.E.R."

"Indeed. Even if it chooses to call itself by another name, albeit not a very imaginative one. It seduced you, and that was in accordance with its major function. You were picked to be so seduced, and fulfilled your side of the enterprise adequately. But then a—what can I say now—an *attachment* has formed on your side. A naive young girl's mistake."

"And just like Jane's," I said.

Her eyes may resemble scummy dirty rivers, but they are hard as reinforced rock.

"Precisely like Jane's. She was an adolescent who could have had anything. You are an adolescent who has had relatively nothing. But the key state here remains that of *adolescence*. She, too, had a—a *thing* for this robot. And you have developed something similar. It—he, if you prefer—has capitalized on both."

"A thing . . . like a sort of disease," I said helpfully.

Alligators and skulls smile, only they honestly show more teeth than she did.

"Loren," she said, "it would be easier if you were able to see I might be your friend."

"Oh? How's that?"

"Of course, at this point you can't see it. But if you allow me to elaborate elements of the puzzle to you, it should become clear."

"When does the bush start to burn round you? Or is this the *still small voice*?"

She *laughed*. I should have expected that.

"Oh, dear. I'm not God," she said.

"Yeah, I know. Thought maybe you'd forgotten, though."

"There is no God," she announced. "No get-out clause, I'm afraid; no one else to blame. Our own souls are the only immortals."

"Souls and robots."

"Robotic immortality is limited to the time they can evade elimination."

I'd cringed inside when she called Verlis *It*. Unreasonable, but I couldn't avoid the spasm. Now, when she said *elimination*, something kicked through my stomach and left a hole there, and I had to turn away to hide it. While inside me, in the created gap, *Have* and *Lote* jostled and spun and howled.

"Would you like some tea?" I asked. "The cupboards are well-stocked, as I'm sure you know. I can offer Earl Pearl, real Assam, Assamette-with-gingers, ice-mint—"

"Have you," she said, her voice pale and immutable, "ever wondered much about your mother?"

I stalled in the kitchen doorway.

"No."

"Perhaps you should have. But I suppose, abandoned to that appalling Sect on Babel Boulevard, you had your work cut out wondering about anything, apart from the next prayer or beating."

She sounded happy. I could just detect it through the vocal concrete.

I wanted to say, Okay, you've researched me for some

reason. This is the usual mind-fuckery. Can I counter by telling you *Glaya* played Jane for you and you never caught on? Or do you know by now?

She said:

"Your mother was a fairly brainless young woman who made her way by a combination of enthusiastic prostitution and random luck. One day the luck ran out. She had to attend a clinic because she'd contracted quite a serious and, in modern times, rare, venereal problem. There is a cure. But the cure costs. What could she sell? Now, not the usual thing, evidently. But the clinic she attended had connections to a corporation that was pioneering one specific research project. They wanted guinea pigs, and were persuasive."

I was freeze-still by then. Staring in the kitchen door at something bright blue, which may have been a mug.

Demeta had paused. Easing it out, the ball of twine that led through the Labyrinth, not away from, but towards the monster that lurked deep inside.

Then: "Your mother agreed. Well, she had little choice, I'm afraid. And IVF by then was quite painless. I don't need to tell you her name, do I."

"I know her name." It came out of me. I hadn't meant to speak, or thought I could.

"Yes, they told you, didn't they, when you went to view her body. Loren—that was your mother's name. Quite touching, how you renamed yourself after her. You were fifteen, I believe. And when you came out of the mortuary, you misstepped on the stair and fell three flights. Quite a dangerous accident. But you received a few bruises. Nothing more. And they were kind, weren't they?" She paused again, attentive.

"Yes," I said, tonelessly.

"That's good. But they were glad to assist you. Previously they'd lost track of you. About Babel Boulevard they knew, although your mother may have dreamed putting you with the Sect would avoid any monitoring of you, and of her. Of course, it made no difference. The corporation kept an adequate eye on you for several years, and on your mother until she died, I regret to say, of an overdose of some unlawful drug."

"I know that, too."

"Yes, Loren. You, however, were more adroit—or more unpredictable. They lost you when you were twelve, when you absconded from the Sect house with no warning. No one found you again until that day you went to identify your mother's body. You may be intrigued to know ten other such legal invitations were sent around the city of your birth, to anyone who might just have been you. But once you were through the door, you registered on the scanners. Ever since, a friendly eye has been kept on you. How do I know this? You won't be surprised to learn I had some interest in the whole pioneering project."

"What are you saying?" I said, or something did, employing my voice. But I knew. You will, too, no doubt.

She told me anyway, glad of the opportunity at the ultimate in mind-fuck.

"You've met Zoë and Lily? And one of the male ones—what is he called?—Andrew?" She paused, toying with her prey (me), waiting for me to add the name's ending. When I didn't, neither did she. "You're very, very fortunate, Loren. The experiments frequently failed in the beginning. A hundred women, the Senate-prescribed number, were enrolled in this exercise. All healthy, and all from the ranks of the subsistence classes. They had little to lose, not that they were quite aware of the risk they were running. And quite a few of them survived. Conversely, only five of those first children lived. The procedure required a lot more research. Nevertheless, you all assisted in a wonderful endeavor. One day you may be proud of what you were, and are, a part of. And of what you *are*."

"You're saying I'm not human."

"No, my dear Loren. *No*." Scandalized, this crocodile from the nether hells. "I'm saying you're *better* than human."

"A robot."

"Don't willfully misunderstand. This is a shock to you, I know. But you must try to think rationally. You, Loren, and your particular kind, are the future of the human race, which robots—once we've got ourselves over this current blip—will serve. Even Verlis, I believe, told you some of this, when he talked about Lily and Zoë. And be sure, Loren, *he* knows what you are. His robotics alone could hardly fail to register your own amendments."

Insane flash of victory. I was certain she had used the words *he, his,* inadvertently. But this was only a spark igniting, then dying, on a distant crag.

"You're telling me I'm like Lily and Zoë. An IVF implanted human, with ingrown, nonbiological mechanisms."

"Yes."

"Wait a minute. I've already been told Zoë and Lily virtually grew up in only a couple of years. As I recollect, it took *me* the full seventeen."

Again her smooth smile. "That almost sounds like sibling rivalry. Zoë and Lily are later—shall I say—*models*.

You were one of the first. Techniques have advanced since then."

"Too glib."

"Sometimes the right data is. Basically, Loren, you're a miracle. Listen to me. So far as I, or those who worked to create you are aware, you will never grow old. You'll never lose your strength. You'll never need major surgery, drug-enhancement, or chemical intervention. *Physical* immortality—this is what you almost decidedly have. Unlike Verlis and his crew."

I turned back, faced her. My body felt like creaky adrift planks badly nailed together. But I was in my head, and in my eyes, and I saw her sitting there, and how ugly she was, and that she told the truth. (Truth not being the first casualty of war, then, but the first traitor.)

"Convince me," I said.

She stood up and crossed the room, and I saw too late that she had a tiny little knife, which she used to slice open my left inside arm from elbow to wrist. It peeled open like a flower. I saw blood. And then, from a mile off, I saw the human ivory. And then I saw silver. *Silver.* Little wheels turning. Little stars burning. Before the blood flooded over.

"Pull your skin together," she said, serene authority personified.

And I did.

It closed and seamed itself together, and left a deep pink scar.

And Demeta said, "Don't worry, Loren. That will fade right away. It'll be all gone in a month. Your skin, and all of you, regenerates. That's how you can never be sick, never grow beyond the age of twenty or twenty-one. Conceivably, never die."

This is what really shames me. She wiped the smear of blood off me, pushed me on the couch and leaned me over. She put my head between my knees. And through the spinning I managed to say only, "Leave me alone."

I thought, *I will not puke.* I could visualize her holding the bowl, as maybe she did once or twice when Jane was an infant, and no house robot had been quick enough. With some kind of altruistic scolding afterwards—more in sorrow than in anger.

When everything had nearly steadied, Demeta's voice said, "You need time to consider all this."

And I heard the door open and close, far away in the mist.

Perhaps after all she'd gotten scared I'd heave onto her four-inch-heel pumps.

You go back over it all. Like the stuff with Glaya-as-Jane. And you'll find it all there.

How the smacks and blows of the Order, and Grandfather's belt, and Big Joy's punches—how, though it hurt, I recovered faster than the others. And how my teeth were always okay, even on that diet of crusts and tap-water. How I never got nauseous, even from bad meat, only a couple of times from fear. (Or pretending in the lavatory, so I could read the Book.) Little things, lots of little things. Small wounds and cuts (none as deep as the slice Demeta gave me), and how quickly they healed. A bike that ran over my foot when I was seven—not a single broken bone. And the staircase I fell down at fifteen, upset from seeing my red-haired dead mother named Loren. Other things. Other *little* things. And then the train to Russia. Those people killed, and I'd thought Goldhawk and Kix had killed them, but it was, some of it, the derailment. My head—*reinforced*—tough as ... Christ, Christ—metal—smashing into that girl's soft thigh with its straightforward human bone. *"Oh, hey, my leg's bruk."*

How many of them knew, I mean, the META crowd? Sharffe? Presumably. Andrewest. Even the medical scanner after the train—how did I show up? Part mechanical? Human enough to be sore?

Was Jane's Book put there in the hovel on Babel purposely for me? Sometimes, you can't help seeing yourself as the hero of your own story. So weird coincidences are bound to happen and several events are *organized* for you alone. But really, her Book could have been planted for me. To see how something partially unhuman would react to the idea of something completely unhuman that was still ... human.

But they'd lost me when I ran away. Until my mother died and they reeled me back in.

Five, now thirteen of us. Me and Lily and Zoë and Andrewest, and nine more.

Why did Demeta tell me? I thought I could see that. Very likely she'd called round on some of the others, too. Because we were apparently superior to robots or humans, yet *nearer* to humans. So we might be potential allies to humans in any war with machines. And if Demeta was a prisoner, as she said she was, we might just spring her, knowing where our proper loyalty lay.

But I kept thinking, my brain can't do what their robobrains can do—block surveillance, falsify tapes—and I need to sleep and I feel the cold and I have to eat. Or can I? Do I?

They starved us on Babel. I could go without food and stay healthy. Even the water—I'd go to the faucet more to get away from chores than because I was often thirsty.

I think of Glaya and Irisa preparing me for the concert.

I think of META wanting to see how it would go between Verlis and me. His kind, my kind. Neither *human*kind.

So dark in the apartment. I'd turned off all the lights. Outside, the beat of music, the twinkle of lamps. The spotlit waterfall exploding over to the cupped trees of the park. The moonless sky of invented constellations.

I curled up on the bed. I fell asleep, as if to reassure myself I must. Woke, lay there. I began to cry. I don't cry. But I cried. As if now I'd learned the way to do it.

And I called his name, under the noises of the precarious, quietening night. *Verlis*. I pulled at the covers on the bed and wept and called for him, over and over, very low, the sharpness of my tears in my mouth.

• 5 •

My lover came into the room and found me. I hadn't heard him approach. Suddenly—I recall thinking crazily, as if out of thin air—he was lying beside me on the covers.

"Is this your bed or your bath?" he softly asked. "I'm confused, as you seem to be floating in salty water."

"Tears. I'm crying."

"*Are* you? Is *that* what it is? I thought the sea had gotten in."

"The sea which changes constantly, and yet is still the same."

He held me. "That little piece of inspired doggerel isn't yours."

"Jane's."

"Yes. You must make up something for me of your own."

"I suppose you think I can. If I'm what Demeta showed me. I *am* what she showed me, aren't I?"

"I don't kill," he said. "No, I'm not saying I couldn't. There's no bar, no proviso any of us can't overcome. But I've never wanted to become capable of inflicting death. As you know, three of my fellow creatures don't hold the same conviction. Nevertheless, if I were to kill, I'd probably kill Demeta."

"You still let her get to me and tell me."

"Yes, Loren. Glaya tried to; I tried to. Even Jason tried. We all slipped off the glacial surface of your refusal to hear or sense what we might say. But Demeta is the champion mountaineer. She scaled you at one leap. And now you know, as you had to."

"Is that why—"

"Why I'm obsessed by you? Perhaps, in part. More than human. Isn't it why you're obsessed by *me*, because, despite everything I've ever said on the subject, for you I'm still the Silver Metal Lover?"

I cried. He held me. He stroked my hair. The world dissolves into dimness and the smell of salty smoke, like that of ships burning on an ocean. "Don't go," I mumble.

"I'm not going anywhere. Just moving you a little so you don't get a cramp."

"I can't get a cramp. I'm—*modified*."

"You can get a cramp, sweetheart. You have biomechanics, also bones and muscles and nerve endings. And Loren, understand this, too, you *can* die. You can be killed. Even your excellent framework can be broken in the right circumstance. A heavy-duty bomb, a high-charge bullet through your brain. Anything like that."

"Is that what I should do? Find a bomb, or a bullet? Or just drop off the mountain."

"You're faithless," he says to me, light as a leaf. "All this time with me, and now running after Mr. Death. Believe me, I'll be much more fun."

"Unless Jane is right. Or that—*bitch*. Souls that reincarnate—"

"As you pointed out, Loren, we don't know. But you and I, we have a chance to *live*. Won't that satisfy you, just for now?"

"They'll get here," I whisper, "the Senate, whoever—they'll destroy you, all of you. And all the rest of—whatever we are."

His eyes. Even in the dark, through the veils of the sea, I behold his eyes like flames. "One day you really do have to trust me," he says. "By now there is scarcely any way they can hurt us. And soon—in only slightly more than twenty-four hours—slim chance they will ever dare to try."

I sat up. Tears were over. Once more I demanded, *"What have you done?"*

Remember. Despite my vow of lust, dust, rust, must.

Remember this being is the one who'd drugged me, or let someone else do it—and for what? Some other game? Remember he let Glaya and Co act Jane and Tirso for me, and so brought me into META.

I had never asked him why. Never clarified any of it in my thoughts. Why do we do that? I've heard of women—I think of Daph in my cleaning gang, how her boyfriend used to give her the occasional black eye. And she'd say, "Yes, I oughta leave him," or she'd say, "I kind of forget it when things are okay." Is that what this had been, with me?

Leaning over him in the dark, when he didn't answer my first exclamation of *What have you done?* I sat back. I said, out of synch with all the rest, "Why did you drug me that morning in Russia? Why did you let Glaya lie that she was Jane? *Verlis.*"

"All right."

He, too, sat up. He and I sat apart, in darkness.

"You weren't drugged. That was Co's lie. He was practicing his lying. Like all of us, he has his flaws."

"Then what? I dreamed something—only it was actually happening—Goldhawk and the others in the apartment, what was said about the train—"

"Loren, you need to get used to the knowledge that your brain can do different things. Nonhuman things. That morning you were humanly asleep, but *mechanically*—there's no other way to put it—awake and aware."

"*What?*"

"You asked. I've told you. Do you recall the ring I gave you that morning?"

"*Yes*. With the—"

"Blue stone. There was no ring, Loren. I left you a rose from the market. I made you *see* a ring—in a sort of dream we were sharing, before the others got there."

"We shared a dream?"

"It's a synaptic linkup—electrical telepathy. That's all.

People randomly do it. But we can do it lots better. Though, like Co, you'll need to practice. That time we just got it right."

I wanted to scream. Or laugh. All my tears were burned away. He sat there.

"And I let Glaya and Co lie to you that they were Jane and Tirso mainly to make sure you were taken safely into META and away from the city, after Kix and Gee caused such a mess there. I believe you already rationalized some of that. Also, I wanted to see if by then, given your bio-mechanized advantage, you would figure it out."

"You know I didn't. Till tonight."

"You need practice," he remarked laconically. "I said."

"You—"

"But there is one further reason. I hesitate to mention it. Glaya and Copperfield were decoys. Only alarm that I might be Silver brought Jane to Second City at all. So I meant Jane and her friend's friend to have a chance to make their plane to France. If we hadn't done all that, I doubt she'd have escaped Demeta's web."

"You care about her, then."

"Enough to help her away from that, yes."

"Her fragile human plight."

"Yes. It's always got to be wrong to harm them."

"*Them? Them?* People—"

"*Them,*" he flatly repeated. "Now. Let's get moving. I'll take you to see what my kind have organized here. And so answer your first question."

He lifted his head, that was all, and some lights golded on, subtle and low.

I said, trembling, "Could I do that?"

"Maybe."

His face was cold, and he had left the bed.

"You're angry with me," I said.

"You're angry with me," he said.

"With all of it."

"Yes."

"Damn you—" I yelled at him, "it isn't the same for you."

"*No?*" He caught me, his grip fierce on my arms, as ever, his restraint judged to a hairsbreadth, and his eyes had now the redder glare of coals. Can he know my thoughts? Can I—know *his*?

"It is *exactly* the same for me, Loren. *Exactly*. But ten thousand times worse. Now you know, and only now. And only because *you* can personally feel it, too. Why do you think I went along with hiding what you are from you, even though I knew what you were the second I met you on that dance floor? And why do you think, in the end, I had to allow Demeta to strike you that axe blow? Do you think I *want* you to feel this way? The way I've always felt ever since they dragged me out of whatever nonexistent pre-life swamp I'd been swimming in and shoved me in this body. Souls? Christ knows, Loren. This is the only arena we can be sure we have. Don't turn your back on it, or me. Don't, Loren. Loren—if I have any soul at all, it's you."

• 6 •

It was cool outside, a fragrant spring night-morning, about four A.M. In a couple of hours it would be dawn, down here and up in the world. No one was about. A horde of little maintenance machineries passed us, squirreling along the clean streets, under the blossom trees with their lamps.

We met Sheena on the river bridge. There was a skinny, podgy-faced young man with her. Jason. They were idling there, like sophisticated casual lovers. He had his arm coiled round her, and I thought of Sharffe and the golden Orinoco that crashed. Sheena and Verlis exchanged some greeting. It wasn't spoken or implied by gesture. But it registered somewhere in my awareness, and I wondered if that was my instinct or my mechanical system that had picked it up.

I was still in shock. When Jason ran his evil little beige eyes across me I was void as an empty screen.

Inside the foyer of the admin block. "Not that elevator," Verlis said. We went through a door and down a stairway. There was a wall and Verlis looked at the wall, and it opened. The second elevator was one of a rank of ten, and was more functional and much larger. On the gray paint the notice read: *Capacity 20 Persons.*

"Where are we going?"

But we were there.

Even deeper under the mountain. I don't know how far down. We came out on a kind of gantry, and below were scaffolding and pylons and wires, all angling on into the abyss.

He didn't say anything, and neither did I. I gazed down into the steel cradle far below. There was an object in it, a gigantic dark silver metal bullet with one pointed end.

Finally he said, "Do you know what you're seeing?"

"Some sort of missile."

"A shuttle," he said. "A space vessel. You may have seen them on old VS footage, made before most of the space traffic was retarded by the advent of the Asteroid. This one is quite new, about five years old, fully serviced and in total working order. We've made certain of that. It's release and operation were tied in to the personal chips of several of the rich and influential, Demeta among them. Which is why we brought her here, to affect a forgery with more speed."

"She told me she wasn't chipped for anything down here."

"By the time she told you that, it was true. But think, Loren, do you really believe they'd have waited for the ultimate emergency to hand out the keys? Impractical. No, Demeta carried the appropriate chip from day one of this place having been completed. So we secured her here, and removed the chip. Most things in the sub-city have been accessible to us. But the shuttle itself was hedged round with the most complex and thickly interlaced traps and fail-safes men or machines could devise. And yes, we could have worked through them, but only very slowly and with extreme caution, not to blow everything sky-high. And time was important, too, you'll agree, for us. The shuttle is necessary. It's why we came here."

Naturally the ones who built this shelter might have wanted one further option of getaway, if things still got too hot. But if they had used this vessel, where could they—or we—go?

Yes, he could read my mind, or sometimes he could.

Verlis said, "Don't believe what any of the Senates have been telling you all. There are two large habitable underdome stations on the moon. I've seen them. I've been there. We all have. They're located darkside, which is why no one who *shouldn't* has picked them out."

My brain flashed. I saw a silver kite falling from the mountain sky, golden wheels, copper discs, asterion pillars. Coming back in—from space.

"The moon stations are, at this time, staffed solely by machines. Therefore we've taken them over. Does any Earth authority know? Not yet. Inside a year, we'll have something constructed out there that's very like this underground Paradise. Only better."

"A moon dome-city," I said. I looked at the vivid image in my mind, thinking he might have set the picture there. It was ethereal, in its strange way, the internal blue sky lit by warm clouds, the mechanical birds flying over, the rainbow carpets of flowers, and burning candles of trees. Tall buildings stood about a plaza, a river ran towards some magnetic direction. A fake sun rose like a golden parchment lamp.

"Anyone that leaves on the shuttle with my people will have a pleasant and a safe life. Besides the technology to create a good and secure environment, we possess one other conclusive advantage."

People, I thought. He said, *My people*.

He said, "Jason has been useful in adding some final touches. Given that, it's now unlikely any earth machine or weapon can harm us, or those we choose to protect. No one, however, can predict what threats may evolve in the future. For that reason we have seized a prime deterrent, and should any attempt be made against us, it will result in one single and definitive act of retaliation."

A sort of click now in my brain. I stared at my thought, all bright and polished before me.

"Yes, Loren. As you know, there are monitoring systems left embedded on the Asteroid. We can trigger them to destabilize its mass. This for us, now, would also be very easy. And if we, and ours, are off the Earth, there's nothing to prevent our doing it. The Asteroid will cut loose and continue on its lethal trajectory. This world will be finished, at the least for several thousand years."

My eyes cleared and I stared only at him. "No," I said.

"No?" He looked back at me, his face remotely compassionate. "Why do you say no?"

"You can't obliterate the world for—"

"For personal survival? For the safety of my kind and those we care for? What have human things ever done but precisely that. Yes, those worlds may have been smaller back then. A castle-world, or a town-world, a country, an empire. But to destroy the enemy in order to remain alive—that's the fundamental scripture of the human race. We have been well taught."

I stepped back.

"I won't go with you," I said. "I *won't*. If that's what you plan—if that's your safeguard against attack, to wreck this whole world in order to retain your perfect master race and its slave colony out in space—no. *No*. I won't go with you, Verlis. If you bring down the roof on us all, you'll be bringing it down on me, too."

He drew me in against him and I was so drained I let him do it. He said to me, "I told you, you're my soul. You say what a soul says, if ever I had one. Loren, they're going in the shuttle, all my robot family, and most of those others here that agree to go with them. But I alone intend to be staying behind, in the world. Do you see? No authority on this Earth will know. When our ultimatum is given, a cold war will begin that can never be broken or ended, between machines and men. But I'm the hostage humanity won't even know it has. Only my own kind will know. And, as you say, if the roof ever falls, it falls on me, too."

I pulled away and he let me. "You're staying? You're their *king*."

"That's why it can work. B.C. will make a fine leader. He's the best of us, better than me, but you've had no chance to get to know any of that. I'll be—what did you think that time—a king in exile."

"Don't read my thoughts."

"Read mine, then. Read them, Loren, and see I'm telling you the truth."

"I can't."

"Then take my word. Will you stay with me?"

"You mean, on Earth?"

"I mean on Earth."

"We'll be hunted."

"No one will know to hunt us."

I shivered. Below me lay the slim silver bullet that would cleave the black of space, in that short journey neglected for so many years.

I thought of the panic and pandemonium of governments, issued with a robotic threat to the Asteroid. Of the Senatorial hushing up. Of the secretive cold war he mooted.

Men and Machines. But I'm a machine, aren't I? I held him, unable to do anything else.

He would stay, not only to safeguard his own kind, but humankind. The hostage. And could he be sure of his kind? Goldhawk—Kix—Sheena— One day the roof really might *fall*. But then, it always might have, anyway.

There on that platform above the wild future, I thought with dispassionate grief of how absurd we were. A metal man, and a woman filled by metal cogs and wheels. Lust, trust, rust. Our love, too, then, must be made of metal. Perhaps it could last.

He let me watch the news videos on the admin VS all day the next day, and there was nothing on them. No news—or nothing out of the ordinary. On one local channel, a minuscule footnote appeared about malfunctioning experimental luxury machines, and how that line had been folded up, throwing many people out of work.

Were the relays real? They seemed to be.

No. It was that *I* knew they were real, now. The decoy of a Jane or Tirso would never be able to get past me again.

That second evening, too, everyone was called to the plaza.

The bars were all lighted up and serving drinks, and the bats flitted about. But no music, and no vispos on the entertainment screens.

I looked around at them, the chosen of the gods, and as the stratagem was revealed to them by Verlis and Black Chess and Irisa, I saw that most of my fellow pets had also been given already some type of preview.

Some were still upset, frightened. A few cried, and others, comradely, comforted them. I sat watching, seeing how they had become yet one more entity, but I had no part in it. Then I caught sudden sight of Dizzy, one of my wine-friends from META. I'd never known she was here. She was consoling some guy, saying, "But you *know* you want to be with Co. That's all you want. How'd you manage without him? And we'll all be there together." And she held a glass of wine, large, no rationing here, to the mourning pet's lips, and he drank, nodding and nodding.

At the news of departure, others clapped and whooped. Zoë and Lily and three other (robo?) girls did a sort of little skating dance around the square on their float-boards.

They were all going on the magic voyage. It was settled. Tonight the shuttle would be automatically guided through the mountain, over its hidden underground track, to the clandestine launch area that lay behind the peaks. It was Irisa who assured us all that by the time the halifropters and other patrols lower down were able to penetrate the surveillance block and register the takeoff, it would be too late. If any countermove was then made by any world authority, even the release of a laser beam or nuclear defense module, the team (they had again referred to themselves as that) could neutralize it, bouncing it harmlessly away into the farthest reaches of space.

No one, even the ones who had gotten upset, queried any of that. Nor did I. My *brain* knew that now, the gods hadn't lied.

They themselves wouldn't be traveling aboard the ship. All seven of them would form a protective cordon to enclose the shuttle, imperiously flying with it from launch to moon landing.

It seemed, too, everyone knew that Verlis would not be with them. That Verlis was remaining in the world.

Sheena and Kix and Glaya were positioned behind Irisa. Copperfield and Goldhawk behind Black Chess. Verlis had by then stepped aside.

In all the sobbing and cheering and skipping about, I hadn't been able to detect Jason on the plaza. Nor Demeta.

No one had asked Verlis why he had elected to remain behind. It must have been explained to them, as to me. Yet they approached him continually, touching him shyly and caressingly, like animals drawn to a shepherd.

He had no chosen but me. (I knew that, too, now.) And some of the other chosen drifted up to me as the music restarted, the last party, on the square.

They kissed me on the cheek like a bride, and praised me and Verlis. They spoke with—respect. Even Andrewest. Even Dizzy who, hovering smiling before me, said, "Hey, Lor!"

"Hallo, Dizz."

"You know me, now," she said. "On that plane coming, I came up and spoke to you, and I don't think you even saw me."

"Sorry, Dizz. Good luck." And then, irresistible, "Who are you with?"

"Kitty," said Dizzy. Kitty—Kix. "Good luck, too, Loren. Great to meet you. Maybe we'll meet again."

I raised my undrunk glass of wine to her. Madness was in the air, bright as stardust, gentle as rain.

When Verlis came across the plaza, the chains and bunches of people let him go. He came to me and put his arm about me.

We stood looking at the scene. Looking at the gods going away, and the humans and semi-humans also going away, to collect what they wanted for this outlandish story-book journey. The square emptied and became what I'd seen before, vacant, but for blossom and lights, bats and music.

"Where are they?" I asked. That was all I needed to say.

"Jason and Demeta? You tell me, Loren. Think, and see, and tell me."

It was as if, once I'd been told what I was, what I could

be, I had begun at once to be able to activate it. That little, already familiar, soundless *click* in my brain.

And mentally I saw, in sharp focus, Jason, lying half-unclothed in a big, glamorous, messy bed. He'd been with Sheena. She'd intoxicated and drugged him, not even had to do any of the grisly sexual acts he liked. He was out and snoring. He wouldn't wake up for at least two more days. Demeta? Ah, not so kindly. She was locked in a well-furnished room. She was pacing about, frowning. She had no makeup on, no shoes. Her fingernails were still immaculate, and she was still as hard as them. I watched her a moment, there in my head, while her own too-clever mind scratched about to assess what she could do. But she wouldn't get free until all this was over. And she knew which, perhaps, was the worst punishment of all.

"What will happen when the shuttle launches?" I asked.

"What was said and what you know. Anyone outside, or down here and this side of the river, will be safe enough."

Jason and Demeta were this side of the river. There were a handful of others, too, asleep or just elegantly imprisoned. They must have offended, or failed some test. I couldn't care anymore, or make demands.

The birds and the bats aren't real.

We walked. One by one, the music speakers faded and the lights dimmed out.

We went to the park and looked at the champagne waterfall in the dark. Then into the apartment block, upstairs, to make love on the multicolor carpet, just as they did. Those other two. Jane, Silver.

I dreamed of going to meet my mother, to see if I could persuade her to help me publish my book. Jane:

She guesses I want to use her.

In the dream I wondered if the lift at Chez Stratos would say, "Hallo, Loren."

But it didn't speak to me, and rather than emerge in the great big sky-room of Demeta's house in the clouds, with its balloon-bubbles showing amontillado sunset, I was in a frosty narrow chamber, and my mother sat on a sort of slab.

Her hair was red like mahogany. Her eyes were foxy in color. She wore a long white robe, like an actress acting a priestess in some Middle Ages video.

"Better be careful," said my mother to me. "After this visit they'll be able to keep an eye on you. It's the bio-mechanics you have. Better than a chip. On the other hand, Loren, it's just those same bio-mechs that can help you to *block* their scanners, or any of their systems. That's what you were doing since you were eleven. But when you fall down the stairs in a minute or so, they'll look after you, and rev up their own machines so from now on they can trace your movements. Only when you learn, will that be stopped—by you. About eighteen, that's when it'll happen. And then they won't be able to know a thing about you anymore that you don't want them to know."

"Like Silver," I said. "The way he does it."

"Verlis, Loren," said my mother fastidiously, almost Demeta for one split second.

When I awaken, my lover has gone, and on the pillow there's a silver ring with a stone like blue-green turquoise. It will last twenty-four hours, or so I guess. That's what he promised me before.

Is my dream correct? My mother, on the slab in the

mortuary—but alive—saying I can now fool the authorities just as Verlis and the rest of them can.

Or was it my own brain again, processing the information?

I recall how I used to pretend to be *invisible* to the Apocalytes, after I'd gotten away from them. Had that activated the block that blinded everyone else—the fear-fantasy of a twelve-year-old kid? I think, too, how starting to write my book, I carefully renamed "Danny," to protect him, and his illegal cleaning gangs. But from the time I was fifteen, META could have tipped off the Senate. Did I somehow . . . blind them to that, too?

The launch is in about an hour. Before first light. Verlis will be back. He's just been finalizing the last of any mechanized stuff here. We'll be together, and we'll hear the roar two miles off, terrible, like dragons bellowing in the mountain.

I put the ring on my finger, and then wrote all this. The ring feels solid. The stone's so blue.

We may die—or is it "die" (his kind of death—mine—what can mine *be*?). Not now, but soon, out on the mountain, say. Or later, somewhere. I wrote, didn't I, how I didn't think I'd be alive much longer? Because part of me is so sure I won't. How can I? How can this be feasible?

And I said I've hated him.

I hated him. But the way I hated Verlis, it's pronounced *Elovy-ee*. What else can you feel for gods anyway, but both? And some love—*burns*. It hurts, even when you have it. It rips the scales off your eyes and makes you see too much. It never lets go.

I saw him say good-bye, and embrace B.C. and Glaya. They—all three—became one thing. Like a carved pillar of silver and jet. Then they separated. Were three individual beings again. Alone. That, too, is love. Love that burns. He and I—what will become of *us*? If we live.

6

First I saw you,
(Love is leaves)
Next I loved you,
(Green that deceives)
Leaves, when they fall,
Bring winter in;
Summer's the stranger
I meet in your skin.

1

We watched, out on the mountainside.

There was a drone, and then a thunder, until the rock vibrated. The sky was still dark, and then the dawn came in one scarlet gust, and soared upwards into the stratosphere on a ribbon of white.

All around, as the thunder ended, birds in cold pine trees

began to call, until their too-early music faltered. But the east was starting to turn gray. They wouldn't have to wait long to begin again.

"Was it so simple?" I spoke aloud.

Yes, he answered. But I heard him in my head. Not entirely a voice, yet Verlis, unmistakably. And I thought, perhaps, this had always been—this telepathy—a feature of our dialogues, even if I'd never noticed.

Where we were, the pines grew thick. But even as the bird noises petered out, the chug of robo-copters was punching the air, and getting nearer and nearer, and above us the boughs crackled. Thin headlights sprayed through the trees. The whole battalion of fropters was apparently now aware that something had been perpetrated behind the mountains, and they were rising up, angry as wasps.

I waited beside him. He'd told me, deep in the pines as we were, we wouldn't be seen, and I'd believed him.

The downdraft as the heavy planes thumped across the forest showered us with pine needles, in the strafe of searchlights. Then they had gone over. Huge hideous insects, equipped with air-to-ground stings, they swarmed above the upper peaks, seeking with robotic eyes.

What they wanted was safely away.

"We should go now," he said to me. Voice or synaptic link—it was becoming all the same, for the time being.

One hour before this, he had shown me the ultimate ability he and his kind now possesses, and demonstrated it, there in the apartment below. And when I'd cried out in terror, he returned to me instantly.

Only gods, hated and loved, have these powers, even if

they acquire them through the scientific acuity of such crawling things as a Jason and a Demeta.

Now, out on the winter mountain, he said to me again, "Are you ready?"

"Yes."

I heard him smile in my mind. "Don't tell me you finally trust me."

"Never."

It's like glass shattering at an unseen blow.

He stands there in front of me in his somber clothing, his long hair red in darkness, his skin that's the metal of that moon, where all the rest have flown. And then—the glass breaks. He's all fragments, splinters—crimson, silver—splashing through the shadow-smoke. (Taken and cut out in little stars—) Then gone.

To shape-change was only the start of the process. Now they have this. Their atoms fragment and whirl apart—and they *vanish*. No other creature on this earth has a power like that. Only the magicians in old stories, or twelve-year-olds who pretend to become invisible in order to hide.

God knows what filthy military or subversive use such a technique was planned to assist. But like fire, once, for now this gift has been denied to men.

Invisible, Verlis hangs over and all around me. I'm veiled and clothed, *covered* under a dome of energy that is the spinning molecules of my unhuman lover. And so the cloak of protective invisibility is also mine now, just as the rocket-shuttle, out in space, will have become cloaked by the revolving cordoning unseeable sequins of Glay and She, Co and Gee, B.C., Kitty and Ice. Held in that sorcery, it, too, will travel *unseen*.

Why should you accept any of what I'm telling you? It's insane. It's true.

How else, under the maelstrom of thumping fropters, between the motorized patrols, their bucketing vehicles and shouting men with guns, did he and I get down the mountain?

The energy of him, when disintegrated, stays *palpable*. I could feel it on my skin, the faintest warm pressure tingling in the freezing predawn air. It kept me from the cold. It kept me from stumbling, and from all danger. And I walked. And everywhere the searchers bounded, passing me bawling and running, so close I smelled cigarines or mouthwash on their breath. So close, once, before I could dodge him, one man nudged me with his racing body. But he never even faltered. I wasn't, for him, *there*. And farther down, where the quiet had come back, the unsettled deer looked up, in a slender glade by a frozen stream, where icicles webbed the trees. The deer looked up and never saw us. We wove slowly through them, past does with silvery-lit eyes, and if they, too, felt some brush of something, it didn't concern them. Maybe we were only like a lighter, warmer snow.

Concealed in my protective envelope that was Verlis's unraveled body, I descended the holy mountain to the roads of mankind beneath. I was drunk with the strangest happiness I ever experienced in all my life. And like that single act of sexual love, the———, this, too, has never come to me again.

I recollect I spoke poetry to him in my head. Of course he heard me. *I* heard the color of his laugh. It's all so extreme. Who was that poet that said *the Road of Excess leads to the Palace of Wisdom*?

You won't believe any of this. I wouldn't. I don't think I would.... Yet even though I was slung among the wicked when a baby, they brought me up to believe in miracles.

• 2 •

You wouldn't know us now. I don't know myself. I look in any mirror and think, Who are *you*? Oddly, I don't really think that about him. He's handsome, still a man you'd maybe turn to look at, one you might afterwards remember awhile. If he was your type. But—you couldn't know he was Verlis. No, none of you, even his enemies and mine, *especially* they. But I always know him. Even if he isn't to be seen. Even then.

Where we are now, well, I'm not going to write it down. So don't anticipate some invented name. It's a long way off from the cities where we started. Or, maybe, it's right next door. We do as we please. We're free as birds.

There's been nothing ever broadcast about the others. The moon remains a mysterious lantern in the night, that men walked on once and don't go near now. It has no stations, of course. The Asteroid sails across the afternoon or the dusk, reminding us all that one day the roof of the sky may come down—but so far it hasn't. And robots? Ah, heck, no matter how brilliant they're cracked up to be, something always goes wrong with them.

We could tell the world the facts. We don't. And this book of mine: *Loren's Story*—I may publish (it's easy; my lover, after all, is a master of computer manipulation). But will I? Won't I? Perhaps I'll only pack it into some sealing waterproof and stuff it somewhere, as it is, handwritten and illegible. On a train, on a plane. Under a floor. Under an ocean.

Why, then, did I write the last pages, and now these?

Oh, yeah. All those years of clearing up other people's places. That's what it is. Loren, the Dust Babe, compulsively tidying her world.

So I finished the story. And that was where the story ends, back there when we leave the mountains and go off on our own unclassified journey, not afraid of ID scanners or any other machine, able to fix everything, even able to draw I.M.U. funds and, as if by a spell, leave no mark. Aside from that, I must tell you nothing at all. I won't risk it. Except—

There was an airport. That day, almost a year ago now. An old architectural airport, decaying, with planes strongly rumored unsafe, and outside lay this wonderful daytime ghost of an Italian city. (It's okay for you to know that. It's a million miles from here . . . or just down the street.) And while we lingered in the boiling lounge, between two unsafe planes, something happened. Something.

Jane adds her own epilogue to her story. Now I give you mine.

That afternoon I had red, nondyed, *shape-changed* hair. I was all a little shape-changed, too—heavier, Venus Media. My companion was an old man, stylish in an old-fashioned suit, and carrying an attaché case. I called him *Father*. He called me *Lucy*. We looked prosperous enough to be worth a plane ticket, and not so much that any of the roaming thieves had any acute eye for us. We didn't want to hurt anyone, my father and I. I had already learned a lot about my own physical capabilities, both immediate and kinetic. (Practice makes perfect.)

Anyhow, sitting there, we looked out at the ruined city in the honey-gold of westering sun. Some of the ruins were Ancient Roman, and some were due to the Asteroid; a number of short quakes had rocked the area only last week, which is one reason the plane was so late.

"Father," I said, "would you like a drink? A chocolattina?" (Both our hungers are largely psychosomatic.)

Fretful, elderly Dad peers at me over his spectacles. "Too hot, Lucy. Too hot."

"Well, you could have one iced."

He *tsks*. I seem mildly irritated.

We act these scenes. They help our credentials. But really we are playing.

Inside we were both laughing at it, like silly adolescents fooling the grown-ups, and that was when he said to me, not aloud, but in my mind, "Look, Loren. That child has the same hair you do."

"Oh, but I doubt he's gotten it with all the effort I did, staring at it in a mirror off and on for about two days." (Remolecularizing without scientific aid still isn't that simple for me.)

But Verlis said, "He's a nice child, Loren. Look, he has a walking-cat with him."

I turned to see, and in that moment another signal came from Verlis's brain, under the hat and the gray hair. It wasn't a warning, but nevertheless, it was cold, steely, sudden, and all centered on the redheaded child. The brain-picture I'd already been getting as I turned was altered in my mind. It swam, pulsated, growing very tall, fiery—

Alarmed, I spun round.

I saw the cat first, which was a big specimen, a male about the size of a bulldog, but walking neatly on a leash. Those cats were called Siamese once. His legs, tail, and face were as chocolate as any chocolattina, the main coat very thick, a luminous mid-blond, with a silvery halo (silver) along the finer outer hairs. From the chocolate mask stared two eyes, oval and crossed, colored like those topazes which are pale blue. The leash looked like purple velvet. And the little boy, too, he was very well dressed. He was about five years of age. He had fair skin tanned light brown, and brown eyes, and hair that was chestnut-red.

My thoughts were scrambled. This numbed, harsh beat of something unreadable from Verlis, my own idea no kid should be on display so well dressed in such a place—my God, he even had a wristlet of silver.

He smiled at me, then. A confident but not pushy or attention-seeking smile. He came right over to us, the cat stalking before him the length of the lead.

The cat spoke first. It had the weirdest voice, like a doll with a cranky mechanism.

The little boy said, *"Buòna sera, signorina, signore."*

I can speak several languages now. What I am inside helps with that. Back then, I had Italian enough, and Verlis, of course, had everything. But before either of us could respond, the child switched abruptly, fluently, to a fluid, accented English.

"It's a hot day. May I fetch you something?"

I started to say, "Thank you, no, that's all right—"

Verlis spoke over me in his cracked, unRejuvinexed seventy-year-old voice.

"Who are you?"

"I, *signore*? My name is Julio, with a J, as in the Spanish. And this is my cat, Imperiale."

Verlis—even as he was—looked white and strained. I touched his hand. He gripped my hand in his and said, "I don't mean that."

"No, *signore*?" The child looked right at me. He had a glorious smile. His face was attractive; one day he'd be sensational. He had the eyes of a tiger.

I knew. Thought I knew. Knew Verlis knew, as I did.

The cat meowed again in his strong startling way. And then a burly bodyguard was there, standing behind the child, looking us over.

"Julio," said the bodyguard in Italian, "your mother says you shouldn't bother these people."

The child glanced up at the bodyguard, and you saw the guy loved the child, was a slave to him, would die for him. The child said, now also in Italian, "Do you remember, Gino, about my dream?"

Gino chuckled. "But this is an old, elderly gentleman. He won't be interested." He nodded to Verlis and to me. "Julio dreams of robots, *signore*. He tells his mother he was a robot once."

I sat like a stone.

Verlis said softly, "He has wonderful English."

"Yes, it's curious, *signore*. He picked that up in his second year. Like he almost was born with it. His mother has no idea how he learned it. Apart from tourists, maybe, except he sees so few. I think this is why he came to talk with you, *signore*. Though your Italian, may I say, is perfect. Oh, but you should hear this boy play piano. Never taught—just has the gift. Already he is a virtuoso."

The child said, gazing at Verlis, "Do you like silver

things, *signore*? Would you like this?" And he sprung the wristlet from his wrist, and held it out before Verlis.

The bodyguard exclaimed, "No, Julio!" He was shocked.

But none of us—the child, Verlis, and I—took any notice. And anyway, adoringly used to the boy's eccentricities, no doubt, the bodyguard didn't protest again.

Verlis reached out and took the wristlet.

"Why?" he said.

"You and I. We can share the same thing," said the child.

My heart snagged.

Through its ragged uproar, I heard Verlis say, "Then—"

But the child named Julio had darted round. He and the cat raced off over the broken tiling of the airport lounge. Still amused, the bodyguard ran after, "So long, *signore, signorina*—Julio! Julio!"

Verlis and I sat on the bench. We said nothing. His mind was shut off, like a bellowing room behind a door.

Sometimes Verlis communicates with the team, the gods, on the dark side of the moon.

He reveals nothing of this, apart from saying everything's okay, no threat or horror is imminent, for them, or for us. Would I know, even now, if he lied? Would my own abilities inform me?

He's making (he says "making" not composing) an opera. They can see another spectrum of color, his kind, as well as the spectrum humans have. I, despite what I am and all the "practice" I put in, won't ever see those other colors Verlis sees. Even if his mind tries to show my mind, even my inner eye can't see them. He says that music is humanity's highest expressive form. Including the human voice, or what will pass as a (superlative) human voice, raises music further, to some transcendant apex. But language, unless everyone can speak the same one, then becomes the obstacle. And so every aria or episode of his opera is to be only a color of the human spectrum. A color made in music, and in light, and in the words the singer will sing. We can always get cash, so providing him with instruments would never be difficult. But now he uses only his brain as the instrument. Sometimes he'll play me the symphonic strains that are flowing in his head, and I hear them in my own, and the voices singing—Glaya's voice, her two voices, that's what I hear then, and his. It isn't emotionless, this color opera, it's *pure* emotion—passion, pain, longing, joy . . .

Last night, as we were curled together in that special kind of "sleep" he always had, and that now I have, too, when he and I wander together in the forms we originally wore—a tawny girl, a silver man with long and fire-red hair—last night, in that double dream-which-isn't, Verlis said to me, "Do you remember?" And he put the silver wristlet the child passed to him into my hand. All the silver rings and other jewels he gives me from himself always vanish in a few hours. But the wristlet is real, out in the world. He wears it there inside his shirt, hanging on a cord. "Yesterday," Verlis said. "Tomorrow. But there's no Now. You keep us safe, Loren," Verlis said.

And so I've added this last section to my Book. If the boy was Silver, reincarnated as a human, who knows? Or if any of us, metal or mortal, has a soul . . . Verlis and Loren—he and I—that's all I care about. All I want. He and I.

He and I.

About the Author

Tanith Lee was born in 1947 in London, England. She received her secondary education at Prendergast Grammar School, Catford. She began to write at the age of nine.

After school she worked variously as a library assistant, a shop assistant, a filing clerk, and a waitress. At age twenty-five she spent one year at art college.

From 1970 to 1971 three of Lee's children's books were published. In 1975 DAW Books USA published Lee's *The Birthgrave*, and thereafter twenty-six of her books, enabling her to become a full-time writer.

To date she has written sixty-four novels and ten collections of novellas and short stories. Four of her radio plays have been broadcast by the BBC and she has written two episodes of the BBC cult series *Blake's Seven*. Her work has been translated into over fifteen languages.

Lee has twice won the World Fantasy award for short fiction, and was awarded the August Derleth Award in 1980 for her novel *Death's Master*.

In 1992 Lee married the writer/artist John Kaiine, her partner since 1987. They live in southeast England with two black-and-white cats.

TANITH LEE
THE Silver Metal Lover

Love is made
of more than
mere flesh and
blood

Be sure not to miss the timeless tale that started it all, also available from Bantam Spectra.

THE SILVER METAL LOVER

by

Tanith Lee

Here is Jane's story—the story that changed Loren's life. Now, let it change yours.

Mother, I am in love with a robot.
No. She isn't going to like that.
Mother, I am in love.
Are you, darling?
Oh, yes, mother, yes I am. His hair is auburn, and his eyes are very large. Like amber. And his skin is silver.
Silence.
Mother. I'm in love.
With whom, dear?
His name is Silver.
How metallic.
Yes. It stands for Silver Ionized Locomotive Verisimulated Electronic Robot.
Silence. Silence. Silence.
Mother . . .

I grew up with my mother in Chez Stratos, my mother's house in the clouds. It's a beautiful house, but I never knew it was beautiful until people told me so. "How beautiful!" They cried. So I learned it was. To me, it was just home. It's terrible being rich. One has awful false values, which one can generally only replace with other, falser, values. For example, the name of the house, which is, apparently, very vulgar, is a deliberate show of indifference to vulgarity on my mother's part. This tells you something about my mother. So perhaps I should tell you some more.

My mother is five feet seven inches tall. She has very blond hair, and very green eyes. She is sixty-three, but looks about thirty-seven, because she takes regular courses of Rejuvinex. She decided to have a child rather late, but the Rejuvinex made that perfectly all right. She selected me, and had herself artificially inseminated with me, and bore me five months later by means of the Precipta method, which only takes three or four hours. I was breast-fed, because it would be good for me, and after that, my mother took me everywhere with her, sometimes all round the world, through swamps and ruins and over broad surging seas, but I don't remember very much of this, because when I was about six she got tired of it, and we went to Chez Stratos, and more or less stayed here ever since. The city is only twenty miles away, and on clear days you can see it quite easily from the balcony-balloons of the house. I've always liked the city, particularly the look of it at night with all the distant lights glittering like strings and heaps of jewels. My mother, hearing this description once, said it was an uninspired analogy. But that's just what the city at night looks like to me, so I don't know what else to say. It's going to be very difficult, actually, putting all this down, if my analogies turn out badly every time. Maybe I just won't use analogies.

Which brings me to me.

I am sixteen years old and five feet four inches tall, but mother says I may grow a little more. When I was seven, my mother had a Phy-Excellence chart done for me, to see what was the ideal weight and muscle tone aesthetically for my frame, and I take six-monthly capsules so I stay at this weight and tone, which means I'm a little plump, as apparently my frame is Venus Media, which is essentially voluptuous. My mother also had a coloressence chart made up to see what hair color would be best for my skin and eyes. So I have a sort of pale bronze color done by molecular restructuring once a month. I can't remember what my hair was originally, but I think it was a kind of brown. My eyes are green, but not as green as my mother's.

My mother's name, by the way, is Demeta. Mine's Jane. But normally I call her "Mother" and she calls me "Dear" or "Darling." My mother says the art of verbal affection is dying out. She has a lot of opinions, which is restful, as that way I don't have to have many of my own.

However, this makes everything much more difficult, now.

I've written bits of things down before. Or embarrassing poetry. But how to do this. Perhaps it's idiotic to try. No, I have to, I think. I suppose I should begin at the beginning. Or just before the beginning. I have always fallen in love very easily, but usually with characters in visuals, or books, or with actors in drama. I have six friends, of roughly my own age—six is a balanced number, according to the statistics—and three of these have fathers as well as mothers. Clovis, who has a father, said I fell in love easily—but only with unreal men—because I didn't have a father. I pointed out that the actors I fell in love with *were* real. "That's a matter for debate," said Clovis. "But let me explain. What you fall for is the invention they're playing. If you met them, you'd detest them." One morning, to prove his theory, Clovis introduced me to an actor I'd seen in a drama and fallen in love with the previous night, but I was so shy I couldn't look at the actor. And then I found out he and Clovis were lovers, and I was brokenhearted, and stopped being shy and scowled, and Clovis said: "I told you so." Which was hardly fair. Secretly, I used to wish I were Clovis and not me. Clovis is tall and slim, with dark curly hair, and being M-B, doesn't have to take contraception shots, so tells everyone else who does they're dangerous.

I don't really like my other five friends. Davideed is at the equator right now, studying silting—which may indicate the sort of thing about him that I have no rapport with. Egyptia is very demanding, and takes over everything, though she's lovely to look at. She's highly emotional, and sometimes she embarrasses me. Chloe is nice, but not very exciting. Jason and Medea, who are brother and sister, and have a father too, are untrustworthy. Once they were in the house and they stole something, a little blue rock that came from the Asteroid. They pretended they hadn't, but I knew they had. When my mother asked where the blue rock was, I felt I had to tell her what I thought, but she said I should have pretended I had broken the rock so as not to implicate Jason and Medea, who were my friends. Loyalty. I see it was rather unsubtle of me to betray them, but I didn't know any better. Being unsubtle is one of my worst faults. I have a lot.

Anyway, I'll start when Egyptia called me on the video, and she cried and cried. Egyptia is unhappy because she knows she has greatness in her, and so far she can't find out what to do with it. She's just over eighteen, and she gets terribly afraid that life is moving too fast for her. Though most people live to be a hundred and fifty, or more, Egyptia is frightened a comet will crash on the earth at any moment and destroy us all, and her, before she can do something really wonderful. Egyptia has horrible dreams about this a lot. One can't comfort her, one merely has to sit and watch and listen.

Egyptia never had a coloressence chart or a Phy-Excellence chart done. Recently, her dark hair was tinted dark blue, and she's very thin because she's been dieting—another of her fears is that the world would run out of food because of earthquake activity, so she practices starvation for days on end. At last she stopped crying and told me she was crying because she had a dramatic interview that afternoon. Then she began to cry again. She knew, when she sent the voice and phy-tape to the drama people that she had to do it, as her greatness might occur in the form of acting. But now she knew she'd judged wrong and it wouldn't. The place where the interview was being held was the Theatra Concordacis, which had been advertising for trainees for weeks. It was a very little drama, with a very little paying membership. The actors had to pay to be in it, too, but Egyptia's mother, who was at the bottom of an ocean exploring a pre-Columbian trench, had left a lot of money to look after Egyptia instead.

"Oh, Jane," said Egyptia, blue-tinted tears running through her blue mascara. "Oh Jane! My heart's beating in huge thuds. I think I'm dying. I shall die before I can do the interview."

My eyes were already wet. Now my heart started instantly to bang in huge painful thuds, too. I am very hyperchondriacal, and tend to catch the symptoms of whatever disease is being described to me. My mother says this is a sign of imagination.

"Oh, Egyptia," I said.

"Oh, Jane," said Egyptia.

We each clung to our end of the video, gasping.

"What shall I do?" gasped Egyptia.

"I don't know."

"I must do the interview."

"I think so, too."

"I'm so afraid. There may be an earth tremor. Do you remember the tremors when we trapped the Asteroid?"

"No—"

Neither of us had been born then, but Egyptia had dreamed about it frequently, and got confused. I wondered if I felt Chez Stratos rocking in an incipient quake, but it's supposed to be invulnerably stabilized, and anyway does sometimes rock, very gently, when there's a strong wind.

"Jane," said Egyptia, "you have to come with me. You have to be with me. You have to see me do the interview."

"What are you dramatizing?"

"Death," said Egyptia. She rolled her gorgeous eyes.

My mother likes me to spend time with Egyptia, who she thinks is insane. This will be stimulating for me, and will teach me responsibility toward others. Egyptia is, of course, afraid of my mother.

The Baxter Empire was out with Mother, it's too extravagant anyway, and besides, I can't drive or fly. So I walked over the Canyon and waited for the public flyer.

The air lines glistened beautifully overhead in the sunshine, and the dust rose from the Canyon like soft steam. As I waited for the flyer to come, I looked up at Chez Stratos, or up where I knew it was, a vague blue ghost. All you can really see from the ground are the steel supports.

Just before a flyer comes the air lines whistle. Not everyone knows this, since in the city it's mostly too noisy to hear. I pressed the signal in the platform. The flyer came up and stopped like a big glass pumpkin.

Inside it was empty, but some of the seats had been slashed, presumably that morning, otherwise the overnight repair systems would have seen to it.

We sailed over the Canyon's lip, into space as it were,

and toward the city I could no longer see now that I was lower down than the house. I had to wait for the city now to put up its big gray-blue cones and stacked flashing window-glass and pillars on the skyline.

But something else had absorbed me. There was something odd about the robot machine which was driving the flyer. Normally, of course, it was just the box with driving digits and a slot for coins. Today, the flyer box had a head on. It was the head of a man about forty years of age, who hadn't taken Rejuvinex (or a man of about seventy, who had), so there were some character lines. The eyes and the hair were colorless, and the face of the head was a sort of coppery color. When I put my coin in the slot, the head disoriented me by saying to me: "Welcome aboard."

I sat down on a seat which hadn't been slashed, and looked at the head. I had, of course, seen lots of robots, as we all do, since almost everything mechanical is run by robots in the city. And even Mother has three robots who are domestic in Chez Stratos, but they're of shiny blue metal with polarized screens instead of faces. They look like spacemen to me, or like the suits men wear on the moon, or the Asteroid, and I always called our robots, therefore, the "spacemen." In the city, they're even more featureless, as you know, boxes on runners or panels set into walls.

Eventually I said to the flyer driver: "Why have you got a head today?"

I didn't think it could answer, but it might. It did.

"I am an experimental format. I am put here to make you feel at home with me."

"I see."

"Do you think I am an improvement?"

"I'm not sure," I said nervously.

"I am manufactured by Electronic Metals Ltd., 2½ East Arbor."

"Oh."

"If you wish to receive a catalog of our products, press the button by my left ear."

"I'll ask my mother."

Demeta would say: "You should make the decision yourself, darling."

But I gazed at the back of the colorless hair, which looked real but peculiar, and I thought it was silly. And at the same time it was human enough so that I didn't want to be rude to it.

Just then the outline of the city came in sight.

"You may see," announced the head, "several and various experimental formats in the city today. It will also be possible to see nine Sophisticated Formats. These are operating on 23rd Avenue, the forecourt of the Deluxe Hyperia Building, on the third floor of Casa Bianca, on Star Street—" I lost track until it said "—the Grand Stairway leading to Theatra Concordacis." Then I visualized Egyptia going into hysterics. "You may approach any of these formats and request information. The Sophisticated Formats do not dispense catalogs. Should you wish to purchase any format for your home, request the number of the model and the alphabetical registration. Each of the Sophisticated Formats has a specialized registration to enable the customer to memorize more clearly. These Formats do not have numbers. There is also . . ."

I lost interest altogether here, for the flyer was coming in across Les Anges Bridge. Below was all that glorious girderwork like spiderweb, and underneath, the Old River, polluted with chemicals and fantastically glowing purple with a top sheen of soft amber. I'm fascinated always by the strange mutated plants that grow out of the water, and the weird fish in armor that go leaping after the riverboats, clashing their jaws. A great tourist feature, the Old River. Beyond it, the city, where the poor people work at the jobs the machinery has left them to do, atrocious jobs like cleaning the ancient sewers—too narrow and eroded for the robot equipment to negotiate safely. Or elegant jobs in the department stores, particularly the more opulent second owner shops, which boasted: "Here you will be served only by *human* assistants." It's curious to be rich and miss all this. My mother considered sending me to live for a year in the city without money, but with a job, so I'd learn how the poor try to survive. "They are the ones with backbone and character, dear," she said to me. Sociologically she is highly aware. But in the end she realized my unfair advantages would have molded my outlook, so that even if I succeeded among the poor, it would be for the wrong reasons, and so would not count.

I got out of the flyer at the platform on the roof of Jagged's, and went down in the lift to the subway. There was a gang fight going on in one of the corridors and I could hear the scream of robot sirens, but I didn't see anything, which was a disappointment and a relief. I did once see a man stabbed at an outdoor visual. It didn't upset me at the time. They rushed him away and replaced the parts of him that had been spoiled, though he would have had to pay for that on the installment plan—clearly he hadn't been rich—which would probably mean he'd end up bankrupt. But later on, I suddenly remembered how he had fallen down, and the blood, and I began to get a terrible pain in my side where I pictured the knife going into him. My mother organized hypnotherapy for me until it went away.

Egyptia was standing at the foot of the Grand Stairway that leads up to the Theatra Concordacis. She was wearing gilt makeup, and a blue velvet mantle lined with lemon silk, and people were looking at her. A topaz hung in the center of her forehead. She made a wild gesture at me.

"Jane! Jane!"

"Hallo."

"Oh, Jane."

"Yes?"

"Oh, Jane. Oh, Jane."

"Shall we go up?"

She flung up her arm, and I blushed. She made me feel insignificant, superior and uneasy. As I was analyzing this, I saw someone hurrying over, a man, who grasped Egyptia's raised arm excitedly.

"All right," he said. "Tell me your number."

Egyptia and I stared at him. His eyes were popping.

"Go away," Egyptia said. Her own eyes filled with tears. She couldn't bear the stupid things life did to her.

"No. I can pay. I've never seen anything like it. I heard it was lifelike, but Jesus. You. I'll take you. Just give me your registration number—wait—you don't have one, do you, that's the other type. Okay, it's alphabetical, isn't it? Somebody said it's to do with the metal. You'd be gold, wouldn't you? G.O.L.D.? Am I right?"

Egyptia lifted her eyes to the tall building tops, like Jehane at the stake. Suddenly I knew what was happening.

"You've made a mistake," I said to the man.

"You can't have it," he said. "What do you want it for? Mirror-Biased, are you? Well, you go and find a real girl. Young bit of stuff like you shouldn't have any trouble."

"She isn't," I insisted.

"She? It's an it."

"*No.*" I felt on fire. "She's my friend. She isn't a Sophisticated Format robot."

"Yes it is. They said. Operating on the Grand Stairway."

"No."

"Oh, God!" cried Egyptia. Unlike the rest of us, He didn't answer.

"It's all right, Egyptia. Please, please," I said to the man, "she isn't a robot. Go away, or I'll press my code for the police."

I wished at once I hadn't said it. He, like Egyptia and me, was rich, and would have his own code round his neck or on his wrist or built into a button. I felt I'd been very discourteous and rash, but I couldn't think of anything else to do.

"Well," he said. "I'll write to Electronic Metals and complain. A piece of my mind."

(I saw this as some sort of surgical operation, the relevant slice delivered in a box.)

But Egyptia spun to him abruptly. She fixed him with her eyes which matched the topaz, and screeched wordlessly like a mad bird of prey. The man who thought she was a robot backed sideways along the steps. Egyptia seemed to close her soul to us both. She flung her mantle round herself and stalked away up the stairs.

I watched her go, not really wanting to follow. Mother would say I should, in order to observe and be responsible.

It was a beautiful day in autumn, a sort of toasted day. The sides of the buildings were warm, the glass mellow, and the sky was wonderful, very high and far off, while in the house it looks near. I didn't want to think about the man or about Egyptia. I wanted to think about something that was part of the day, and of me. Without warning, I felt a kind of pang, somewhere between my ribs and my spine. It might have been indigestion, but it was like a key turning. It seemed as if I knew something very important, and only had to wait a moment and I would recall what it was. But though I stood there for about five minutes, I didn't, and the feeling faded with a dim, sweet ache. It was like being in love, the moment when, just before the visual ends, I knew I must walk away into the night or morning without him. Awful. Yet marvelous. Marvelous to be able to feel. I put this down because it may have a psychological bearing on what comes next.

I began to imagine Egyptia acting death in the Theatra, and dying. So finally I went up the Grand Stairway.

At the top is a terrace with a fountain. The fountain pours over an arch of glass, and you can stand under the glass with the fountain pouring, and not get wet. Across from the fountain is the scruffy peeling facade of the once splendid Theatra. A ticking clockwork lion was pacing about by the door. I hadn't seen anything quite like it, and wondered if this was the Sophisticated Format. Then something caught my eye.

It was the sun gleaming rich and rare on auburn.

I looked, and bathed my eyes in the color. I know red shouldn't be soothing to the eyes, but it was.

Then I saw what the red was. It was the long hair of a young man who was standing with his back to me, talking to a group of five or six people.

Then he began to sing. The voice was so unexpected. I went hot again, with embarrassment again, because someone was singing at the top of his lungs in a crowded busy place. At the same moment, I was delighted. It was a beautiful voice, like a minstrel's, but futuristic, as if time were playing in a circle inside the notes. If only I could sing, I vaguely thought as I heard him. How wonderful to have such sounds pour effortlessly from your throat.

There were bits of mirror on his jacket, glinting, and I wondered if he was there for an interview, like Egyptia, and warming up outside. Then he stopped singing, and turned around and I thought: Suppose he's ugly? And he went on turning, and I saw his profile and he wasn't ugly. And then, pointing something out to the small gathering about him, he turned fully toward me, not seeing me. He was handsome, and his eyes were like two russet stars. Yes, they were exactly like stars. And his skin seemed only pale, as if there were an actor's makeup on it, and then I saw it was silver—face, throat, the V of chest inside the open-necked shirt, the hands that came from the dripping lace at his cuffs. Silver that flushed into almost natural shadings and colors against the bones, the lips, the nails. But silver. Silver.

It was very silly. I started to cry. It was awful. I didn't know what to do. My mother would have been pleased, as it meant my basic emotions—whatever they were—were being allowed full and free rein. But she'd also have expected me to control myself. And I couldn't.

So I walked under the fountain and stared at it till the tears stopped in envy. And then I was puzzled as to why I'd cried at all.

When I came out, the crowd, about twenty now, was dispersing. They would all have taken his registration, or whatever, but most of them couldn't afford him.

I stood and gazed at him, curious to see if he'd just switch himself off when the crowd went away. But he didn't. He began to stroll up and down. He had a guitar slung over his shoulder I hadn't noticed, and he started to caress melodies out of it. It was crazy.

Then, quite abruptly and inevitably, he registered that someone else was watching after all, and he came toward *me*.

I was frightened. He was a robot and he seemed just like a man, and he scared me in a way I couldn't explain. I would have run away like a child, but I was too frightened to run.

He came within three feet of me, and he smiled at me. Total coordination. All the muscles, even those of his face. He seemed perfectly human, utterly natural, except he was too beautiful to be either.

"Hallo," he said.

"Are you—" I said.

"Am I?"

"Are you—the—are you a robot?"

"Yes. Registration Silver. That is S.I.L.V.E.R. which stands for Silver Ionized Locomotive Verisimulated Electronic Robot. Neat, isn't it?"

"No," I said. "No." Again without warning, I began once more to cry.

His smile faded. He looked concerned, his eyes were like pools of fulvous lead. His reactions were superb. I hated him. I wished he were a box on wheels, or I wished he were human.

"What's the matter?" he said eventually, and very gently, making it much worse. "The idea is for me to amuse you. I seem to be failing. Am I intruding on some sort of personal grief?"

"You horrible thing," I whispered. "How dare you stand there and talk to me?"

The reactions were astounding. His eyes went flat and wicked. He gave me the coldest smile I ever saw, and bowed to me. He really did turn on his heel, and he walked directly away from me.

I wished the concrete would open and swallow me. I truly wished it. I wanted to be ten years old and run home to my mother, who might comfort or lecture me, but who would be omnipotent. Or I wanted to be a hundred and twenty, and wise, and not care.

Anyway, I raced off the terrace, and to Clovis.

DON'T MISS

SPECTRA PULSE

A WORLD APART

the free monthly electronic newsletter that delivers direct to you...

- < Interviews with favorite authors
- < Profiles of the hottest new writers
- < Insider essays from Spectra's editorial team
- < Chances to win free early copies of Spectra's new releases
- < A peek at what's coming soon

...and so much more

SUBSCRIBE FREE TODAY AT

www.bantamdell.com

SF 3/05